BYZANTINE HONEYMOON
A Tale of the Bosphorus

BYZANTINE HONEYMOON

A Tale of the Bosphorus

by

PHILIP GLAZEBROOK

LONDON
VICTOR GOLLANCZ LTD
1979

ISBN 0 575 02589 1

Printed in Great Britain by
The Bowering Press Ltd,
Plymouth and London

CONTENTS

I

The Devil's Current

I T W A S I N the summer of 1895 that I first heard the nightingales singing in the cypress woods of the Bosphorus. My situation was a delightful one as I strolled now in sun, now in shadow, in the white dust of a track which wound upon the wooded heights above the Castle of Rumelia; and in my companion there was that hint of strangeness, of mystery even, which well suited the romantic expectations which such circumstances arouse in the traveller's breast. He was an old man, and my idea of his nationality altered with almost every word he uttered : a Bulgar? A Macedonian Greek? A Georgian? A Persian? Or, since that unfortunate nation is so much in one's mind, especially in Turkey where its people lie under constant threat of massacre, an Armenian? I did not know. The sunlight which fell in shafts between the dark columns of the cypresses, and which warmed me, did not appear to warm my companion. A wide-brimmed dark hat kept his face in a climate of its own, a climate un-affected by the sun or by the scented breeze of these resinous heights. A long snuff-coloured dustcoat enveloped him. Cracked slippers seamed with dust shod his feet. Sallow, his cheeks sunken, the skin thin-stretched over the bony architecture of nose and chin, a mouthful of black teeth; in Italy I would have taken him for a friar of some mendicant order, rudely disguised, who was either making off with the abbot's plate or else hunting down the miscreant who stole it. For I sensed a dualism in the creature; I could not determine whether the pull which I felt attracting me to him was the magnetism of good or of evil. In the same way, as we walked, I experienced at one moment the warmth of a southern summer in the sunlight falling upon me, and at the next a chill breath of the north wind which blows across the Black Sea from the wastes of Crim Tartary beyond. The two climates of

Constantinople, against whose treachery the traveller is warned, were better personified in my interesting companion than I then knew.

Earlier that day I had been lounging in stark idleness at the rail of a Bosphorus steamer, watching the wonderful array of craft which crowds that majestic waterway dividing Europe from Asia, myself travelling nowhere in particular. My discontent was extreme. Such a membrane of busy life connected these craft, these boatmen flying hither and thither; diverse as they were (and nowhere on earth, I suppose, is there greater diversity than among the peoples who cluster upon the shores of the Bosphorus) they shared much with each other, whilst I shared nothing with anyone in the world. It seemed to me that the commodity they shared was Life. As I gazed, a red-sailed felucca dashed by; I glimpsed its interior, heard its helmsman's cry, before it was snatched from me—strain as I might to experience the life of the Bosphorus, it remained as remote from me now, though my eyes beheld it, as ever the idea of it had been. I gazed upon the scene which seemed quite as cleverly painted as the active and crowded canvases of Mr Frith, and quite as lacking in the essence of life. Of what was this armour-plated glass composed, which so insulated me? A phrase attached to our foreign policy of recent years—a phrase in which I had hitherto taken pride—occurred to me : splendid isolation.

Splendid isolation! Was it perhaps that what this diverse, desperate, rascally population shared with one another, and did not share with me, was that they were urgently engaged in gaining a living, and that I was not? Obliged to strive or starve, they hastened to and fro upon the face of the water; whilst I journeyed nowhere in particular because my quarters in the hotel at Pera, and the company of my wife, had been more than ordinarily irksome that morning. Necessity linked them : necessity is not an influence an English gentleman cares to admit in mapping his course, especially amongst foreigners. I had in my hand Redhouse's *Turkish Vade-Mecum*, for I had hoped to inform myself of the language of the place, but I replaced it dejectedly in my pocket and continued to stare out at the straits which the ferry clove between wooded shores a gunshot apart. To and fro over the water, restless and swift-winged, in flocks insubstantial as ghosts, fled flights of sheerwaters; never resting, never touching

8

the surface over which they skimmed, it was these *yelkovan* rather than the human traffic of the Bosphorus which seemed to me like myself, and I was contemplating our shared insubstantiality when I became aware of a hand—a gnarled hand—closer to mine upon the boat's rail than mere accident could have explained. Out of the corner of my eye I made out a snuff-coloured coat, a dark hat, a presence more or less sinister, before a voice spoke :

'*Sheitan akindisi.*' The hand uncurled its fingers from the rail and gestured downwards at the swirling waters cut by the ferry.

I moved away. Despite my discontent with life for passing me by, one is bred up to dislike life even more when it is importunate.

The creature closed the gap I had opened between us. '*Sheitan akindisi,*' he repeated. I took him for one of the Jew money-changers who frequent the ferries, and was about to drive him off with a curse or a kick when he spoke in excellent English. 'The Devil's Current, it is called here,' he explained, 'yes sir, the devil's own current, and the devil's own business too, what these waters must sweep from the Sultan's shores.'

I looked now at the owner of this dark, guttural voice for the first time and was at once struck by something almost gentleman-like about his looks and bearing. His height, too, quite above the mean stature of the Levant, made a favourable impression of manliness, despite his threadbare garments. I was debating whether or not to encourage the fellow by replying, when he spoke again :

'*Dites-moi, excellence,* tell me, sir, can there be pictured a régime more splendid than the Ottoman's, who has *le bon dieu* himself upon the throne, and the devil employed as his street sweeper?'

'You are neither Mussulman nor Turk I take it,' I replied, 'for I think only a Christian sees God and the Devil sharing the world's work between them.' (The facts of my upbringing have made it impossible for me to refrain from darting into theological dispute.)

'And only an Englishman, excellency, only an Englishman condescends to share his thoughts with a fellow traveller upon the Devil's Current,' he replied with some semblance of a bow which seemed the tattered relic of a courtly past.

I warmed sufficiently to him not to continue creeping away from him around the brass rail. The ferry was now passing through the straits at their narrowest, between Rumeli Hissar whose walls drop steep into the water, and the ruined Castle of Anatolia upon its wooded shore. That fierce tide from the Black Sea, here swift as a river in flood between the two promontories, sucked and curled the water's surface into a thousand vicious whirlpools racing past—an infernal current indeed if one fell into its clutches. We both gazed down upon it in silence.

'You have a house perhaps? It is to your excellency's *yali* that you are travelling?' he enquired presently.

Indeed the notion of taking a *yali*, one of the summer houses of the Bosphorus, either upon the waterfront or amongst the gardens and groves of the hillsides, had occasionally tempted me. Thinking that he might be of use in the matter I asked him if he knew anything of the mechanics of renting such a property.

'*Pas moi*,' he replied, holding his old hands wide in disclaimer, 'these questions are beyond *un tel viellard* as is your slave. But indeed—yes indeed—were I young and rich, an Englishman, handsome—' (here the vestige of a bow applied these epithets to myself) 'why then I would take me a house, a *yali*.'

'Where?'

'At Emirghian, excellency, where the ferry calls next.'

'Why would you choose Emirghian?'

He was silent. He looked at me, as if to assess my worth, and then drew a large and absolutely clean white silk handkerchief from his sleeve with which to dab his beak of a nose. Behind him drifted the European shore. The water hissed against the ferry's sides as we slid swiftly towards the dark bulk of Anadoli Hissar beside the Sweet Waters of Asia which there flow into the Bosphorus.

"Why Emirghian?' I repeated. In the silence the place had doubled its attraction for me, like a benefit offered, then witheld.

'*Eh bien*,' he said, as if reluctantly, folding away his handkerchief, 'it would not be a place to recommend to a married man, to a family man, and I do not know what is your excellency's situation. So, I hesitate. But for the man who is romantic, is without *les liens*—why sir, imagine to yourself how it would be to have a house, a retreat, upon the water's edge at Emirghian— on a night in summer, let me tell you, the lighted *kaiks* dart to and fro *comme des mouches à feu*, the air, sir, the air is *vibrante* with the singing of Greeks, the music of guitar, the scent of magnolias—ah!' he sighed, seeming to relapse into contemplation of past delights.

'No doubt one can hear guitar music in other villages,' I said, hoping to prompt a fuller explanation of the peculiar delights of Emirghian. I certainly had often enough wished heartily that I was not a married man.

'At Emirghian there are few Europeans,' he said.

'Well?' I replied, not content with this tersity.

He looked at me keenly. 'The Osmanli has arranged for himself sources of every kind of pleasure.'

Now followed a silence in which, I must confess, my mind elaborated with alacrity upon his suggestive statement. My wife was, or pretended to be, in delicate health, almost an invalid. The notion of Byzantium's delights, and fabled decadence, swept in upon my mind like a glimpse over a cliff-edge. The ferry meanwhile, with the exquisite skill of those Bosphorus helmsmen, had slid up against the quay of the Castle of Asia, where I had intended disembarking, and now hovered there as if waiting for me to make up my mind as to my future. Which was it to be? Here I would only walk to and fro, drink coffee and smoke cigars, until another ferry took me back to Constantinople, and to that darkened and mahogany-filled suite of rooms with its invalidish smells—whereas if I travelled on as the stranger suggested, what might I not find at Emirghian? *Every kind of pleasure.* The boat trembled at the quay. Which?

The gangplank rattled away upon its rollers, the ferry hooted, thrashed water, swung swiftly offshore and was under way again. I had chosen—inaction had chosen for me. My heart lifted. I recaptured for a precious instant that sense of heightened life which was the chief delight of breaking bounds at school. As if in response to my changed mood a *kaikji*, propelling his craft inches from the ferry's cutwater, grinned up at the narrowness of his escape and made the gesture of cutting his throat with his fore-finger. That villainous grin welcomed me aboard his frail boat—welcomed me into the quickness and life of this romantic channel.

Now the glistening water, the stern mountains rolling upwards from the shore, the channel winding now broad and now narrow between wooded or fortified headlands on either hand, the craft moving this way or that under sail or oar or steam—all this struck

11

me afresh, with a liveliness I had not as yet experienced from my travels. I had only consented to undertake our tour to the Levant on account of the romantic imaginings with which I had looked towards Asia all my life, and I had been disappointed. Now I could for the first time imagine myself in the very pages of a storybook, and not merely looking on at the spectacle of Asiatic life.

I would have liked my companion to have talked, to have told me more of Emirghian, whose waterfront could now be made out as we approached it, the line of sparkling façades dividing dark water from the darker cypress groves above. But he was silent, sunk in reflexion at the rail beside me. I stole a glance at him. In repose his features took on a haughty, even cruel, demeanour. The impression that he was in some sense incognito formed in my mind. He was playing a rôle. I could not tell whether his hands really trembled on the rail, or whether the boat's vibration made them shake. Nor could I still the speculation which he excited in my mind. Was he Turcoman or Caucasian Russian, or Persian perhaps? The whole Aladdin's cave of races which people Asia seemed hinted at in him. Satisfied that he was, by origin at least, a gentleman, I remained at his side.

By now details of the approaching village could be distinguished. There rose from the water a line of the fantastical wooden houses of the Bosphorus, wrought and carven, balconied, gabled, chimneyed—the whole apparition dancing in the waterlight whilst its reflexion trembled below it in the liquid mirror of the water. These were the ordinary dwellings of the place. Set apart in their own gardens, fronting the straits with stone quays, stood the summer mansions of Stamboul merchants. At a distance these *yalis* had an abandoned air; their windows shuttered, their planks starved and weathered to greyness by salt and sun. Nearer at hand, as the ferry rushed along the shore towards the quay, one saw that the dilapidation was illusory, for the gardens were neat as pins on paper, the houses sound, stone and marble gleaming on balustrade or stair. Everywhere great magnolias grew richly and profusely. The idea of renting such a retreat was vastly attractive.

'Tell me,' I said to my companion as the ferry bumped the quay, 'how might a fellow set about engaging a house in such a place as this?'

He seemed to start out of his dream and speak at random. 'What? Take a house? Step ashore, excellency, trust yourself to fate.' When I hesitated he urged me further : 'If you are to descend, it must be now. *Chabuk!* So. *Allah ismarladik.*'

I felt myself hustled off the ferry, although the boat was not upon the point of departure. I gave up my ticket and found myself in the village square. Plane trees shaded the beaten earth, there was a fountain, a number of idlers smoking or drinking coffee cross-legged upon the ground against the house-fronts, and innumerable dogs. At one corner of this *meidan*, where a white road led out of the village, two or three infinitely dejected horses stood for hire in a cloud of flies. Because of the deadening dust, and because there is little wheeled traffic, the quietness of a Turkish scene is remarkable. I heard the ferryboat hoot and churn water as it departed; the small animation of its coming seemed to pass; peace, or inaction, resettled upon Emirghian. The impetus of my own arrival petered out. I began to walk aimlessly across the *meidan*.

Evidently the inhabitants of the place were unused to the spectacle of an Englishman crossing their square. I was the cynosure of interest. A certain consciousness of superiority attaches merely to being watched. Going out to bat at cricket, succeed or fail, one has at all events been chosen to play; and so too here, an Englishman watched by these beggarly Turks, I was aware that simply by virtue of race one has been marked out by the Great Selector. As I crossed that dingy square I thought of the countless millions of native eyes fixed at that moment throughout the globe upon the figure of an Englishman, often young, often alone, often all-powerful over life and death; I thought of the manner in which a handful of our fellows had removed Egypt whole, to all practical purposes, from the dying clutch of this effete empire at whose centre I stood; and I felt as proud to belong to that island race whose empire is the most powerful the world has ever known, as if I had been chosen by the Doctor to bat first wicket down for The Gentlemen of the world against the Players. αἰὲν ἀριστεύειν καὶ ὑπείροχον ἔμμεναι ἄλλων.

When one's personal and private situation is unhappy, or weak, it is of comfort to partake of the wider esteem which attaches to being an Englishman abroad. In the same way one's financial dependence upon others (in my case upon my father-in-law's fortune) is exceedingly irksome in England, where the flimsy melts through one's fingers, whilst abroad a gold sovereign or two in one's pocket (however obtained) makes one master of the situation. Of course I don't intend to convey that this complacency attaches properly to all Englishmen—nothing is so ludicrous as the self-esteem of a little fellow such as the Lord Mayor of London, Reinalls by name, whom we had seen at Paris, whither he had come with his gilt coach thinking to make a splash, and had ended up the laughing-stock of any Frenchman of breeding who had noticed him—of course it is only to an English gentleman that such complacency is proper.

These reflexions soon reconciled me to my situation as I strolled through the *keui* whilst a tail of villagers with interests to forward attached itself to me as cats attach themselves to a seller of fish, or seagulls to the plough. *Every kind of pleasure,* the old traveller had promised; well, as a commencement I wanted luncheon, and the moment my wishes were known they provoked suggestions, quarrels, even bloodshed, amongst my entourage as to where I would be served best. My good humour was restored. It is impossible not to feel a lively interest in a personage so fêted and followed as was I.

An hour or two later I was seated amongst bolsters and cushions on the balcony of a waterfront house, the remains of an excellent meal on the discarded brass tray at my side. I had begun with a bowl of *chorba,* and progressed to grey mullet, a fish which in winter resorts to the lagoons of the Euxine and grows enormously fat; then *dolmas* of mutton rolled in quince leaves, and sweet-meats and *helva,* had made me feel as fat as a mullet myself. Before me lay the waters of the Bosphorus, as lively an entertainment as could be contrived by the greatest duke in England to accompany his luncheon. I reclined amongst my cushions in the warmth of the sun, sipping the deliciously sweet coffee of the Turks and smoking one of the cigarettes provided for me, also so sweet and pungent that I suspected the admixture of *bhang* to the tobacco.

Under the influence of this *luxe orientale* my mind had strayed back to the idea, so tempting and suggestive, of an independent establishment in this indulgent spot—a retreat in which to forget the heavy curtains and heavier furniture which darkened my

14

wife's rooms in the Pera Palace Hotel, to forget the fringed lamp-shades and the smell of sal volatile, and the dry scratch of her nib as she wrote letters, or her journal, or whatever it was she wrote—a retreat in which to forget what we had become to one another in the short months of our marriage. So I dreamed, almost dozing, regrets and desires rippling my mind as the wind's catspaws rippled and darkened the waters which separated me from Asia, until a voice behind me spoke the Turkish grace :

'*Afet olsun, effendi.*'

Turning, I was somewhat startled to find my acquaintance from the ferryboat. Looking up into his face I again received the impression of haughtiness and cruelty from his aquiline features and curiously light-coloured eyes. Above his head danced a string of pilchards drying in the sun. 'Well my friend,' said I, 'what can I do for you? I thought you had travelled on.'

He fell at once into his meek, almost fawning manner, hands concealed in sleeves, coat buttoned in the manner of Asiatics who wish to show respect. 'Excellency,' he said, 'in the moment that the boat was quitting the quayside I have recollected how I might after all be of help to you.'

'In what way, pray?'

'I forget, with this old head, always forget. So, when the ferry reaches to Stenia what do I do? Excellency, I take a boat back, if you believe me!'

'Listen,' I said, my mind somewhat clouded, 'tell me what it is you have remembered, old man.'

For answer he produced from the sleeve of that long snuff-coloured garment a large iron key of elaborate design. I do not know how, but I knew at once the key's use. Nor was I sur-prised; perhaps on account of the narcotic effect of my cigarette, which lent to these happenings a fitness and order they really lacked. I listened whilst he explained how he had recalled a small house empty at Emirghian, had discovered the owner, obtained the key—I listened, but it was as though these were lies I had thought up myself to explain his possession of that key. Although in his long robe and in his manner there was something of the wizard, it seemed to me evident that he had an article to sell me, which put our relationship upon a plainer footing.

'Come,' I said, holding out my hand that he might help me

to my feet, 'arrange with these fellows how much I am to pay for my luncheon, and we will look at this house of yours which has appeared so conveniently from nowhere.'

We were soon walking through the village towards a row of wooden houses sleeping by an inlet of the Bosphorus. To one of these my cicerone had the key. Once inside, he preceded me through the empty rooms, throwing wide the shutters so that one room after another was filled with the mysterious reflected light of Venetian palaces. The house faced upon the straits and had an inlet or creek at its flank, so that two sides gave upon water. I was attracted by the place. This watery half light had the tone to illuminate the notion forming in my mind. I went to a window, my English boots tramping loudly on the bare boards. Across the creek a decayed façade confronting me, and the slime upon its water-stairs, again put me in mind of Venice. The creep of water was everywhere, in one's mind as much as in one's ears, filling the high empty rooms with unformed ideas.

Of course I assumed that the house belonged to the old polyglot, who pretended that it didn't in order to make more room to manoeuvre in the matter of rent. Doubtless he would sketch in a greedy landlord who would turn down my offers. I was considering how best to negotiate—and how indeed to raise the necessary at all without interesting my wife too closely in the project—when my eye was caught by a scene in the walled yard of the house across the creek.

Above the wall, striking at some object on the ground which was hidden from me, a hammer rose and fell in the hands of a singularly repulsive individual. Bull-necked, his large pale head quite hairless, this creature grasped the hammer in huge hands and struck with dull ferocity at whatever lay at his feet. There was about him some gross deformity which I could not readily identify—in the slackness and whiteness of the flesh something monstrous—which was utterly repugnant. The sound of the blows coming across the water to me was sickening; and what aroused a sense almost of horror in me was that beside him, watching, stood a very large rough-coated dog. This brute watched the work without interest; one had the impression of an appetite already satiated. I tore my eyes from the scene and went in search of my guide. 'Tell me,' I said, 'who lives opposite to you?'

'No one!' he screeched out, 'the house is empty!' Yet he was at the window in a trice. 'See? Empty—closed, shuttered—empty,' he said with plain relief.

I went to the window and looked down. Of the scene I had witnessed there was no trace. Was its disappearence explained by a difference in angle from this viewpoint? Or had that deformed creature and his wolfish hound been a presage or omen visible only to myself?

'This house however, excellency,' the old man now corrected me, 'is not belonging to me.'

'Doesn't it though,' I said, laying my hand upon his arm, 'but I'll wager it belongs to a friend of yours who has authorised you to negotiate for him, eh? Come, we will take a turn about the village and talk terms.'

This we did. He professed not to know what the owner would accept by way of rent, but advised me to offer 2,000 francs, about 80 gold *lira*, for a year's let. When I said that the house must be furnished he replied that I would do well to appoint an agent to superintend the furnishings and to control the household in my absence. I supposed that he meant himself for this rôle.

'There must first of all be a household to control,' I said.

'You will send down servants from Pera?'

I avoided his eye. 'I had thought,' I said, 'of keeping up a purely Turkish establishment. Such as you spoke of. When recommending Emirghian.'

Every kind of pleasure: I did not know how openly to speak.

'What do you want?' he enquired.

I found I could not produce any very exact picture of what I desired : I conjured either an Arabian Nights company of kohl-eyed houris disposed upon silken cushions—a company into which I couldn't project myself except in a fancy dress of turban and curly-toed slippers, a dagger at my waist and a *narghilh* at my side—or else I saw myself as I am, in which case the lovely captives of the harem were replaced by a tiresome Cockney from the chorus at the opera. If Emirghian was to be no better than a Turkish St John's Wood I may as well have stopped in England.

'What is it that your excellency wishes?' he repeated.

'I want—I want——' It is only when there is an immediate chance of one's desires being realised that one perceives their inexactness. 'I want—every kind of pleasure,' I finished, making a grand, if vague, gesture.

17

'Even pleasures must be chosen,' he said, 'even at the *yessir bazar* a choice of pleasures must be made.'

'The what?'

'The slave market.'

My blood ran cold, then hot. Yes, that was what 'pleasure' signalled to my blood : a slave, a female slave, a woman absolutely in my power. Feeling my face redden and my heart thump, I could not trust my voice to answer the old man.

But he read my silence. 'A slave? That is your wish? Is soon arranged——'

'Yes, yes, later!' I replied rapidly, unwilling to face the subject all at once. 'Come, I must return to Constantinople. I will consider the whole project and let you know my decision.'

He bowed, that fine old hawkish face of his turned from me— yet lit, I thought, by a smile of triumph, as though a trap had sprung.

At the landing quay all was confusion. The Turkish method of time-telling, in which sunset must always be at twelve o'clock, makes the reading of time-tables an almost impossible feat. My companion came away from his tussle with these oracles with the news that no further steamer would call that day, and that we were obliged therefore to walk to Bebek, where a ferry called at a later hour.

'Come, excellency,' said he, buttoning his long coat, 'it is no great distance and we will talk upon the road.'

So it came about that we were walking together upon the heights above the Castle of Rumelia, in the mingled sunlight and shadow of those cypress groves in whose depths the nightingales sang, whilst my companion told tales which seemed to transport me into the world of Scheherazade, so fantastical and mediaeval did they sound to an Englishman who had but recently quitted the modern London of 1895. Apropos of my anxiety to regain Constantinople before dusk he had commenced by telling me that when he first knew the city its gates had been shut between dusk and dawn, and that a traveller arriving by night would not be admitted save upon a *firman* signed by the Sultan himself. 'I well remember,' he said, 'reaching to the Adrianople gate at the end of a journey I once made with a Tatar from Belgrade— riding post, you understand, many leagues covered quick, all

18

riding like the devil through villages and all yelling—Tatar, *sureji*, me—all yelling! Well—at the end of that journey we reach to the Adrianople gate an hour or two before dawn. In no way can we make the gatekeeper to listen and open his gate. Not the Tatar even, for his *firman* was not for Stamboul but the Dolmabaghcheh. Let me tell you—I wrap my cloak about me, I lie on the ground, I sleep under the stars till a traveller wakens me at dawn.'

With the pride which these doings evidently aroused, there came into his step and his gestures an elasticity which surprised me. Wondering about his age I enquired, 'What year was your journey made in?'

'That journey? Ah, I made so many in the 1840s.'

'And you have lived continuously at Constantinople since those days?'

'Sir, I have lived—that is all.'

I soon ceased to tease at the puzzle he posed, and gave myself over to listening to his stories until we began to descend towards the sparkling blue waters of the Bosphorus again. He told me that he had been in Bokhara when the two English officers, Stoddart and Connolly, had been murdered there, and had met the mad preacher, Wolff, who had come in search of them; he had been at the stronghold of Gunib, in Daghestan, when the Lesghian chieftain, Shamyl, had surrendered to Prince Bariatinski; he had seen, so he averred, a sackful of severed heads tumbled onto the ground as purchase money for a Hindoostani princess in the old slave market at Khiva; he swore that he had travelled in the first train to run from the Caspian to Samarkhand on the railway built by Annenkov; he mentioned Penjedh, where the Russians had run up against the Afghans in the mid-'80s, and he spoke of the Kizilbashes at Kabul as though he had friends amongst them.

I listened entranced. Those names, those tribes, those tracts of central Asia, had been the inspiration of all my childhood's imaginary travels, and of its terrors too. My companion was a storybook come alive, and I was a child again, listening to his tales; the child I used to be, spurring my hobby horse into flight from the little girl who was to become my wife, she urging her horse and her horde of Turcoman cut-throats in pursuit—both of us imagining the pleasure grounds of her father's house to be the

19

wastes of Crim Tartary, and imagining the fate which awaited me to be that obscene outrage which neither of us had puzzled out : 'a fate worse than death'. Had I met a man who had told me that he had dined with Arthur at Camelot, or who had seen the very beanstalk Jack climbed, I would not have experienced more strongly the sensation of a remote age, and remoter lands, being suddenly at hand. In his tales were realised what I had thought to be fables.

Because of the railway (which had reached Stamboul only five or six years ago)—because of the mahogany comforts of Pera—because of the electric telegraph and the steam ferries and the presence of Mr Cook's egregious tourists—because of all these modernities I had regarded 'old Turkey' as a land gone forever; or at any rate only surviving in a Bowdlerised and hygenic form, as our own Dark Age has survived in the needlework of Mr William Morris. But it was evidently not so. From Grand Vizier or Kizlar Aghasi down to the meanest palace spy, the apparatus of old Turkey yet ruled the fate of 35 millions of subjects between the Nile and the Danube. History—the fantastic history of the Levant, whose treacheries and cruelties I had gulped down greedily as a child—was not over, as history in Europe is tamed and done with by the Spencers and Huxleys and Darwins and Colensos of our progressive century. My companion's tales of travelling in the Sultan's domains, of his reception at the hands of Kurdish chieftains in the Caucasus, or of his miraculous escape from infection by the plague-stricken Jews inhabiting the ruins of Tiberias—such adventures have no parallel in England since the adventures of King Arthur's knights.

And he—who was he? I placed him now as probably a Persian or Turcoman from east of the Caspian, possibly an Uzbeg from Tashkent; at any rate as a native of the borders of that immense plateau out of which all the races, and all the history, of the world are said to have emerged. Evidently he had been a soldier of fortune, had lived upon his wits—had probably acted too the spy's and the assassin's part—he had, in short, been a pretty fair representation, in his own person, of the human race. That he had been valorous and quixotic I did not doubt, and the panache and high good humour of his tales made one wink at their morality, for it was apparent from his handsome features and refined manner that he had all the instincts of a gentleman.

I longed for such adventures to befall myself, and counted upon my acquaintance with this rare old rascal to help bring them about. Of course there ran through all his tales the crimson thread of fierce torture and ugly death. Does not the same thread run through the fairy stories all children love? Certainly the 'fate worse than death', and impaling, and exposure, had all added zest to my childhood games with Rachel; and I experienced now —a mere 75 hours by train from modern London—a *frisson* from the notion that scimitar and bowstring were as active as ever within a few miles of me. The anticipation of a flogging never lessened the attractions of crime at school—sharpened it indeed, for a fellow of the right sort, and became an indivisible part of illicit delights.

We were now entering Bebek by way of its *champs des morts* (amongst whose cypresses the nightingales sang quite as cheerfully as in the wooded heights we had traversed) and my companion pointed out to me signs of the Europeanisation of the town— indeed, its Englification, for he assured me that there was a Church of England community and its clergyman established here—which made Emirghian by contrast, for a true traveller and no mere Cook's tourist, vastly the more attractive location. There might in this Anglican community be protection from the mediaeval fears of old Turkey such as spiced my companion's stories; but as punishment for the pleasures I intended to indulge I preferred the threat of the bowstring to the threat of the sermon, for I am (you must know) a parson's son.

Arrived at the waterfront of Bebek we repaired to the ferry station. Learning that a steamer would call within the hour we made our way to a coffee shop and there discussed the arrangements which needed making if I were to lease the house at Emirghian, as I was now determined to do provided I could induce my wife to come down with the flimsy without questioning its use. It was agreed that I should bring an advance payment, in gold, to a certain house which had been pointed out to me as the landlord's. Furnishing could then go ahead. My companion now seemed disposed to disappear from the negotiation, making me wonder what his part in the business really was. Though I could not make out his interest in my taking the house, I was certain that he had one, and a strong one too. I would have felt easier had I known what he stood to gain. I was anxious too that

21

one suggestion he had made should not lapse—the *yessir bazar*—but I feared that my hauteur over certain insinuations of his against our Ambassador, Sir Philip Currie, (whom he had accused of causing Armenians to be put to death to furnish an excuse for his bringing the British Fleet to the Marmora) might have made me too upright a personage in his eyes for the matter of slaves to be reopened between us. There are difficulties in preserving the dignity and fair name of an Englishman and yet admitting to the human weaknesses. Not until the ferry was at the quayside, and I was about to step aboard, did I broach the subject:

'You will not forget your promise?'

'Promise, excellency?'

'To furnish—to arrange—the *yessir bazar*,' I whispered into the shade of his hat, feeling myself flush.

He stood back from me. For an instant, I know not why, I felt that I had fallen alive into a trap prepared for me. With a low bow, and yet with disdain, he retorted, 'All will be as his excellency desires'.

I watched the gangplank rolled ashore. I felt the screws shudder the ship. I raised my hand in farewell to my rascally acquaintance, be he who he may, who stood upon the quay. Then —it caught my eye—I saw that same rough-coated dog I had seen in the walled yard at Emirghian. Not a pi-dog, it was rather of the type kept by shepherds at Angora to protect their prized flocks, a large fierce animal of the reddish colour of the jackal. This brute came bounding towards the quay whilst behind it hastened two Turks. Neither of them was the horrible creature I had seen wielding the hammer. When they found that the ferry had put to sea they slowed their pace—it had been very remarkable to witness a Turk running—and ambled towards the water. Both were fat, dressed shabbily in the cloth coat and red fez of their kind, the thinner of the two having an unrolled black umbrella besides. Then I saw that they were acquainted with my old companion. They came up with him, one on either side, just as he turned to quit the quay. I could not see his face, and the distance was increasing every moment as the ferry slid away from the shore, but the impression was conveyed to me that the old ruffian was surprised, and not pleasantly. Had the Turks looked less criminal—and had the reappearance of the hound not caused me a tremor of alarm—I could have believed that he

22

was a fugitive and that they were officers of the law. I strained to make out more as the scene receded; but met for my pains only a long hard stare flung at me in no friendly fashion across the water by the fatter of the two Turks. Though I turned quickly away, I was aware that my appearance was now printed indelibly upon the memory of one of the most villainous customers I have ever seen.

II

Acquaintance with a Sweep's Daughter,
and how I set her Papa to clean my Chimneys

DUSK WAS FADING colours out of the vaprous light when my
ferry entered the Golden Horn, where the bustle of the waterway
meets the bustle of the street, below the famed skyline of Stamboul. Along the hills' brow that skyline writhes like an immense
dark serpent twined amongst the minarets, its humped coils the
mosques it has swallowed. From the water I heard the thin crying
of the muezzin which pierces the sky, and pierces one's heart,
precisely as do the bells of an English church across cornfields and
woods at evening : that call to prayer which, in these last years of
the nineteenth century, when the modern world has progressed so
far from Faith towards Doubt (that dark serpent swallowing the
mosques upon the skyline), it seems a betrayal of one's modernity
to answer, and a betrayal of one's heart to ignore.

But if the fading light, the screaming of the swifts, the long
sob of the muezzin, were melancholy, the bridge which spans the
Golden Horn at Galata was a receipt to revive one's spirits, and
restore one's faith in life and humanity, if not in God. I stepped
ashore onto the rocking platform under its spans and pushed my
way up the ladder-like stairs to the bridge itself. There I payed
my ten *paras* to one of the collectors who flit through the throng
like so many Charons gathering tolls from those who cross the
Stygian stream, their white smocks ghostly in the dusk. Certainly
no passage in this world carries a traffic more representative of
the human race than the bridge at Galata. I could scarcely make
my way for the press of the crowd : merchants driving their
donkeys; water-carriers so awkward to pass, here a Tartar's van
with a wheel off and its load spilled, there a group of dervishes
—naked, ash-smeared—wailing and striking out with their staffs,
hamels whose spindly shanks seemed like to buckle under their

vast burdens, occasionally a pasha's carriage moving more swiftly in a storm of blows and curses dealt out by its coachman to part the crowd; shouts and cries, lights and flares reflected in the water; and everywhere, of course, the human débris of the East, beggars and cripples, wretches without hands, without noses—without faces or souls one might say, if one had ignored the muezzin's call. In travelling, however, an outlook inured to distress, like a digestion proof against foreign cooking, is essential to the traveller's enjoyment of the varied scenes of Asiatic life. I felt my spirits rise at the realisation that I formed part of this multi-farious crowd. It was indeed the realisation of a childhood dream —or the coming-to-life of the child within my bosom—for the Levant, as I have said, had ever fascinated me, and as a child I had pored by the hour together over an atlas of Asia, learning like a magic spell to transport me thither the names of the tribes that inhabited these lands, planning expeditions (with Marco Polo for dragoman) to be undertaken on hobby horses by myself and Rachel, now my wife but then my comrade. In the traffic upon the bridge my eyes at last beheld, as I believed, Tajiks and Hazares, Druses, Magyars, Yezzites, Tates and Bashkirs in their high lambskin hats, Kalmucks, Kurds and Lazes, Cherkess, Armenian and Jew. Rogues and robbers I imagined them to be, and I felt that the experiences of the afternoon had connected me to them, so that I too had earned my right to swagger across the Golden Horn not as a mere tourist but as a personage with an intrigue on hand to match the intrigues which swarmed around me.

Finding that I had exhausted all my small change (keeping one-self supplied with *metallik* in Turkey is as ticklish as keeping one-self supplied with sovereigns in Mayfair) I was obliged to walk up the Grande Rue to Pera instead of taking the funicular. Even this I enjoyed, dirty and ill-made, and worse lighted, as the street is. By the time I reached the hotel night had fallen, and I was an hour beyond our time for dining. I might have been robbed or murdered for all my wife knew. To discover whether any alarm had been felt as to my safety, I went first of all quietly to my own rooms—in lieu of any open display of affection, constant tests and experiments must be made (so marriage had taught me) to deduce circumstantially what is one's worth to one's spouse. My evening clothes were laid out. No agitation ruffled the air.

Through my dressing-room I approached my wife's quarters. And as always happens—as though my heart would not learn by my head's experience—I walked faster and threw open the door eagerly, calling as I entered :

'Rachel! Rachel! Are you there?'

And there came, as there always did, an excited response, a feminine flutter, then her light-footed dark self rushing towards me : rushing, alas, only to stop, the urgent forward incline of her body checked, before we were within reach of one another's arms. 'Ah,' she sighed, 'it's you. Hello.'

There we stood. In her puddle of light, sewing, Nanny watched. Nanny—! Day and night, it seemed, she sat sewing or mending for Rachel, a surrogate Penelope whose never-finished task kept suitors at bay. Was it because of Nanny that Rachel did not continue her run into my arms? Or was it for Nanny's eyes that she made the pretence she did of welcoming me? I looked into Rachel's eyes; deep and dark, they had gone dead of feeling, as I knew my own had done. And yet our two hearts had almost met.

'You have eaten your dinner I take it?' I said coldly.

'Yes. You were so late. We didn't know.'

'I had better find something to eat I suppose. I won't trouble you with coming in again. Goodnight.'

'Goodnight. One or two letters have come—but we can speak of them when you are more at leisure, perhaps tomorrow. Goodnight.' Now she kissed my cheek, now that there was no emotion between us. She turned away, and so did I. I did not like to close the door between her rooms and mine. But in a moment Nanny rose and closed it for me.

I dressed, and dined alone in the tall and empty gloom of the dining-room, thinking of Rachel and myself. It often happened, I am sure, that when my footstep approached her room—when she heard my voice—both of us half believed that a miracle had taken place, and that we would come together not coldly, as we had parted, but in the innocence and comradeship which we had shared together as children. It was never so. If nothing else interposed, there was sure to be Nanny. All my life I had associated Rachel's nanny with the disagreeable sensation of being caught *in flagrante delicto*; the crime I cannot recall, but a distinct picture

26

forms of Rachel frogmarched away by Nanny, whilst guilt settled upon me . . .

We had been uncommon thick, Rachel and I, and had shared everything in life until I had gone away to school at eleven or so. Whether raiding a caravanserai beyond the Oxus, or sacking bazaars along the Golden Road, or flying as fugitives from the treacherous Bakhtiyari, with a fate worse than death upon our heels, we were essential to one another. I do not exactly recall what comprised the 'fate worse than death', but I have a notion that certain bodily functions were involved, and it is possible that it was some innocent proceeding of this kind that Nanny interrupted, dragging Rachel away and leaving me at the mercy of guilt. It is strange that my memory is occluded upon this issue . . .

What I do recall with tragic clarity, however, is the very moment of my severance from Rachel—I might say, the very moment when adulthood began. I had returned from school, and eagerly did I make the crossing from our rectory garden to the lawns and pleasaunces of Rachel's home, that vast queer erection of her father's, there to meet her as we had settled by letter. I found her in the cedar's shade. She was flying upon me out of the darkness on the swing, the wind of her coming blowing her hair from her face and her skirts from her legs—never swooped hawk or Harpy more predatory upon its prey. I stopped appalled. In my mind was knowledge picked up at school which made carrion of my mind for her to swoop upon. Rachel was a girl. That was my realisation. Rachel must suffer the disgusting indignities which had been whispered in my ear at night. I turned from the swing and ran as if for my life—and it was, it was indeed out of my childhood and into life that I was running, pursued by that fate worse than death which was now revealed to me.

Of course I returned, then or later, and of course we played; but never again innocently on my part. I could not forget what I knew. It was not quite the first piece of knowledge to separate me from Rachel—learning that Father Christmas did not exist, and that her papa was a Jew, predated this incident—and it was not to be the last: most of the knowledge drilled into the head of an English boy of the upper class serves to separate him (as is proper) from all but a handful of the human race. But learning that she was female was the most fundamental of these stages of separation by knowledge. I could not be in her company without the rankness of her sexual nature reeking in my mind like a dog's mess she might have brought into the drawing-room on her shoe. Indeed in my head I can still see her swinging out of the dark of the cedar, bare legs wide and feet hooked out like talons swooping upon me.

To this barrier is now added another, subsequent upon our marriage : money. Since we were wed I was never in her presence, I believe, that I wasn't contriving how best to abstract the needful from her without submitting myself to the indignity of asking, or to the humiliation of thanking. There were thus strong deterrents to my passing much of my time in Rachel's company. To dine alone, drinking Champagne without the sensations of guilt I underwent when consuming luxuries in her presence, was a pleasurable finish to a day which had opened up enterprising prospects of pleasure to come—when I should be master of an establishment at Emirghian.

The relationship between Rachel's family (or her father, for she had no mother) and my own might appear on the face of it a simple one. Her father owned the parish of which my father was rector. Yet for the persons involved this simple fact bristled with complexities and with those social anomalies, where fortune is not matched with breeding, which cause so much distress, especially in country districts. For one thing, old Dolfuss had purchased the estate of my father's elder brother, a profligate so deep in debt that house and land were sold on his succession without his ever inhabiting them. For another, this fine Mr Dolfuss had pulled down my father's old home, a plain brick mansion built at the beginning of this century, and had erected in its place a perfectly enormous structure in a style averred to be Byzantine. A third aspect of the situation which exasperated my father was that old Dolfuss, who had of course purchased the advowson with the estate, and was therefore my father's patron, was a Jew. This I always found rather funny, but my father (who had left off hair shirts and the use of the 'discipline' when Newman went over to Rome in '45) was chafed in spirit to hold his living from an Israelite. I call Dolfuss 'old' but he was a very much younger man than my father, not above 40 when he bought up the estate in the 1860s, whilst my father was then 50 or more. Dolfuss was widowed almost at once (his wife passing away in giving birth to Rachel, their only child) whilst my father was newly wed, the bachelor habit thrown off (if briefly : by the time I knew him he epitomised bachelordom once more) under an impulse as much precipitated by theology as by biology, I believe.

It will be seen that there were complications in the relation of rectory to manor, the more so when my mother's character is considered. Almost 40 when she was married, having earned her bread for many a long year as an amanuensis in North Oxford, her enthusiasms were of the most arid kind—the Oxyrrhynchus sayings of Jesus, iconography in the Protevangelium, the Sassanian kings—and the style of her mind was such that she viewed inter-course with Mr Dolfuss as the owner of a china shop views intercourse with a bull. Plainly neither my mother nor my father wanted to have to do with their neighbour—and if they met they fell out, for I remember high words over the Bulgarian massacres in '76, Dolfuss being a Gladstonian and my father an Anti-atrocitarian, like all people of breeding at the time—but they quietened their Christian conscience by making sure that my brother and I accepted all invitations to the manor. We doted upon it. We were not offended by the Eastern turrets and looped windows which rose upon the site of my grandfather's old home; we were not oppressed in spirit by the glinting domes and minarets which bore down up on my father like the ordnance of an infidel army encamped at his door; we were not frozen to death in the vast and lofty halls and colonnades, a fate my parents claimed to fear should they accept to dine there. On the contrary, the newness of the toys, the shininess of marble stair-ways, the vulgarity of statues and suits of Turkish armour and vast canvases depicting battle and pillage in the East—this Aladdin's cave appealed to all those instincts in children which make a child the despair of parents who think that their genteel tastes should be inherited. My father was always eager to hear details which would confirm Dolfuss as 'impossible'. He considered that Dolfuss by his lapses of taste—above all by building his improbable house—'gave himself away' : in fact of course the reverse was true, the house making as plain a statement of the truth about Dolfuss as the nose on his face. We children saw only advantage in vulgar display, and in this pleasure dome which the feeblest imagination could convert into the court of Kubilai Khan. I had not yet been taught what it is to be a Jew. I envied Rachel her

29

father's trade, for on account of it she had tin working models of his ships which we sent on voyages across his lakes. I envied her the Turkish pavilions, the marble-latticed kiosks amongst bamboo thickets, and above all the stone elephant up to his knees in the lake. Not until I went to school did I learn to despise all this. By then too I had heard the rumours put into circulation as to the nature and conduct of Dolfuss' business. A fact was discovered, or invented by the County, which caused a great deal of derision, namely, that the foundation of the creature's fortune had been laid upon extensive imports of dog's excrement from the Levant, a substance apparently necessary to the preparation of leather for fine ladies' gloves.

However fastidious the County felt about Dolfuss, those with marriageable sons had few objections to Rachel. As my own awareness of her sex—and of her fortune and race—ended our old comradeship, these same attributes gained her many new friends, my elder brother amongst them. I do not suppose that she understood my withdrawal (for she of course retained her innocence) but she did occasionally chide me, in the laughing happy style she had, with standing too much upon my dignity and refusing to admit that I remembered the childish games we had shared. Once she told me that when I had ceased to play with her she had continued our adventures alone by writing down tales of our travels. I enquired stiffly if I was still her companion in these expeditions. 'No, no, poor Archie,' she replied in her teasing manner, 'I'm afraid you lost your leg to a lion in the Dasht-e-lut and can't keep up with me any more.' I was obscurely offended at this, and often puzzled over my ill-luck in the lion's jaws. . . But Rachel had the knack of upsetting my dignity, so that I avoided being alone with her. I was then acquiring, too, as I rose to power at school, the superior and élitist instincts of an English gentleman, which must of necessity sever one from inter-course with those of inferior race or social station—sever one, it might be said, from intercourse with the inferior sex. Then, when I was sixteen or so, there occurred an incident which put my relations with Dolfuss and daugther upon the footing they were to retain.

Dolfuss was by this time Master of Foxhounds, a position much relished by Jews for the license it affords as to riding roughshod over the property of their betters, and hounds were to draw a cover near the rectory one September morning. Since my brother had first call upon my father's only horse, I had walked across the fields in the early light to see the fun. Glorious as was the morning with gossamer and dew, and the sunlight aslant the magnificent shabbiness of autumn trees, I soon became conscious of the indignity of my position, on foot amongst people of a rough class. I escaped them by entering the wood where, of course, I fell into the danger of being discovered and told off by a hunt servant. My agitation was extreme until at last the hunt left the cover, having killed a leash of cubs, and I was free to return to my breakfast. But the sound of an approaching horse caused me to shrink back amongst the bracken and brambles of the glade where I had been hiding from the hunt. Nearer and nearer drew the horse, and lower and lower I sank among the herbiage; when it became evident that the horseman had entered this very glade, I was committed to remaining hidden if I could. The horse stopped, a saddle creaked. I peeped between the bracken fronds and saw—Rachel. I was debating whether or no to rise before her from the brake, as did Pluto before Proserpine of old, when I took in aghast the meaning of the activities I watched. She had dismounted. She was wrestling with her garments. I closed my eyes, but not alas my ears, against this scene of shame. Worse was to come : I opened my eyes at last to find that Rachel had begun to pick blackberries, which would inevitably bring her to my hiding place. What was I to do? Retreat was impossible. As a gentleman I could not advance and betray that I had witnessed her degradation. I fell back upon a ruse. Shrinking lower into the bracken I carefully extended my limbs and feigned sleep. Before long the brambles forming my cover were shaken. There was a shriek.

'Archie ! Whatever are you at?'

'Miss Dolfuss !' I started up, amazement imprinted upon my features, dashing my hand through my hair. We were very close, her lips parted in surprise, her colour high, her bosom heaving. I shrank away, stammering that I had been overcome with fatigue and had dozed off—'These London balls, you know,' I finished, 'knock a fellow up no end.'

'I don't believe it,' she replied.

'Upon my word, Miss Dolfuss,' I assured her earnestly, 'I saw nothing.'

'I meant I don't believe you have been to a London ball in

your life, Archie,' she retorted, laughter colouring her voice, 'now admit it.'

'Of course, if you require me to,' I said. I could not see my way to escaping from my brambly den without touching her, for she stood in my path picking and eating the berries whose ripeness stained her lips. Ordinarily still a schoolroom miss in short skirts with her hair down—she was no more than sixteen—her riding habit lent her the formidable aspect of a mature Diana of the Chase. She was right: I had been to no London balls. I had no experience of the sex. I could not meet her dark humorous eyes in which child and woman seemed blended—a happy mélange very far from the stiff conjunction of child and man in myself.

'Come Archie, how absurd you are,' she said, the laughter breaking out in her voice like a brook into sunlight, 'have a blackberry at least, if you've time before the next court levée.'

Awkward to stay, awkward to go; in my mind I cursed her, and the whole world, for the succession of awkwardnesses which made up my life away from the certainties of school. Her fingers approached my lips with a ripe berry. Affecting to see a slug upon it I took the fruit and hurled it from me. I was breaking past her out of my prison of briars when I heard a horseman enter the glade behind me, and a voice call out:

'By heaven, what is this!'

It was Mr Dolfuss, his voice squeaky with rage, bundled up on his thoroughbred in his usual grocer's style of riding. I turned, expecting him to apologise immediately he recognised me. But his anger did not subside. 'So it's you, young fellow, eh? You on foot are you? Blackberrying, is that it? If you was looking for more than blackberries, sir, with my girl, why—I'd skin you alive so I would!'

'I suppose I have a right to walk through this wood if I please,' I said, disliking his tone.

'I don't know as you have,' he shrieked out angrily, 'I don't know as you've any rights except them as you can pay for.'

The vulgarity of this was of course beyond anything, so I turned my back on the pair of them and began to stroll off, well pleased that the opportunity to extricate myself without loss of dignity had presented itself. The Jew then started in to abuse his daughter, telling her she wasn't a child that could run loose any longer, but an heiress whom he counted upon to do him honour when the

32

time came. I would have left them to it had a cry not made me turn my head. What had happened I am not sure, but Rachel lay sprawled upon the ground. Were it only that the cad had chosen to knock his daughter down I wouldn't have troubled myself, but her horse had broken free and was trotting towards me. Not to have caught the brute might have looked like cowardice, so I seized the bridle and led the animal back to the spot where Rachel lay. Her pallor, her ivory neck, contrasted most becomingly with raven tresses strayed from their pins. Dolfuss had hopped off his horse and was kneeling by her, all the coxcomb knocked out of him.

'She ain't strong, that's where it is,' he said, 'tumbles quick as wink into these queer goes when a thing happens as upsets her. Oh dear!'

One couldn't help being put in mind of a tinker whose dog has been knocked over, the way he rocked to and fro and squeaked out little wails. I stooped down. 'I'll take hold of her legs,' I said 'and we'll lift her——'

'You keep your hands off her legs!' he piped up fiercely; and then, in a broken-down tone, continued, 'Don't mind me, Archie, I know you was always friends, and handsome I thought it on your pa's part to let it be so. But now she's a right to look—to aspire—if you take my meaning, her an heiress. Oh dear, oh dear.'

His patting of her hand had taken no effect, so up he bounced and trotted across to his horse where he set about fiddling loose a flask. I was gazing down at Rachel, torn between pity for the child in her and desire for the womanly form abandoned at my feet, when her eyes suddenly opened. Meeting my gaze took her aback. Her faint was a sham, no question. Swiftly she moved a slim forefinger to lips still stained with fruit, enjoining my silence, and then her long-lashed eyelids, veined it seemed with the same purple dye as her lips, closed once more over her dark eyes. Evidently she found the swoon a convenient trap-door through which to drop out of inconvenient situations. I saw no reason to give her game away. If Dolfuss chose to beat his daughter, or if she chose to funk the chastisement, it was all one to me : one doesn't, I suppose, expect from the weaker sex that heroism in the matter of standing firm under punishment—of taking your medicine like a man—which is amongst the chief virtues inculcated by our great schools. I left the two of them that morning with quite a new-formed notion of each of them, and of their relationship. In glimpsing Dolfuss with his temper up I had seen a very different article from Rachel's jolly little papa who used to slide down his marble bannisters to make us laugh as children; I felt I knew now what he was like when he was at his bucket shop, and I saw too that he regarded his daughter—his 'heiress'! —as a commercial property from which he expected profit.

I rose out of their sphere at that time, for I was a successful schoolboy and consequently moved in a set of rank and fortune. At school, like the heroes of old, we ruled a world which was a universe *in parvo* (whether the school world had been constructed according to the blueprint of Creation, or whether the *alumni* of the school had altered Creation to fit the school's blueprint, makes scant difference to the fact of the matter, namely, that the ruling of that school, and subsequently of the British Empire and so of the world, was in the hands of a dozen or so families). Arm in arm we swaggered through the streets, looked upon with the same fearful respect by scugs as was felt by the inferior races of Egypt for Lord Wolseley, or by the Afghan savages for Lord Roberts. For prowess in battle we substituted success at games; we practised the heroic capacity to withstand pain, misfortune, and death, by our readiness to submit to punishment without question, or murmur; indeed we would submit to a flogging or administer one with the rare indifference of a soldier who submits himself to the chances of war. We had laws and customs quite as ancient as any enacted by Parliament, and for these we would flog or be flogged as readily as ever soldier or missionary slew or was slain in darkest Africa for the sake of the Ten Commandments. We learned that unquestioning obedience which taught us to obey with equal alacrity the rule forbidding us to walk upon the left-hand pavement, and the rule forbidding us to steal; or, if we broke either rule, we learned to sustain our punishment with the fortitude of an English gentleman in the hands of the enemy. A simplified system no doubt, which might be accused of blurring nice distinctions between morals and manners (by punishing lapses of both with the same rod) but the proof of the pudding is in the eating, and I take it that none of us who underwent the system (save a few renegades and degenerates) would quarrel with the assertion that the world is better ruled, and ruled by a finer set of fellows, under our system than at any time in its history.

Aye, and it was an Empire *in parvo* that we ruled at school. For subject races we had the Lower School, for the socially inferior administrative class we had King's Scholars; objection might be made that in this Creation of ours which formed our characters we had no females, but a moment's reflexion will show the triviality of this cavil, especially when the peculiar sweetness of the intercourse between master and fag is considered. In his fag, the young proconsul had a being utterly timid, utterly within his power, an unformed and tender creature in whose innocent mind he stood as a God incarnate—what better preparation could he have than this for his dealings with the young maidenhood of England? Over our fags we learned to exercise the benevolent despotism which alone ensures a peaceful hearth. By showing an interest in their childish pursuits, by sitting on their beds and encouraging them to falter out confidences as to home and parents and early history, one could be sure of receiving from them a slave's devotion. The occasional beating was of course necessary . . . No relationship in subsequent life has ever quite gratified me as did that sweet relation between master and fag.

I have digressed, but it may be seen from this how far I had risen above the sphere of a Jew pedlar and his daughter. Dolfuss seemed exceedingly small beer from the circles I moved in at school—as indeed (*res augusta domi*) did my father's rectory. It had been my father's view that the decline of our family's importance—the loss of the estate—made it more than ever essential for his sons to display the superior education and habits of gentlemen. When my elder brother emigrated to New South Wales, where he went into paint, my father would close his eyes and shake his head at all mention of his name thereafter, as though praying in his mind for a lost soul. As a result of my brother's defection I had a good deal of grace in the matter of overdrafts and long bills from the tailors, the unspoken threat between Father and me being that if he didn't stump up the blunt, then I too would go into paint.

There are wonderfully few things a fellow can go in for, and remain a gentleman. I couldn't afford the Army or the Diplomatic. The Church of course was the obvious choice. The Church attracted me—its obvious fitness in my case apart—on account of an enduring vignette stored in my mind from earliest times : the picture was of myself bathed in the golden light of a summer's evening at the window of our day-nursery, watching the swifts wheel and dive in the heavens and listening to the sad clamorous tongues of the church bells. I was hiding behind the curtains from the summons to bed. The day escaped upwards, slipping through my fingers like happiness or gold, borne upward on the bells and the swifts' wings, ascending from the darkening earth into the wonderful clarity of the empyrean. Then I looked down and saw my father as, following his curate, he made his way with due dignity through the shrubbery to the churchyard. I saw the white-ness of his linen extinguished by the vestry door, and I heard the bells cease. Their summons had succeeded; my father had an-swered it. That then, the path he took, was the path to heaven. The dark, silent earth only remained. On the ceasing of the bells, a great emptiness and darkness and silence filled the world. Now I might as well go to bed, for the light had gone . . . This image would, I fancied, pass muster as a vocation with most bishops, and of course the moral principles of Christianity were already familiar to me as an Englishman and a gentleman. Unfortunately, Father had more or less lost his Faith about this time, and put any number of obstacles in my way. His intellectual obstacles I could leap or circumvent—mounting Archbishop Pratt to jump Colenso, relying upon Professor Browne to carry me clear over the double-oxer of Bradlaugh and Besant—but Father's temporal impediments were another matter. If he had chosen to come out strong against the Church and make a rumpus, he would have put paid to my chances of securing a decent billet after Ordina-tion.

Father had a history of losing his Faith, or at any rate of mis-laying it for years at a time. The first of his Doubts came along within months of Ordination, I suppose in the early 1840s, and concerned the Efficacy of Good Works in procuring Salvation. He wrote off pell-mell to Dr Newman, who replied with an invitation to join his community at Littlemore. Here numerous clerics with Doubts and Tendencies were gathered, like spiritual hypochondriacs clustered at a railway station from which trains ran frequently to Rome. No sooner did my father cure one Doubt than he was infected by another, and with these he wrestled grimly, applying the 'discipline' to his shoulders, spreading his

36

bedding upon the floor, and assisting in compiling the biographies of ever more improbable saints, until Dr Newman himself went over to Rome and left them all flat. My father was offended, feeling that Newman's behaviour had not been quite gentleman-like, and in his umbrage he became an out-and-out High-and-Dry man. There were still a number of years to wait before the incumbent of the living in his father's gift made way for him, and he took up one or two curacies; but the subordinate nature of the work didn't agree with him, and he rapidly discovered scruples which led to resignation. In the end I believe a lump sum was offered to the incumbent of my grandfather's rectory, who retired to a chaplaincy at Nice, for there was little or nothing in the Church of England's canon which my father had not Doubted, and he threatened to begin again at Good Works if his mind was not stabilized by a comfortable rectory house and £2,000 a-year. However, the habit of upending his intellectual positions stayed with him. By temperament, by nature, by custom—and, unfortunately, by philosophic conviction—a bachelor, at 46 he suddenly reversed his whole intellectual stance upon the question of Virginity. Hitherto (like Hurrell Froude whose *Remains* was his bedside book) my father had entertained 'a high severe idea of the intrinsic excellence of Virginity'. Now he abandoned this position. I do not know what exactly occurred to overturn him, but the year of his marriage (1864) was the year of Dr Newman's public debate with Canon Kingsley, and it is possible that my father (still smarting perhaps from Newman's apostasy) felt bound to support the Canon's stand against every aspect of Jesuitry, their celibacy as much as their casuistry. A true intellectual, the body's wishes and needs entirely unconsulted in the mind's decisions, he was married, within weeks of reading *What Then Does Dr Newman Mean?*, to the only single female of his acquaintance. More, my brother was conceived. Had he but delayed till Newman had written his reply, the *Apologia pro vita sua*, it is probable that he would not have acted with such pro-miscuous haste, for that book soon joined Froude's *Remains* at my father's bedside, indeed replaced my mother in that intimate position. He took once more to sleeping on the floor, an evasive posture in a married man, although as it happened my mother too slept upon the floor (of another room) to accustom herself, so she claimed, to the discomforts she must expect to endure upon her projected, but never executed, travels in the Holy Land. The reader will not need to be told that their two children never saw the inside of a high bed until sent away to school.

The penalty which Providence had exacted from my father for his momentary dereliction of Virginity was a heavy one. He intimated as plainly as he could that children and family life were a punishment richly deserved but almost intolerable, and a punishment in which all the family could share. Canon Kingsley's works were burned. Like Pusey in 1848, my father formally gave up smiling.

The Church, then, did not seem the ideal career for me; the more so because our family living was now in the gift of old Dolfuss, and I had no idea (at that time) of being beholden to an Israelite purveyor of dogs' excrement for my bread. There remained the Bar. This had the advantages of being in London, of taking three years to prepare for, and of requiring little capital outlay apart from the expenses of living in Town. I calculated these expenses, doubled them for good measure, and put the screw upon my father for the sum total. He approved the Bar (in part to flout the pronouncement of his long-dead *bête noire* Dr Arnold, that Advocacy is incompatible with the pursuit of Truth) and came down with the flimsy. I took rooms in Berkeley Street, began to eat the requisite dinners at the Inner Temple, hired an usher to cram me one morning a week, and set to work to enjoy the London of the late '80s.

It was amazing how quick I found myself in Queer Street.

I recall that I came in one night from playing dummy whist, not a year from the date I had reached London, and concluded that I might as well put a ball through my brain at once. The way the expenses had mounted up was the very deuce. I had attempted to recoup by plunging on the quads, and the long and the short of the matter was that I was plucked. The crammer had gone long since—the very first of my economies—so I had no prospect of passing the bar examination, and consequently no chance of earning a living. Besides, there could be no question of *earning* the sort of tin which supported the round of dinners and balls and country houses in which I had joined; one had to inherit or marry that size of income—unless you are some sort of commercial fellow like Dolfuss, and then you ain't invited anyway. The thought of old Dolfuss stirred up an idea in my mind

38

as I sat in my rooms drinking gin-and-water that summer night, the windows open upon the rumour of pleasure still animating the London streets. It seemed to me that this was the only kind of life worth the name of living, and undoubtedly it was the style of life I had been bred up to by birth and education, if not by fortune; all I stood in need of was a means of financing it. Well, thought I, it ain't a bit of good knowing sweeps if you don't make 'em clean your chimneys. I resolved to make a stab at Dolfuss' money, and, if I failed, to blow out my brains directly. Upon this resolution, and gin-and-water, I slept surprisingly sound.

The existence of Miss Rachel Dolfuss was not entirely unknown in London. Large in the provinces, Dolfuss' fortune wasn't such that it made a splash in Mayfair. But he had hired the spinster daughter of some tumbledown earl to present his daughter at Court, as well as a house in Bruton Street and a brace of footmen prepared to wear powder, and from this he had hoped to float off Miss Rachel rather as he launched his ships. I had kept clear. If ever I did run across her, she seemed to quiz me in a way which wouldn't allow that I had grown quite beyond and above the childhood we had shared. She had a sharp humorous look in those dark orbs of hers which went a good way to deflate me. 'I remember you when you wasn't a dandy drawling after that fashion,' her eyes told me, 'and if I was to get you alone out blackberrying again, by George you'd be the same hobbledehoy you was before!' Her lack of obsequiousness—her want of gratitude— stood powerfully in her way as far as her father's hopes of a brilliant match were concerned, and she had been obliged by him to return year after year to the charge upon that ageing warhorse, Lady Mary Oxton. Her failure was gratifying to me on all counts —I found I couldn't cut a dash while she was by, and nothing turns one against a girl quicker than that—and her fortune was still in the market to be played for.

A day or two later I was knocking a billiard ball about a table at the club when Muffet, Lord Tupper's heir, walked in and rang the bell for brandy-and-soda. 'Hundred up, old fellow?' he drawled out, thumbs in his waistcoat and cigar between his teeth. 'Guinea a-point, eh?'

We began to play. Of course the deuced luck ran all his way, as luck always does for a man who is as rich as a Jew and a lord to boot. Wondering how I was to pay him (if he reached a hundred in his second break, as seemed likely) I asked, 'Know anything of a fellow name of Dolfuss do you?'

'That the Jew from Liverpool got the daughter?'

'That's the article. Know him do you?'

'My dear chap!'

'Know the girl I mean to say, met her have you? She's been taken about a good deal I believe. Lady Mary Oxton looking after her I'm told.'

'Met her, yes I have,' he replied, strolling round the table between shots, 'awful flat. Clever, poor health, invalidish sort. Awful flat. Lies about on sofas, don't you know. Nanny with her half time, taking her in, taking her out, a fellow couldn't come near her the time I saw her, stopping at Lexboro a Saturday-to-Monday that was. Stunner though,' he added, after dropping Black yet again into a pocket.

'She sweet on any one is she?'

'Didn't show at Lexboro. You thinking of entering are you?'

'Don't seem it's easy to get at her, this nanny you say, Lady Mary too.'

'Lady Mary don't signify,' he replied. 'Give her a pair of gloves and she'll bring the girl to tea. Give her a pair with a £5 note in 'em and she'll take herself off after tea and leave you the girl. It was her being in Lady Mary's charge put me up to thinking I'd have a dart myself, don't you know, for they say there'll be £10,000 a-year for the sportsman who puts his saddle on her. But the moment I got a little spoony with her in an arbour there at Lexboro, hanged if the girl didn't faint! Deuced awkward, girl fainting. Quite cut my hamstrings. Well old fellow,' he concluded, straightening up from the table, 'that's a hundred to your sixteen, so it's 86 guineas you owe me.'

It looks a little sharp if you correct a fellow's arithmetic, especially if he's a lord—smacks of the counting-house—so I let him enter the amount in his betting book whilst I rang the bell for more brandy-and-soda. 'How about a return?' I said. 'Suit you if we double the stake? Two guineas on the points?'

He was chalking his cue, quizzing me through his damned cigar smoke. 'You got the tin if you lose have you?' he asked.

Of course I had to laugh his insolence off, but I now knew that the doubt existed as to my ability to pay my debts of honour. If that doubt was confirmed, Society would close its doors to me.

What then would I have to live for? For one who may leave cards when he pleases upon a half dozen of Duchesses—who has been nodded at by a Royal Personage—who has hopes of an invitation to Londonderry House—there is nothing but dissatisfaction in the society of mere mortals. All the precepts I had learned since quitting childhood had fitted me up with the outlook of an English nobleman upon £20,000 a year. I might dislike Muffet—might resent his insolence—but I didn't dislike it half as much as I should have disliked the society of his inferiors. The deuce of it is that one may be bred up to share Society's sense of exclusiveness, and yet find oneself excluded; then indeed one has nowhere to turn.

With all this upon my mind I played wretchedly and lost again. As Muffet stood marking up the final debt in his book, he cut through my apologies for not having the blunt on my person by saying: 'I tell you what it is old fellow, you'd best settle up when you've got the Jew's money in your pocket, what?'

'Easier said than done,' I objected, my back to the fireplace and my hands lounged in my pockets; 'I've met the little brute, and he's dead set on a baronet at least for his tin.'

'You've nothing to offer the father Jew, so you steer clear of him,' Muffet advised. 'You cotton on to the daughter, that's your game, should be. You invest in some haberdashery for Lady Mary, keep her sweet, that's your first dodge; then lay in a stock of sal volatile to bring the young lady back to her scratch when she swoons on your chaise longue, and I'll be hanged if it don't all come right for you at last. Devilish keen on their daughters these commercial gents. Devilish keen. How'd he make his stiff, eh?'

'Why, shipping dog shit into Liverpool I'm told.'

'That's bad.' He shook his head. Then he cheered up and clapped me on the back. 'Never mind. It don't taint the tin.'

One of the letters Rachel had spoken of on my return from Emirghian the night previous proved to be from her father. He wrote that he projected a visit to us at Constantinople, should we remain there any length of time, for he had found his thoughts returning to a city which he had once known so well, and now wished to see once more. 'I don't see why we shouldn't stop on here,' I said to Rachel when I had read the letter.

She was lying on the sofa in her darkened sitting-room. Nanny stitched away at some female garment in a cranny of light at the window. I often thought that the old woman (having let a suitor slip under her guard and seize her charge) occupied herself with sewing undergarments rather in the remorseful spirit which might have caused an armorer to continue with his work of forging chastity belts although his châtelaine's virtue was compromised. Rachel said nothing, ivory hands crossed corpse-like upon her bosom. I never could quite make up my mind as to whether Rachel had chosen Nanny as her maid, or whether her father had wished the woman upon her.

'It don't seem to signify where you are,' I went on, 'so we may as well stop on here as move. A sofa at Pera is as comfortable as a sofa at Rome I suppose.'

'Upon my word, Mr Caper,' spoke up Nanny—who had listened I believe to every word I had ever spoken to my wife—'upon my blessed word, Rome would be the death of Miss Rachel it would! Yes, and I'm wondering at the heartlessness of them as can mention that Sodom of wickedness to us!'

'There is no question of Rome again,' I told her. At Rome I had made an attempt to possess myself of my wife's body. We had by then been married quite a month—but a month spent entirely upon the road, a night here and a night there, so that it had been possible to evade the physical issues of marriage in quarters which fell far short of story-book expectations as to the hymeneal bower. Rachel had delighted in travelling (a real journey reawakening her childish wanderlust) and had expected nothing beyond the kisses we had shared as children when travelling in our imaginations. At Rome however we had reached our destination. Excuses were at an end. Reality must be faced. It became necessary to confront the fact (long suspected, if only from the promiscuous freedom with which Rachel kissed me) that she was not cognisant of the rights of a husband over his wife's body. She appeared to think that kissing, which gratified only herself, quite discharged her duty towards me. And here is the dilemma; whilst insisting that one's wife's mind is pure, one must insist also that her body is prepared for its subjection to male needs. Rachel had no mother, and evidently Nanny and Lady Mary Oxton had told her nothing. At Rome, having dined *en garçon* with a Secretary of Embassy and visited one or two places of entertainment, I resolved to attempt the assault. Uproar was the result. I with-

42

drew, leaving Nanny racing about on the verge of hysterics with burnt feathers to revive her charge, the hotel blazing with lights, doctor sent for and a crowd of sightseeing chambermaids clustered at our door. Next day we had left Rome, and we had continued to travel until fetching up at Constantinople a fortnight since— as far as one can journey without quitting Christendom altogether. Rachel's health had remained low. 'No,' I repeated to Nanny, 'we will not return to Rome.'

'I should hope not indeed,' muttered she over her needle.

'Constantinople seems to suit you as well as anywhere, don't it?' I said to Rachel's prone form. She murmured something. I asked her to repeat it.

'Except my home,' she gasped out.

What had become of her passion for travel? It seemed that everything had been knocked out of her at once by her confrontation with the facts of married life at Rome. And what did she mean by home—that absurd Eastern palace of her father's, where I should have been little better than a lodger?

'Your home,' I reminded her, 'is where I choose to be. However,' I went on, seeing a way of securing my object, 'since you pine for the country, and since your father is bent on visiting us, I have no objection to taking a summer house somewhere upon the Bosphorus. Of course it would take time. I imagine such places would take a month or more at least to make habitable. The expense would be heavy too. But if you are determined to stay here, and if your father is determined to follow us about, I really see no other way. I shall have to give up most of my time to it I suppose.'

This speech of mine met with silence, as indeed had most of my speeches to her since our marriage. I do not know why I had fallen into this ceremonial, even perhaps pompous, manner of addressing Rachel. It seemed to have descended upon me unsought, a gift of tongues, when I was uncertain how to address Rachel as my wife. Uncertainty as to every aspect of marriage had assailed me the very moment that the door of the four-wheeler carrying us away from the wedding breakfast had closed upon us. This *vis-à-vis* with a strange female was a situation nothing in my education had prepared me to encounter. When, earlier, I had contrived a *tête-à-tête* with Rachel, by buying off Lady Mary, it was for a purpose. Each moment gained—each glance of those dark eyes—each kiss snatched or further liberty unscolded—had been another inch of ground gained towards my chief objective : marriage. Married, I found myself in the situation of a commander whose very success in war precipitates him into the unfamiliar circumstances of peace. Kisses need no longer be won—seclusion did not require contriving—interviews were not limited to half hours : before the growler had reached the Victoria Station Rachel's head had seemed to weigh exceeding heavy upon my shoulder, and our journey had seemed prolonged beyond all reason. I had set out to marry the money, and I found myself married to the daughter. From the first of the meetings I had sought with her, Rachel had resurrected the language of our shared childhood. Until I had made sure of her she might have talked in Hebrew so long as it was to me she addressed herself, but in a wife such language clearly wouldn't serve. Its whimsy aside, references to our early games and travels proposed an equality between us which struck at my authority as a husband. Thus I had cast about for a manner of addressing her rather as one might search for a common tongue if shipwrecked upon a desert island with a Hottentot; and I had settled upon a syntax and vocabulary quite removed from ordinary intercourse. Perhaps it was copied from my father's style of talking to my mother— not that I admired him for it, only that I knew no other way in which a husband might address his wife. What one inherits from a parent has little to do with intention, on either side.

At all events, having spoken, I walked from the room with a frown of disapproval. If Nanny thought I disapproved taking a house on the Bosphorus, she would encourage Rachel in that course. Upon Rachel my frowns—like my desires—were wasted as if upon an alabaster image. And in Berkeley Street she had used to make such light and happy work of kissing!

I gave up the conundrum of female behaviour and strolled down to smoke a cigar at the Cercle d'Orient, quite a decent sort of club on the Grande Rue, and to plan my manœuvre towards Emirghian. Dolfuss spoke of travelling out in September, and I counted upon a clear run at Emirghian until he arrived, for Rachel would be sure not to trouble me there. The lease and the furnishing must be settled, and then—my stomach turned over with that sensation of excitement I had but rarely experienced since leaving school—and then I would visit the *yessir bazar* with my old acquaintance of yesterday. A slave——! The very word suggested sweet submission. Money I did not for the moment trouble about, for Rachel would expect to entertain her father *en prince*, and would have to pay according. I had not found old Dolfuss altogether a bad sort in our new relationship. Lady Mary Oxton, whom I had been at no end of expense to keep sweet, had persuaded him that to see his daughter a countess was quite beyond the scope of a fortune such as his. She had, too, pointed out to him the fitness of his estate returning to my family, its rightful owners, so that before long he had quite knocked under and accepted his daughter's choice.

I reconciled myself as best I could to becoming son-in-law to a Jew pedlar. Now that I looked into the matter I discovered that Jews are not all of one sort, as I had supposed, but have many divisions and sub-divisions of which they are quite vain. The Sephardic Jews, for instance, whose descent is from their race's expulsion from Spain in 1492, regard themselves as altogether a superior type, both in personal dignity and by the extent of their commercial enterprises, to the Ashkenazik Jew, German by origin, for the most part mere hawkers in retail trades. I made up my mind that Dolfuss was certainly of the Sephardic division. Besides, Jews of all kinds were everywhere making progress in Society : the first Jew judge had recently been appointed; a fellow called Goldsmid had been made a baronet, I discovered, as long ago as 1841—why, with Rosebery's influence one wouldn't have been at all surprised to hear of the number of Jew peers being multiplied, especially from amongst the Prince's toadies and moneylenders (though they were inferior representatives of the race, for the most part German or Austrian, where there exists a tradition of 'Court Jews' made or broken by princelings in return for huge bribes). No; I was quite satisfied that there was nothing disgraceful in allying myself to the daughter of a substantial shipowner of Levantine descent. Nowadays it is only Christians of a very old-fashioned sort who regard the Jews with the contempt one was brought up to think they merited.

My father, unfortunately, was a Christian of just this sort. His prejudice made the question of taking over the estate from Dolfuss, and living on his doorstep married to a Jewess, too hazardous for comfort. I therefore decided to take a wedding tour—a journey unlimited by time or extent—in the hope that all difficulties would somehow resolve themselves in my absence. Aside from the question of where we were to live (and I could not imagine myself comfortable shut up in the country for long) there was the delicate question of my relationship to Society now that I had encumbered myself with Rachel. There lay in an immediate departure, too, escape from my creditors, who of course had pestered me to death when my marriage was announced. So we had left England, Rachel embarking on the Channel packet with the glee of a child—for it was in truth our childhood adventures she thought now to enjoy as a grown woman. Had this influence caused us to make our way eastwards, towards the mountains of Kurd and Circassian, the plains of Turcoman and Uzbeg where those early adventures had been set? Now we stood upon the very shore of Europe, Asia within view of our windows, where one step further would carry us over the Devil's Current into regions of peril and barbarous dark such as Europe has long forgotten. Here we had halted. There seemed no prospect of our travelling on together. For a creature unable to face the reality of life at Rome, the reality of Asia Minor was not to be risked. Even as far as Emirghian I had travelled alone, whilst Rachel moped and scribbled, and pined for home.

The problems of 'home' had in no way resolved themselves. A further irregularity in Dolfuss' household—putting him past praying for in my father's eyes—was the presence there of a child of five or six years, spoken of as a nephew, a lively, dark-skinned little fellow who seemed amazingly out of place in the English countryside, especially in winter, and who served to remind one, with his quick foreign ways and his un-English speech, to how distinct a race the whole family of Dolfuss belonged. Since Nanny was attached as a body servant to Rachel, the little boy (his name was Ben) had a young nursemaid of unidentifiable Asiatic origin. When this girl had first arrived in the village she had been the very image of the shy, shrinking inmate of the *zenana*, but a very short contact with English manners (or perhaps with English menservants) had sufficed to emancipate her most thoroughly. My father hinted darkly that the relationship of 'uncle', 'nursemaid' and 'nephew' covered a sinful liaison. I liked old Dolfuss for it, whatever the truth of the matter. I should have liked to have enquired of Rachel exactly who the boy was, and how he came to be there, but I did not

46

find it possible to speak to her on intimate subjects since our marriage. I had fallen into a somewhat dismissive way of speaking of her father and her home, which was not consistent with showing interest in the boy's origins. Rachel was extremely fond of him. I wondered if he too—and his attractive nursemaid—would be travelling to Constantinople. Stories my father had told of her scandalous behaviour in the village had whetted my appetite . . . She was of the languorous, odalisque type, full-figured and large-eyed, and I realised, now that I thought of her, that she represented exactly my notion of the inmates of harem and slave market, whose unclothed charms, in the paintings of Ingres or Solomon, make such an appeal to Western imaginations.

I could wait no longer. I jumped up from my cane chair at the club and set out directly for Galata, whence I intended taking the first ferry to Emirghian. I descended by steep streets towards the Golden Horn. It was a brilliant day, the glitter of light on blue water glimpsed between wooden houses, the sun illuminating domes and marble in Stamboul. Boats off Seraglio Point dipped their bows in the white spray heaped up from the Marmara by a southerly breeze. I was aware of an appetite for adventure. *Cras ingens iterabimus aequor!*

III

I encounter a Welsh Zealot,
and obtain a Sinister Introduction

THERE WAS NO difficulty about leasing the house at Emirghian. The business was of course interminably long-winded, lakes of coffee and mountains of sweetmeats must be consumed in the owner's charming garden at the water's edge, or cross-legged upon his divans indoors; and the cheerful attempts to rob me by inserting or deleting clauses (in the translation of documents by scribes in his pay) quadrupled the time needed for such a transaction. But at last the money was handed over, a half year's rent in gold, and I was master of the little house upon the creek.

In furnishing it I determined to follow altogether the Turkish style, being much taken by the voluptuous appointments of my landlord, a respectable Armenian, upon whose silk rugs and bolsters I had found myself inspired to feel quite pasha-like. With the hotel dragoman I visited the Grand Bazar which, though much injured by the earthquake of the previous year and in parts ruinous, still presented an astonishing spectacle. With Persian shawls, with rugs from the Caucasus and Qum, with the metalwork of Khorassan, with silver and gold wrought in Beyrout and with antiquities from Persepolis or Sidon, with Brusa silk, or with ivories brought through the passes of the Pamirs from China—here was the end of the Golden Road, and here existed a mart from which one could fit out a background for all the fantasies of the Arabian Nights. London is an extraordinary market, reflecting the extent of Empire; but in London what is remarkable is abundance and cheapness of Brummagem articles. The tribute of the Ottoman empire, however, hinted at that jasmine-scented luxury of the East with a faint tremor of menace about it, such a tremor as I had always supposed must disturb and thrill the Persian gardens of the cruellest of all kings. It is the secrecy, and

48

corruption, and privilege, of Asiatic courts—the bribes of Artaxerxes which had tempted Themistocles to Susa—which an Englishman responds to in the markets of Stamboul.

At any rate I fitted out the house in accordance with my notion. Upon two inches of clean white sand laid on the floor I strewed my choice Persian rugs, colours and substances interleaved, the whole yielding deliciously as the sand gave way to one's step. Against the walls I placed low divans made comfortable with bolsters and cushions covered in Damascus silk. I lighted the rooms with hanging lamps of pierced metalwork. On the first floor I made my own apartments, and above them, identically furnished, I made my harem. I had determined to employ none but female servants to minister to me.

And there lay my difficulty. The house was furnished, the scene set; but for want of a female companion, or servant, or slave, I was obliged to sit smoking upon my cushions all alone. The old polyglot of the ferryboat had never reappeared. Up and down the Bosphorus I travelled, hoping to encounter him, until I was weary of it. Where else could I search? And who else did I know whose aid I could solicit to procure me slaves? For a number of years slavery had been outlawed in Turkey. I had no curiosity as to the inside of a Turkish goal.

More than once on the bridge at Galata I had imagined that I had spotted the old traveller—a long cloak disappearing, a broad hat on the landing stage, the glimpse of a hawk-face which might have been his. But it never was he. My mistakes only served to show how typical of the flotsam of Stamboul the old man was, and how impossible to find. I began to fancy that he had been some *genius loci*, or djinn, the spirit of Asia sent to tempt and trick me.

Returning one evening from a day passed alone at empty Emirghian, consumed with desires fostered by my voluptuous furnishings, I was walking disconsolately up the Grande Rue when it occurred to me that the ill-lit side streets above the quays must certainly house brothels. To think was to act. I entered a steep alley. The Grande Rue itself is scarcely lit here, and exceedingly ill-paved; the lane I now ascended was dark as night, its surface all mud-holes and heaps of ordure. The houses, mostly wooden, were built out overhead so as almost to close out the sky's last glow. Constantinople, on account of the want of wheeled traffic, strikes the European as a strangely silent city. I could hear a tram ringing and clattering far off below me, and the sound of several dogfights rose above the town. In the dark lane where I walked, though, I heard only my own English boots (I did not wear the galoshes worn by most inhabitants). But I was not alone. My eyes soon made out in the dusk numerous human wrecks of both sexes slumped against rotting house-walls or upon the steps the alley now climbed. They were neither Turks nor Arabs, but Europeans. Then a ship in the port below hooted, and I was reminded at once of Liverpool. Far from reassuring me, the familiar alarmed me : I knew what could befall a man who strayed into the slums of Liverpool. The notion of Turkish ruffians, Eastern desperadoes, was all storybook to me; but the fear I felt of the dregs of my own Western world was real as six inches of cold Sheffield steel between my shoulder blades.

Could I extricate myself from the rat-trap I had entered? I slowed my pace. At this hesitation in my step the heaps of rag stirred. I saw eyes flash white at me. I quickened my pace. By turning right and right again might I not come out upon the Grande Rue? I climbed more steps. I passed the glare of a ghastly interior : its flare revealed, to my horror, a wall closing the street some twenty yards ahead. My heart hammered at my throat. I turned on my heel and strode back the way I had come. Light feet, ragged cloaks, skinny figures, scuttled aside. I was through these pursuers before they knew it. With the latest gleam of the sky in my face the alley seemed less gloomy. I hoped to escape.

I believe I might have done had I not tripped on a cobble. As I stumbled I was pushed, then caught by the shoulder and spun round. I had boxed a good deal at school, and at once put up my fists to defend myself. But the scoundrel who had spun me, though he wasn't above five and a half feet and could never have got inside my guard in the ring, knew nothing of a fair fight. I had only the time to drive home a couple of straight lefts before the brute kicked me exceeding hard. I doubled forward. He seized me by the hair, for my hat had tumbled off, and dragged me to the wall. Here he began knocking my skull against the house-front, fortunately of timber, and rotten at that. In a trice the rags of sacking which served for curtains were jerked aside and a woman's head poked itself outdoors as if to answer the knocking of my head.

50

'Help!' I yelled with all the force I could, hoping that the female might not be altogether pitiless.

Quite ignoring me, she bellowed at my attacker in what I took to be a Maltese or Indian dialect, at the same time pushing him away from her house-front with a long broom handle. It was her property she was alarmed for, and not my head, but her blows had the effect of impeding the fellow's attempts to murder me. In a moment more sacks were pulled aside, more bellowing female heads were thrust into the alley. From their number, and the nakedness of their shoulders, I realised that I had found what I had come in search of. It was a brothel, this verminous house-front pierced by women's faces which my attacker seemed bent upon demolishing with my cranium.

I had a plain view of it because the creature had dragged back my head till I thought my neck would crack. Now he slammed me up against the knocking-shop. Doubling my arm into my back he went rapidly through my pockets. The smell of him was so offensive that I thought I should faint. I wondered how he would serve me when he had robbed me—if he had a knife surely he would have used it—when a blow at the base of my skull lit the world for me like a white firework, before a waterfall of darkness tumbled me down.

I came to my senses cold and wet. Arm and head ached abominably. It was the cold on my legs informed me I had been deprived of my suit. Only my shirt, drawers and homburg remained to me, the latter jammed upon my head. I examined my surroundings with caution, fearing further punishment if I stirred. Wondering why my shirt and drawers were wet I looked down; when I made out that I was lying in a drain I scrambled to my feet, disgust stronger than fear. No response came. The alley was dark and empty; I looked up, and the silent façade of the bordello looked untenanted too.

It seemed that the sudden violent scene which had been enacted was like a travelling show which can be folded into a cart when it is finished, and driven away; next morning the common is bare where last night sideshows flared. The sudden irruption of action into one's adult life is unreal in this way; if I am to be truthful, I regret its passing. A little pain has ever seemed to me a low price to pay for the matchless thrill of action. A broken bone never dissuaded any but the feeblest scug from playing the Field

51

Game, nor did a flogging taint the sweetness of stolen fruit; rather the reverse, for injury or punishment supply occasions for the display of Fortitude, which is the soul of Heroism. Evidently the fun was at an end, so I drew my shirt tails about me and made my way downhill to rejoin the everyday world at the alley's bottom.

In a very few moments I recognised the Grande Rue where I had left it on my excursion—all too successful—to discover a brothel. But I regained it in a somewhat altered case; even by the feeble lamplight of this quarter I could perceive that my appearance was not going to pass muster nearer the hilltop of Pera. In an alley my half naked and filthy condition would have gone unremarked—my shirt, though smeared with ordure and torn, reached my knees, and my legs, feet, face and hair were so indescribably dirty that I looked quite like a native of the Sultan's empire—but, however eager for action, I did not care to try and find my way to the hotel by way of alleys. I hesitated at the street corner, my hat in my hands, uncertain of which course to take.

Then my problem was solved : a passing citizen, only a little less shabby than myself, dropped a coin into my hat. Thus shown the way, in the character of a beggar I hobbled and slithered up that interminable street with my hat held before me in a humble and inviting posture, keeping under the darkest walls, where my feet from time to time explored a pile of that commodity upon which my father-in-law is said to have based his fortune. I may remark that if there is one way more certain than another of rendering oneself invisible to persons of the better class, as I wished to do, it is to appeal to their charity. Of those few who noticed me sufficiently to drop a mite into my homburg, there was not one pair of eyes looked into my face. Success—under such a régime as Abdul Hamid's where only corruption succeeds—does not care to look failure in the eye. Or is it that some shameful passage ever exists in a man's road to fortune, and it is that very passage that every beggar he meets with seems to know of? Thus philosophising I proceeded.

But near the entrance to the hotel I hesitated. How was I to enter? When I made out the doorman, a stout Greek dressed like a field marshal, and around him his flock of urchins in buttons, the matter of my dignity—both of person and of race—came strongly back to me. I did not see how I could maintain the character of an English gentleman as I walked through them. Then, whilst I watched from a street corner opposite, there bounded out of the hotel a thin, mincing kind of fellow upon spidery legs which carried him across the street directly towards me. About his darkish suit and his unrolled umbrella was a hint of the missionary. A parson! I began to hobble rapidly off. But with a couple of strides of his heron-legs the fellow's hand was upon my arm. Heaven knows what language he preached in, but through it I recognised the low church, tin-chapel drone; and if I wasn't mistaken, his accent was Welsh. I had kept my face turned from him until he commenced dragging me along the road, doubtless to some dreadful Baptist mission where I should have been force-fed upon cocoa, whereupon my temper would stand it no longer.

'Be good enough to take your hands off me,' I ordered him in the most imperious tone I could summon, turning upon him.

He fell back, his mouth opening and shutting, astonishment puffing his moustache in and out like a net curtain at a draughty window. I had to follow up my *coup*. I walked boldly across the street towards the porter, who had watched the scene, and strode up the steps of the hotel.

'Good evening,' I called out, 'lend me your coat would you, there's a good fellow.'

I had my hand on the collar of his coat, and had helped him out of it, before he realised what was up. This splendid garment I threw about my shoulders. Then, dropping into his palm the coins I had collected in my hat, and settling that article upon my head, I walked through the entrance halls and slowly up the marble stairs.

As I strolled down to the club next afternoon I realised that I had been lucky to escape from that alley so lightly. I had lost but little—a sovereign or two and a suit of clothes—and I had been reminded of how the mere survival of an ordeal underlines one's own reality, and inspires that physical self-confidence which is at the bottom of confidence in other aspects of oneself. In early life one is constantly being knocked about, and one's idea of one's own stoutness of character must learn to survive—indeed to feed upon—physical abuse. You must come away from a flogging as a soldier comes out of the firing line, your self-esteem enhanced by your display of courage. But after school one goes through life increasingly alarmed at the thought of being knocked into the gutter; only when you are knocked into the gutter, and survive it, do you realise how little a tumble signifies. Indeed, life in the gutter can look most awfully jolly from behind the plate-glass windows of the clubs which blood and breeding oblige a fellow to belong to.

I turned in at the Cercle d'Orient and looked about for someone to give me a game of billiards. In clubs abroad, of course, none of the members are ever gentlemen—and one's disdain is bred in too deep to be got rid of simply by wishing it away—but I contrived to light upon a military gent who wasn't impossibly vulgar. He was on furlough from some sheikh or other's army and styled himself 'General', and had cultivated a broken-veined countenance and set of whiskers to match this rank. Any of these fellows are ready to talk the hind leg off a donkey on the subject of Asia, and the ruffians they work for in its deserts, their chattering always interlarded with scraps of Arabic or Hindi or Turkish; and talk he did, my *bimbashi*, with a little steering, about the native women his kind resort to.

'Ever hear of any slaving going on nowadays do you?' I asked.

'What's that?' He missed his shot. 'Slaving? Gad yes, half the blighters about the place do nothing else you know. Gad yes. I recall a time——'

'Which blighters?'

'Bring em down from Galabat you know, lovely creatures those, bring 'em down to Tajurra, run 'em across the Red Sea. Do it in dhows you know. Or run 'em down to Zanzibar. *Habash* they're called, lovely creatures.'

I made my shot and said, 'But the Zanzibar market was closed down in the '70s.'

'Don't pay no heed to that, your slaver don't. Remember once——'

'Who are the slavers?'

'Oh, merchant-johnnies you know. Box-wallahs. Perfectly open.'

'The *habash* are darkies aren't they? What about white slaves?' I asked.

'Two a penny. Not snow-white, they aren't. They'll be Kurds,

Circassians, Russian Jewesses, your white slaves will be. Not snow-white.'

'And where did you say they sell them hereabouts?'

'All over the shop. Black, white, nigger-boy—you pays your money and you takes——'

'But where?' I demanded, ready to shake him with impatience.

'I say, steady on old man! You trying to set up shop are you?'

I played a shot before I replied coldly that my interest in the matter was that of a Christian gentleman in savage customs.

'Ah yes, yes, to be sure,' he said, stroking his whiskers. 'Speaking of slaving,' he went on as I continued my break, 'I well recall a little negress, pretty little thing, running into my kiervan one time. . . .'

And so forth. I didn't trouble to speak to him again till I told him what he owed me; I could almost have made my living out of billiards at the Cercle d'Orient, for I suppose some of those fellows who lived in the desert went months on end without having a cue in their hands. But I had come no nearer the slave market—if such a thing existed at Constantinople.

A day or two later I came back to the hotel in the early evening from a trip I had made to Bulwer's island (no more than a few rocky acres with a huddle of ruinous buildings upon it, though one bedroom yet contained, let into its ceiling, the mirror in which the Princess Ypsilanti had been used, I suppose, to inspect her charms) to hear voices from my wife's sitting-room. I entered. As usual it was all but dark, my wife on her sofa under a fringed lamp, four or five persons chattering upon chairs and drinking tea, Nanny there too of course, nodding and pecking over the cakes. Before I could make my displeasure felt I found myself pushed down into a hard chair, a cup of tea put into my hand, and a voice speaking hot in my ear from behind :

'Just in time! About to begin!'

'Begin what, pray?' I enquired.

'Mrs Caper and my lady wife. Telling of their experiences.'

'And what experiences are these?'

'Why, their visit to the harem, man!'

The accent was Welsh. I half turned. Settling back in his chair was the missionary who had approached me (in my beggar's rôle) a few nights previous. The woman I took to be his wife, a sturdy female with cropped hair, was already upon her legs in the lamp-light by Rachel's sofa, holding up a formidable pair of arms to secure silence.

'I will commence my remarks,' she said, 'from the moment of entering the women's quarters, the so-called harem, from the *selamlik* of the house, where of course we had left our galoshes and capes. It will be best if there is silence until I have done. Very well?' Her tone was brisk, her eye severely upon us. Pains had been taken to suppress her Welsh accent. She took a sip of water in quite the practised style of the orator and proceeded. 'Very well : at the end of the passage conecting *selamlik* to harem we were met by a relative of the *hanum*—the wife, that is to say—and by a number of young girls, slaves I am afraid, who linked their arms about us in such a way that we were lifted and rushed along the passages to the *hanum*'s apartments in a jolly, rapid kind of way. Nothing remarkable in the furnishing line—usual divans and so forth of wealthy folk—cordial greeting, most cordial—and down we all sat. No conversation, smiling seemed sufficient. Then along come more chattering slave-girls, scampering along with the smoking requisites——'

'You've forgotten them undressing us,' broke in Rachel.

'Silence till I finish, dear. *Kaleons*, water-pipes——'

'Two of the girls,' went on Rachel unsubdued, that old laughter I had almost forgotten bubbling eagerly in her voice, 'two of them took ages trying to get my clothes off, pulling and tugging and giggling—they couldn't believe all the strings and buttons—it was so funny !'

'*Narghiles* were offered,' continued the other, raising her voice, 'coffee and sweetmeats of course——'

'And tell about the girls trying to pull off your——'

'My dear,' said the formidable female, turning upon her inter-rupter with a rustle of bombazine, 'pray be silent, or I shall not allow you to accompany me about my work.'

This procured silence, and her description continued. The picture she drew—jolly little slave-girls scuttling in every direc-tion—was a taking one. When I thought of my own empty harem I could have wept with vexation.

Nevertheless, that Rachel had run off to such a place—for a pure-minded young lady should surely not have cognisance of the harem—in company I could not approve, was a serious offence.

I hadn't given any thought to what Rachel did with her time, but I had supposed that she would occupy herself in a lady-like fashion—indeed I had made sure that her low health compelled it. Instead I found this indecency. When her companion was describing how the slave-girls had played upon instruments and danced, Rachel again broke in :

'And they had a pillow fight! That was the Circassian ones, really beautiful, and slim—you should have seen! Music makes them fight.'

'What were they wearing?' piped up a seedy little fellow in a rusty suit sitting near her.

'Oh, practically nothing,' Rachel replied, 'just a sort of little waistcoat flapping open, and trowsers you could see everything through.'

The immodesty of this beat all. There was a silence. Her companion cloaked our imaginations more decently by saying briskly, 'It is regrettable that the unhappy wretches are compelled to wear this diaphanous clothing. But now my friends,' she went on, 'I will come to the purpose of our visit, which was of course to clothe our poor sisters both in body and spirit.'

She continued, but she had lost her audience. The low persons in the room all scrambled to be near to Rachel's sofa—to hear more of her shameless language, doubtless. I confess to a strong feeling of irritation : that my wife should attend a pillow fight between near-naked Circassian slave-girls, and that I should not, seems amongst Providence's worst blunders. I was ruminating thus when I found that the Welshman had taken the seat next me.

'How do,' he said, pushing his hand at me, 'Watkins by name.'

I ignored the hand. 'Caper,' I ejaculated.

He peered with his weak little eyes. He tapped his teeth. 'But,' he said 'didn't you——?'

'Yes.'

'And may one ask——?'

'Enquiries,' I said tersely, 'making out how the natives live, don't you know. Disguise essential.'

He withdrew his long thin face, nodding it slowly. 'Ah. Ah. Research is it. Ah. What outfit are you with, Mr Caper, eh?—thought I knew all the labourers in the vineyard.'

'I work rather on my own account.'

'And the fair Mrs Caper——?'

'Is my wife, and these are my quarters. So good day to you,' I said, for I did not intend that his wife's insinuation into Rachel's company should give him any claim to my notice.

'Stay,' he said earnestly, a large coarse hand laid on my sleeve, of all gestures the most awkward to disengage, 'my labours too, sir, take me among the most afflicted of souls in this Gehenna.'

'Oh ah?' I said, tugging away to get my arm back.

'Among slaves, Mr Caper, and the devils who deal in them.'

I ceased to struggle.

'I'm sure the plight of the captive must affect you, sir?' he said. tentatively relaxing his grip to see if I would yet escape him. 'Souls in bondage no less, Mr Caper. Sold into bondage not a mile from this very room where we is taking our ease, sold body and soul,' he said, removing his hand from my arm altogether; 'think of it, sir—young females sold as you sell a pig, sir.'

I thought of it. 'Yes, well, bad I know—still, I daresay the young ladies are better off in the clutches of some pasha or other than living in tents and caves and so forth. Better fed, don't you know. I mean to say, I believe the Arabian slave don't have too bad a time of it. No outdoor work, and indoors kindly treated. Besides, the Turk's domestic life is based upon it you know— cause a revolution if you put every slave out on the street. And where are they to go, eh? Why, Aden and Bombay are already swarming with freed slaves I'm told, swarming with 'em. You read the *Pall Mall Gazette* on the subject have you?' I asked him, having quite worked myself up in favour of slavery, 'The Arabian slave is best left alone, that's their conclusion; happiest as she is.'

'Happy slaves don't justify slavery, sir,' he responded, those weak eyes beginning to flash with zeal. 'Why, it's happy slaves holds up progress indeed. Their souls it is that's in jeopardy, Mr Caper, them and their owners' souls both.'

'Not the Mussulman's soul. Slavery don't put the Mussulman's soul in jeopardy, Mr Watkins, for it's all square with the Koran, is slavery.'

'Aha, sir! Just where my lady wife comes in that is!' he said triumphantly, gobbling up another sweet cake from the stand by him; 'it's the job of the Zenana Mission to make Christians of them!'

'She converts them to Christianity so as to tell 'em they're damned does she? Well that don't seem quite fair,' I said. In fact it seemed infernal impudence, but I didn't say so to the fellow, for I had been struck by the possible benefits of his zeal to myself. 'Tell me,' I said, 'how close to the slave traffic here in Constantinople have you come?'

'Close? Why, in and out of slavers' houses I am the whole time. Know me you see. In their hearts I suppose they think I can't do them no harm, see. Even so the wicked paid no heed to the cloud no bigger than a man's hand, did they now?'

'No more they did,' I agreed. 'I tell you what it is Mr Watkins, I believe you and I should help one another. Make common cause of our resources. You shall have access to the results of my enquiries amongst the poor seamen, and I—well, you shall help me. What do you say?'

For an instant I thought he would call my bluff. But he only looked solemn, and extended his hand, which this time I took. 'I thought we was destined to labour in one yoke,' he said, 'clear feeling I had when I saw what pains you was at to disguise yourself t'other night.'

Probably he scented money—subscriptions for the charities he doubtless touted for, subsidies for his own schemes, who knows what—for he did not question my own 'work' closely. Before he and the other guests left I had exacted from him a promise to show me the workings of the slave trade. Where the lubricity of the Cercle d'Orient had failed me, this Welsh Abolitionist had turned up trumps. Elated, I went over to Rachel's sofa.

'Archie! Come, welcome; were you here through all that?'

She held out her hand, and I would have taken it had Nanny not pushed her back into her cushions. My mood changed. I spoke irritably:

'It would have been courteous to have informed me of your intention to visit a—a place of that kind,' I said, unable to use the word harem to a lady, 'but of course you do as you please. Perhaps you thought I would have expostulated at the immodesty of visiting such a place. Well you might. After all there is a good deal to be said for the Eastern practice,' I said bitterly, 'of locking their womenfolk up.'

'They are not locked up,' she murmured.

'Do not contradict me!'

'But they're not, truly. They put on that long thing they wear,

59

so you can't see a bit of them, and they flit off wherever they like. Of course the rich ones take a eunuch with them.'

'Silence!' I shouted, appalled that she had employed such a word to me, 'if your language is to be that of a Billingsgate fish-wife you had better hold your tongue!'

Irritated beyond bearing I left her.

IV

The Slavers' Khan

WITHIN A WEEK I received a message from Mr Watkins stating that he would wait upon me at my hotel the following day so that we could 'commence our work together'. At the hour fixed I was ready. He appeared dressed in what I took to be a cycling suit, a small cap in matching tweed clapped onto his head, and a string bag in his hand.

'Statistics for you,' he said as we set out, patting the bag, 'a pamphlet or two of my own you can study too.'

I had equipped myself also. I drew from my pocket a folder of papers relating to housing conditions in Stamboul, all copied from files at the British and Foreign Bible Society's rooms. Thither I had gone confident that they would have collected such information—from contrariness if from no other motive, for the Ottoman suppresses and proscribes all such data. But I had troubled myself needlessly. Watkins was an egotist and there is no need to substantiate an alibi when hoaxing an egotist, for he is insufficiently interested in others to notice discrepancies in the front you present to him. As we walked my companion plunged at once into his own affairs.

'You see, Mr Caper, I'm not one to complain about things—take the rough with the smooth is my way of looking at the world—but by rights I shouldn't be here at all, not lost to the world I shouldn't be.'

He had apprised me that there was a fair step to walk. 'Where should you be Mr Watkins?' I enquired resignedly, stuffing my folder into his reticule.

He fell upon the opportunity. 'You'll have heard of the Reverend Isaac Taylor I daresay?—sitting in his glory! Well, sir, where he sits, I should be.'

From what I could make out of the story, this Isaac Taylor

had pirated Watkins' scheme for unifying the Reformed English Church with Islam, no less, on the basis of their common monotheism. 'Who was it had the ear of Mirza Bakr? Who was it went to Syria? Who had the two big men of the Klemer in Damascus sign the letter?'—he fired out these questions wrathfully at me. It transpired that before this momentous event could take place, the Sultan had vetoed such a union on the grounds that our Queen would outrank him, and supplant him as Caliph. That the planned unification did not come about worried Watkins less than did his loss to the Reverend Taylor of the fame of the thing.

'You have no great objection then to Islam, I take it,' I said.

'None in the world,' he agreed.

'You except their approval of slavery though?'

'Saw an opening in slavery, see, was how I came to it. Antislavery I should say.'

He gave away a good deal of his hand by this. Fame—to rise by any means from obscurity—was what the fellow wanted. In slavery (or anti-slavery: the terms were synonymous to his purpose) he saw the chance of reputation. I believe he would have hailed any vehicle that promised a ride to that end. Indeed I soon learned—what I had surmised from his garb—that he was as zealous about spreading the sport of bicycling in the Turk's dominions as he was about ousting slavery from them: for he had the representation of a Birmingham bicycle manufactory, and to this he pinned his hopes of fortune. His weak eyes glowed with fervour as he spoke of the velocipede. He intimated that the two Yankees, who last year had pedalled from Kuldja to Pekin had been his protégés.

I confess that I was intrigued by this spindle-shanked Welshman trotting through Pera in his cycling knickers. He seemed to me a high example of a modern type. He believed in his capacity, and his right, to rise through the ranks of settled society by virtue of his Brummagem articles of faith (*vide* his anti-slavery) or his articles of Brummagem manufacture, the bicycles he sold. Thank God that settled society is unscaleable with such trumpery tackle. No ingenuity would have procured this Welsh creature a place at my side in London. For he, and his wife too, were as rank a pair of opportunists as ever stepped; she, I learned, combined her Zenana Mission with representing a button firm, and peddled her

62

wares to inmates of the harem who had very like never entered a shop in their lives. So the two of them went on, travelling in buttons and bicycles about the Sultan's dominions, filling his subjects' heads with unsettling notions, and all the while lightening their purses with wonderful indifference to creed and colour. Perhaps after all it is fellows like Watkins, and not our heroes at all, who have acquired us an Empire.

Slavery and cycling did not exhaust his enthusiasms. There had been homoeopathic medicine ('I was a high-potency man,' he confided) and Mrs Besant and no end of others; all abandoned, I don't doubt, as soon as the rigidity of their existing hierarchy blocked the rapidity with which he had hoped to rise to power in them. He spoke of plots and jealousies withholding his true position ('Well, I've started to say it so I may as well go on : they're scared of me in Theosophy, Mr Caper, from Bangor to Madras they're scared of me'). When every venture had failed, he had fallen back upon 'my Powers'.

'What powers are those?' I asked.

'Abandoned by the medical men I was then, Mr Caper— fatally ill on seven counts they said. That was on the Wednesday I lay dying. Then it come to me.'

'The power?'

'The cat, sir. Come in the door and sat on my chest where the pain was bad. A solemn moment.'

He shook his head. We observed a moment's silence. Suddenly disturbance and shouting came up with us from behind. Through the steep narrow street came bustling a crowd, and an urgent high cry : *'Yangin var! Yangin var!'*

Fire ! In the centre of the throng loped the firemen, wooden boxes of equipment carried on four men's shoulders, all of them uttering their discordant cries. The crowd of idlers, their long garments looped over their arms, jogged eagerly with them down the street. Believing that a conflagration in an Eastern town is a spectacle which the traveller should contrive to witness, I called to Watkins, who had taken refuge in a doorway across the street, and set off with a view to keeping the crowd in sight. Though I had sometimes heard the explosion of the cannon at Kandili which announces fires, and had seen on the tower at Galata the flags which signal the fire's whereabouts, I had never before been in the way of seeing the blaze.

We had not gone far, although a few turns in that confounded labyrinth served to lose me utterly, when the crackling of flames could be heard above the crowd's hubbub. Thin smoke hurried across the roofs, and the smell of burnt paint cut through the street smells. In a moment I was upon the scene. The street was narrow, and the heat of the burning house had split the crowd in two. In each group was a team of firemen : Why were their boxes still unloaded?—why were they still shouting 'Fire'?—why did they make no attempt to attack the blazing house, or even to prevent the flames spreading? Already the air was crackling with sparks, the parched timbers exploding in fountains of fragments as the flames leaped through the structure, and in a street of wooden houses a vast conflagration must ensue. Still the firemen stood idle, shouting like hawkers with wares to sell. Now from the burning house came tumbling down bundles flung into the street. At once men sprang forward out of the crowd, fierce-looking fellows fighting one another for a chance to snatch up a bundle—to snatch up a bundle and make off with it! Thieves! I turned to Watkins in horror. But his face, and many another I saw glaring in the flamelight, had become a mask greedy with delight, lips curled back from cruel teeth, eyes alight with the fire's heat. It was not a crowd into whose hands I should care to fall. Now I saw fingers point, and laughter cackle, as if at a spectacle yet more diverting. I looked.

A family with children was upon its knees round the firemen in the Eastern attitude of abasement which weakness must adopt towards tyranny. Whilst the unhappy father held out a purse the women touched the dirt of the street with their foreheads. It availed them nothing. Their house burned behind them.

Then through the crowd another man pushed his way. He thrust into the firemen's midst a purse of larger size. The trick was worked. At once the four firemen followed him to a house three or four doors from the seat of the blaze. Here they began to unpack their equipment in the leisurely style of picnickers who have found a quiet spot. But a show of money such as that is apt to attract disaster in the East. I was aware of a fresh stir in the crowd—shouts—horses' hoofs—wheels rumbling—soldiers! Soldiers armed with long-handled axes and immense long poles shod with grappling-hooks. They drove through the confusion. Smoke billows were by now darkening the scene, and clouds of ash fell, whitening robes and cloth coats, turban and fez. At the house which the firemen were feebly dowsing the troop halted. In a moment their intention was plain : with axe and hook, unless they were prevented, they would pull down the house to make a firebreak. Now the householder who had paid the firemen to drench his house applied his energy to persuading the military to leave it standing. Distractedly he pulled at his beard or beat his clenched hands against his forehead. The *bimbashi* seemed intent on ensuring a sound hold for the engines of destruction. The house front had begun actually to creak forward before its owner drew another purse from his robes. This effected his purpose. The soldiers retreated from the heat to pull down at their leisure some other house whose owner was too poor to defend it from them.

But too much time had been lost in bargaining. In a moment or two the rich Turk saw the roof of his dwelling catch light, and his whole property doomed to destruction. Now the smoke rolled down upon us and obscured the sun. In intervals of darkness and flame I saw outrages performed. The house of the rich Turk fell victim first to the mob. In and out its smoking mouth the ruffians staggered under silks and carpets and ornaments loaded onto their victim's own trays. Scuffles and quarrels over spoil spread through the crowd as fighting spreads through the pack when hounds have broken up their fox. Meanwhile the houseowner, resigned now to the absolute loss of his property, sat impassive and stoic, cross-legged upon a fine carpet which he or a servant had preserved, in a space before his blazing home which even the looters respected. Touched beyond anything by this fortitude in the face of ruin—the one impressive virtue of the Mussulman—I could stay no longer to watch mere pillage. I drove a way out for myself through the crowd. For all their air of savage rapacity, I felt in myself that superior height, and a hardness as of iron assailed by feathers, which distinguishes an Englishman amid the bird-like limbs and flutterings of an Eastern crowd. I soon saw Watkins, bobbing up and down on tiptoe for a clearer view. The fellow disgusted me, but I had need of him.

'Come,' I said, 'I find this makes me pretty sick. We'll be getting on if you've quite done.'

'Watch, Mr Caper, will you !'

He gripped my arm and indicated a couple of murderous-looking rascals hastening into a house quite away from the fire's range. 'Thieves I suppose,' I said.

'Arson, Mr Caper, arson's their game. Coals they got with them, red hot, I seen them—set fire to the house they will!'

'Who does such things!' I exclaimed as he followed me away from the fire. I was profoundly dismayed. I did not see how property, or the propertied class, could survive in such circumstances as prevailed here. In England one has become so used to the preservation of Property being the fundamental concern and purpose of Law that it is an unpleasant shock to discover that no Natural Law upholds the propertied class in a less advanced society. 'Who can be so depraved that they'll spread fire?' I demanded.

'Politics it is,' he answered. 'So they say anyway, all politics these fires and riots.'

'Politics? To destroy property? I don't see it at all.'

'The Armenians is blamed, Mr Caper. This Secret Committee they got, see, that's what makes them riot and burn, causing disorder like. Then it's these here Russian Nihilists is booked to step in, see, and take over.'

'Russian Nihilists? Ridiculous!' I told him. 'The Tsar has put paid to Nihilism once and for all, you may depend upon it. Russia at least is a country where property will always be respected.'

Politically he was evidently uneducated. We walked on in silence. Then he said, 'Now, sir, hope you was able to keep your valuables safe in the crowd was you?'

My hand flew to my pockets. Gone! Money, watch, handkerchief, all. I was plucked clean. Mr Watkins meanwhile was abstracting a greasy purse from the inner band of his cap. Even a Turk is hard put to it to rob a Welshman, I reflected. However, to be robbed is the more gentlemanlike course, if the alternative is to wear a cycling cap full of sovereigns jammed down about one's ears. I now felt myself very much in Watkins' hands for the rest of our expedition. It was he who led, and I who followed, when he turned left-handed at the Galata quay and walked between the warehouses and the water's edge towards Topkhaneh.

Neither Mr Watkins' political concern nor his charity were aroused by the loss of property or by the suffering we had witnessed at the fire. I recognised in this immunity the single-minded nature of a man dedicated to his own advancement. Because the fire did not have to do with his immediate interests—cycling and slavery—he was permitted not merely to ignore the suffering caused by fire, but actually to enjoy the conflagration as a spectacle. It did not touch him, in pocket or heart. No doubt whilst engaged in jockeying for position amongst the Theosophists he had read tales about slavery, or had glimpsed slaves, with that same voyeur's salacity which I had observed on his face at the fire. In myself, on the other hand, I recognised the quickly aroused—and quickly subsiding—sympathy with suffering, and disgust at depravity, which sees in the misfortunes of others an infringement of one's own right to be happy. What I saw worried me, but my mind did not picture miseries hidden from my eyes. Thus, in all the concern I had expended upon the question of obtaining a female slave I had given no consideration to my likely emotional reaction when confronted with the facts of slaving; as one might long to be in America without considering whether or not the Atlantic would make one seasick. Now, upon the quay where grimy Arabian feluccas manned by their murderous crews lay moored, I was glad to discover that I had the stomach for these facts.

I had been at the landing stage at Topkhaneh before—curious to watch the fashioning of *kaiks* nearby—and had walked over the wide esplanade which is crowded with new-made cannon cast in the foundry which abuts on the square. I feel myself exhilarated, as I suppose every true Briton does, by these engines of war, and excitement again quickened my pulse as I followed Watkins past the guns, past the horses standing for hire under the plane trees, and past a white marble fountain in the florid style the Turk so dotes upon. I felt that I was engaged upon an adventure, the first for years, and the sensation put me in mind of the carefree marauds of my schooldays.

But what a companion Mr Watkins made for an adventure! —dodging along at a great pace on those grasshopper legs of his, feet working away at the road, reticule swinging, and stamped on his features an expression of singular earnestness, as of a mongrel with a famous bone buried in the neighbourhood. Yet I reflected that between us we fairly represented the Empire, he with his creed of self-help and his desire of fame and fortune, I following upon the efforts of such fellows as he in pursuit of sport or pleasure.

We crossed the carriage road that leads to Yildiz—how strange to step over tramlines amid these ancient scenes!—and plunged into the warren of houses and lanes clinging to the slopes of Pera. Watkins fell back and we climbed the hill abreast under houses whose jutting upper storeys almost joined overhead.

'Caution, Mr Caper,' he advised in a low tone. 'I've not been here for a week or two to tell the truth, and there's been one or two things has happened I don't like the look of.'

'What kind of things?'

'Straws in the wind you might say. A colleague gone missing like. Elderly person I knew pretty well indeed, old gentleman he was, Russian or Persian I believe. Odd old fellow. Up and down the Bosphorus he'd go, nosing out the evildoer, and then a queer plan he had for settling accounts with them I can tell you. Half-cracked he was—well, not surprising either, his daughter I believe was taken for the slave trade, or wife was it?'

'And he is looking for her?'

'Looking for revenge more like. When he gets in his power some person who has slaves, Mr Caper—my God, sir, but I do pity that man, evildoer as he assuredly is. Terrible cruel the Persians is.' He shivered.

I said, 'And now he's disappeared you say?'

'Vanished. Now look out, Mr Caper, don't pay those scallywags no heed,' he urged me, for a rabble of ragged boys had begun to follow us, hooting and pitching handfuls of dirt, the bolder ones darting up to tap us with sticks, one of which I had seized. 'Lay a hand on those little lads, Mr Caper,' he said 'and we'd be torn in pieces very like.'

I looked up at the houses. Was it possible? Hostility which parents veil, their children avow; and in the belligerent animosity of these infants one could take a truer reading of the state of Turkish feeling toward us—of the Mussulman's abiding fanatical hate of the *feringhi*—than one could learn from an adult mob. What drove these children to insult us could yet inspire their parents to pull us in pieces if they had the chance of performing the feat with impunity. I had not before been frightened of a crowd of Turks.

I judged that we had penetrated deep into the Fundukli quarter when my companion stopped at a closed pair of high doors in a windowless wall which fronted the street. Upon the age-whitened wood of these doors he hammered with his fist. At that heavy, hollow knocking the ragamuffin children at our heels fell silent; and when an iron grating in the doors rasped open, they fled like a flock of sparrows when the cat opens an eye. We were very much alone in the street. I was aware of scrutiny through the grille—I had the sensation of being picked up and held close to the scrutinising orb, of myself turned over and examined in every particular, as Ulysses was catechised by the horrid eye of Polyphemus. Then bolts were drawn and the doors parted.

We entered a pleasant courtyard surrounded by an arcade whose lintel rested upon antique columns. In the centre was a garden of stone paving and rose bushes, its air cooled by a fountain, its stone seats shadowed by palm trees. Upon their perches in this garden sang and twittered innumerable birds. I thought them tame, but as we walked I saw the sunlight flash upon their chains. We followed the ruffian who had admitted us, a black-bearded, fierce-looking fellow, his baggy trousers pushed into soft high boots, a cashmere shawl wound round his waist to receive knife and pistols, a rakish lambskin hat on his greased locks. Lounging on rugs, or resting against columns, were other wild-looking desperadoes pulling at their *kaleons* and regarding us sardonically as we picked our way amongst their legs and the butts of their ancient rifles. No stranger sight than Watkins tramping through this setting in cap and cycling suit can possibly be imagined.

We were led by way of a crooked passage into another court, smaller than the first, in whose centre shone a placid tank of water around the minatory finger of a single tall cypress. Here the silence was profound. Not only was the confused loud singing of the birds from the outer court excluded, the never-sleeping cries and tumult of an Eastern city were silenced too. Above us the silent blue sky, framed by the stone arcade, might have been the sky above *konak* or *caravanserai* in the remotest provinces of mountain or desert. Here we were left. I realised that we counted upon our hosts to show us out : there was no chance of those who entered this court ever leaving it without its owner's permission.

In a moment a door opened—or I deduced from the sudden

burst of menagerie-like noise, which ceased as suddenly, that a soundproof door must somewhere have opened and closed—and a huge man swaggered under the arcade towards us. He too was dressed in the somewhat operatic fashion of the guards, under a turban as marvellously contrived as an eagle's nest, and he swirled and fluttered towards us on soft boots slapping the stone, calling out in a loud, good-humoured voice :

'Watkins! Enter! Come, you are welcome!'

Watkins submitted to a bear's hug which lifted him off his feet. When he indicated me, I too was clutched by the shoulders and had that bearded hairy face thrust close to mine, and suffered the breath from foul teeth to flood over me.

'I am pleased, I am happy, I am glad!' he roared. 'Come, smoke, eat. No vines, sirs! I am good Sunni. Good Isauvi no slaves eh?—good Sunni no vines!' Thus bellowing and gesticulating he preceded us along the arcade to a corner where bolsters and rugs had been laid down. Here we arranged ourselves. I looked for slaves to serve us but saw none.

'No!' cried our host, his shrewd eyes upon me, 'no slave! If he sees slave-womans our friend is hurt, poof!' (he banged his heart) 'so no slave-womans. Soon I change him—soon I make him good Mussulman with harem—or I kill him. Eh? Is it so?' He leaned over and banged Watkins on his cycling cap with the flat of his hand. 'I like him. I love him. I kill him I think, unless he run off and tell Sir Currie how happy is slave-womans. Yes Watkins! You put it in Sir Currie's ear, off he writes to tell in Inglistan the slaves is happy. Yes, yes!' he shouted through Watkins' disclaimer.

I remarked that when that wild countenance was in repose, which was rare, the eyes were notable for their impassivity, their coldness, as are the stone eyes of savage gods. His bombast was a catspaw on still deeps. When he caught me studying his face he reanimated the features.

'You know, sir, you know what is worst unhappy in all trading of slaves?' he demanded fiercely. 'I tell you : is when Ingleez gunboat chase dhow of slaver. Yes, in Arab sea. For how he do, the slaver? Puts slaves on shore to starve, puts slaves in sea for fishes—only then slaves die off dead.'

'They don't ever get hurt or killed when your fellows are capturing them in the villages, I take it?' said I.

70

He thrust his beard in the air and laughed. 'You know what happen? When a slave captain land on the shore? Comes running to him mans and womans, running to be slaves!'

'Running with your accursed whips behind them,' said Watkins.

'Oh Watkins,' said our host sadly. 'This is from old times you hear this history. From times when you Ingleez came catching slaves. Yes, you bring whips and chains you Ingleez did. Now is all different. Now is happy. Now slave is only chance a poor womans get, of big man, of good house. You know Mussulman law. One baby born in harem, mother of baby is wife. Wife of pasha! How else is possible poor girl be wife of pasha? You know truth? I tell you. I take *baksheesh* many time just for accept poor mans' girl for slave. Many time. Now is happy. Come, you see my happy slaves?'

He rose from the rug and we followed him. Walking along the arcade I said to Watkins, 'Heavy weather we make of slavery don't it seem, according to him?'

For answer he gripped my arm and indicated the further corner of the arcade, where a yellow rose climbed the wall. Beneath it I saw a long pole to which two rope loops were attached. Beside it bundles of twigs soaked in a leathern bucket. Rose petals were scattered everywhere.

'The *felek*!' whispered Watkins.

Before I could ask the purpose of the instrument, a door had opened and through it flooded the babel I had heard earlier. Through this door, which was soundproofed by a hanging of heavy leather screening it, we entered a low dim chamber still resounding with the shrill chatter of girls' tongues—or rather with their echo, for silence had fallen at the instant of our entering. With an immense sigh arising from the rustle of cambric and jaconnet, the roomful of females subsided upon the floor at our feet. Tiled walls were revealed as they sank down. The room was lit by lattices pierced in arched windows, and was delightfully cool, scented too with the heavy sweet odour of jasmine. The slaves, of whom there were eight or ten, differed much as to size and colouring, there being abased before us the broad backs and tawny locks of some northern race, the glistening skin and curly wool of three negresses, as well as the slender torsos of fair-skinned girls with hair thick and yellow as corn.

There now arose to her feet a squat elderly female who toddled

71

towards us. That she, of the beauties present, should be alone in facing us, was the worst of ill-fortune, for she was arrayed with appalling simplicity in a single transparent garment. Watkins she evidently knew.

'Can't keep away, Mr Watkins, eh, that your tune is it?' said she. My astonishment was great to hear the plain language of the English midlands issue from her. 'And you, sir,' she said to me, 'you share his views do you, or would you be come to buy?'

'Of course he buy!' roared our host, thumping my back with a fist like a Bradenham ham, 'you show him all, he buy! Eh my friend?' he enquired of me somewhat threateningly.

I muttered something non-committal. Though I had not lost sight of my intention of furnishing my harem, I did not see how I was to buy a slave-girl with Watkins at my elbow.

Evidently a tour of the establishment under the direction of this *déshabille* Miss Pinkerton was unavoidable. We left the lower room and ascended by a narrow pair of stairs to the upper floor. Here was a fine apartment, the panelled walls painted with fruits and birds and cypresses, where we were offered *baklava*, and coffee in cups held in little enamelled holders of filigree work set with brilliants. A stout young female of peasant type carried round the tray. 'A Georgian girl,' our hostess told us briskly, 'carry a donkey and no trouble.'

The girl's robust physique was plain to behold. I found myself wishing that both females' clothing was less diaphanous, and looked at Watkins. The expression in his weak pained eyes was unchanged, unseeing indeed, as he blew his straggle of moustache in and out with sips of coffee. To his surroundings he was impervious. My opinion of him rose. He enquired whether the drudgery of the place fell usually to the lot of Russian girls.

The woman shook her head. 'It's the blackamoors must fetch and carry. Where brain's not the requisite,' she amplified, tapping her veiled head whose dyed black hair twinkled as if dusted with glass-chippings.

'And what is the Georgian's work then?' I asked, merely for the sake of politness, as one might ask at a morning visit where one's hostess obtained her pugs.

'Wherever there's dependability called for you'll find them,' she replied, 'anything in the housekeeping line. Thrift—why, if there's three sixpences can be got from a shilling, that girl'll get them. And honest—Lord alive, you could walk through all of Georgia with a tray of gold on your head, so the saying goes.'

'You teach housekeeping?' I said, committed it seemed to this catechism.

'That I must,' she responded warmly, 'teach them everything I must, young madams. Azeez, he's a one, sir : brings me in all sorts. Every egg a bird, and every bird a whistler—that's his notion of it. Well, sir, it's not human nature. Of course there's girls as will be castaways, sure as there's eggs will never hatch. That's my way of thinking. But I'll take my solemn oath to this, that a girl I've kept a twelvemonth—a girl I've taught personal—why, sir, her you could leave in your house, sir, you and your lady, and travel to China and back, and you'd find all right as a trivet when you come home.'

I felt somewhat let down by the respectability of all this. Whatever I had expected, this was not it. 'And apart from housekeeping?' I suggested. 'Apart from these estimable Georgians? What are the accomplishments of the Circassian girls for instance?'

'Courtezans they sell for,' she replied promptly, her plain words (like her plain person) robbing the notion of its allure. 'There isn't a ruler in Asia, sir, but that you'll find a Circassian slave is his mother. Controls the East, the blood of them mountain savages. But I won't touch them here. All skittles and swipes, that's their idea of life, idle things. No, to a gentleman looking for a concubine, sir—especially if he's elderly—and not just looking for laced mutton—I'd say, Wait until I can put my hand on an Abyssinian direct from Gojjam.'

'Why?' I asked, my interest excited.

But Watkins was on his feet brushing crumbs off his knickers. 'Have a look round, shall we?' he said, 'see all's square.'

We toured the establishment. Whether Watkins' visits acted as checks, or whether he was in some sense in league with the slavers, I could not determine; I suppose that those who support an evil, and those who oppose it, depend about equally upon the evil for their livelihood. We were shown the *hammam*, where the slave-girls learned the art of the bath and of massage; the kitchens, so unscientific in Turkey, where cooking is but one step advanced from the nomadic messes prepared in tents since Jacob cooked for Esau; the slaves' sleeping quarters, their bedding rolled in blue covers and stacked round the walls; the terrace used for drying and preparing tobacco, an art much esteemed in a slave : in short we were shown everywhere. By the time we were returned to our host Azeez—not amongst the slave-girls, where we had left him, but at another doorway giving upon the arcaded court— I stood persuaded that slavery was a most workmanlike institution. And yet I found that my enthusiasm for owning a female slave had declined.

'So?' demanded the slaver, raking his moustache fiercely upward and making his countenance glower at me, 'so, you like? You love? You buy? Of course!'

'He's not here to buy, Azeez, any more than I am,' Watkins put in.

'What?' roared the giant hoarsely, his veins bulging, 'What? Whose dog is this—whose dog is he, that he make us eat his dirt? Eh?'

'Now then, Azeez,' said Watkins with impressive firmness, 'you know you've done all you want, got Mr Caper thinking it's a Girls' Friendly Society you're running here. Going to show him your other place are you? Before he makes up his mind like? Are you?'

'Watkins, my friend, I am your servant to be trod under your boot, but what other place are this?' Despite elaborate gestures of abasement his eyes remained untouched by humility, were lit only by craft from within. 'Here, there, all are happy.'

'Then set them free,' suggested Watkins. 'Them in your cellars on the quays too, and them boys you're making eunuchs of, as is like to die, and them you've half beaten to death, and them you've given over to your Kurd devils, for to take and crucify when they've done with them—will you set all them free will you?'

'Watkins I like you. I love you. I warn you. I warn you, my friend,' he growled, his bent finger tapping forward like a bill pecking, anger on his brow, 'do not look where nobody ask you. Please do not. Or some sad things will happen. Is time now you go.' He turned to me. 'You will come back I think. Yes. I know. You come, you make your slave Azeez happy like a sheep.'

We passed in silence by the narrow passage to the outer court. The tribesmen lounging amongst their weapons—in the garden the birds singing to the fountain's music—the picturesqueness of the scene was delightful. Azeez had led us round three sides of the colonnade when, near the steps up to the gates, we almost stumbled upon a heap of rags against the wall. It was Watkins' cry of horror which made me look again at the bundle. It was a man, the remains of a long dark coat flung over him. His feet were hugely swollen and wrapped in rags soaked in blood. Another bloodied rag bound his head and eyes. Azeez had walked on to the doors.

'Poor old mans,' he said, 'poor old mans. Some sad thing happened.'

The next moment we were alone in the roadway without, and Watkins' excitable voice began at once :

'The old Persian that was! Or old Russian if Russian he was, him I told you of—will you look what they done to him? Will you look at what they done?'

I saw that he was ghastly white, poor Watkins. 'Why——?' I began.

'Saw his feet then? Showed you the *felek* didn't I?'

'What is the *felek*?' I felt a thrill of horror which anticipated his description of that barbaric torture. When he had satisfied my questions I asked him why the old fellow had been dealt with so harshly.

'Oh the evil ones!' he said. 'Caught him queering their pitch I suppose they did. Devils they are and worse, very Molochs in their wickednesses,' he spat out, whistling venomously on his 's's' in the Welsh style.

As we retraced our way through Fundukli, and emerged once more upon the broad highway beside the Bosphorus, I considered whether the picture I had myself seen, or the one Watkins would have me believe, was most probably the truth of modern slaving. As if to drive his mediaevel tableau before it, a tram came ringing and rattling along the boulevard. No, in Constantinople as in London it was after all—I might say, alas!—the year 1895. I clapped Watkins on the back to buck him up.

'Come, Watkins,' I said, 'I believe you have let your imagination get the better of you, eh? Come, don't brood upon it. The old fellow was in a traffic accident you'll discover, and our friends are making him comfortable. That will be the truth of the matter, you may depend upon it.'

We caught the tram, and were transported in a moment to

Galata. As we waited amongst European men of business, and Europeanised Turks from Pera, and Mr Cook's excursionists, for the excellent little funicular to run us up the hill, Mr Watkins too seemed able to shake off his forebodings.

'Not a bad idea,' he said to himself, scratching his nose.

'What idea is that?' I asked.

'Buy a slave,' he said to my surprise. 'Buy one, see, take her on back to England, use her on lecture tours. Illustration like. Bigger draw than a magic lantern any day, eh? You'd want one as had been knocked about a bit wouldn't you? More sympathy like.' Zeal re-lit its lamp in the dingy windows of his eyes. 'Half-starved, chains too,' he added, beginning to swing his string bag cheerfully to and fro.

'You assume she'd consent to being carried about the lecture halls, and half starved and loaded with chains, once you'd set her free,' I said.

He looked at me uncomprehendingly. 'Well,' he said, 'owe it me, wouldn't she? Have a duty like, if I'd paid money for her.'

V

How Recollections of a Poached Cock induced me to make a Momentous Purchase

I CONFESS THAT I grew exceedingly weary of Constantinople in the ten days which followed this excursion. At the club was nothing but low merchants, and long-faced Scots shipwrights come out to build for the Sultan his own ironclad (they had made sure that the Turk had in the end a very dear article, an out-dated battleship which had cost perhaps more than any vessel afloat, for every item of its manufacture, as well as the ship-wrights, had been imported from Great Britain). With these square-toed Puritans, and the Church of Scotland minister who had the cure of their souls, I dined or talked until their cant and their complaints drove me to abandon the club. There was no pleasure in dining with Rachel. Perhaps out of nervousness at my irritability she advanced her opinions behind a barrage of excul-pation—she was sorry to bring it up, etc. etc., but did I think of establishing her father and herself altogether at the house upon the Bosphorus; should she not perhaps look out for a house to rent at Pera, though she hoped not to trouble me, etc. etc. Nothing is more enraging than this tone, of a cur expecting kicks.

'By Heavens!' I rejoined, 'are we to ruin ourselves utterly over this visit? Really I should say two houses is a little excessive. But of course the money is yours to waste as you wish, I haven't a word to say about it if you are set upon a course so unnecessary and vulgar.'

'Have you taken a house yet on the straits?'

I stood up and pitched down my table napkin. 'If I am to be pestered to death with questions I will not trouble you by dining here,' I told her, and left her rooms to complete my meal down-stairs.

The aggravation of being asked about the house at Emirghian

was beyond anything. Empty it stood, furnished to the last particular save one : a denizen for the harem. I had been obliged to hire as caretaker for it a Greek female found for me by the hotel dragoman, and occasionally I took myself down there to eat my luncheon in those empty rooms haunted by water-light, or to lounge under the magnolia tree with a novel. I was reading, I recall, *The Prisoner of Zenda* which had come out just previous, and I found it damnably irritating that such a tailor as Rassendyll should stumble upon adventures without end in his Ruritania, whilst I was obliged to sit in mine as glum as a mayor in his parlour.

I did my duty by the sights of Constantinople, and even took places to witness the *Selamlik*, as the Sultan's Friday visit to the mosque at Yildiz is called. This is a curious spectacle. At first there congregates at the palace gate an immense mob of ragamuffin soldiers, Albanian and Arab *zouaves*, Turkish cavalry, all sorts; even then a double line of police and Yildiz spies puts itself between the spectators and the Sultan's route, which is no more than a hundred clear yards from palace gate to mosque. You receive a notion from all this of how oppressive Abdul Hamid's tyranny is, and it's said he fears his *Selamlik* each week as if he were sure to be shot upon showing his face outside his fortress. At last we heard the gates rumble open, there came a rattle of tin trumpets, a huzza from the soldiers as ragged as their breeches, and I glimpsed an agitated, seedy-looking little oriental carried along in a light carriage with a child on the cushions opposite him. Round the mosque door (where they'd been dropped out of a covered cart earlier on) was assembled a half dozen of dwarves, and these poor little devils set up a shrill piping at the Sultan's approach which meant to say (our dragoman told me) 'Do not become overproud, Padishah, for Allah is greater'. It was hard to say which looked the more timorous, dwarves or Sultan, as the so-called Drinker of Blood scuttled up the steps into the mosque. Rachel accompanied me to this, and was quite put in spirits by our excursion together, but the manner in which a European woman is quizzed by every low rascal is a decided bore for her escort, and I took her nowhere else.

In the hotel's public rooms, handsomely enough fitted up in the modern style, one could observe a cross section of those who visit Constantinople. For want of an occupation I passed many an

78

hour on a sofa in one or other of those lofty saloons, amid palms and mahogany-and-leather dimly lighted from on high. In the foyer was situated Cook's bureau for the reservation of sleeping berths on the Orient Express, and it used to amuse me to speculate on the status or intentions of those who came to take their tickets. There was the Cockney tourist, jaunty enough until some hitch occurred, whereupon he would break out into hysterical ana-themas upon foreigners and all their doings—having made up his mind to take Mr Cook's medicine of a fourteen days' tour abroad and drink it down like a man, he would not for anything have the dose increased. There was the commercial trade, very direct in pot hat and alpaca jacket, stating their demands and slamming down their money, fingers drumming upon the desk whilst the clerk delayed their wonderful and rapid progress around the world promoting the sale of Manchester shoddy and India tea to the tribesmen of Luristan. Occasionally came the case-hardened traveller, rough-bearded, self-reliant, who had perhaps ridden in from Tabriz, or come from Kazakhstan by way of the Volga, now pursuing this last easy stage of his journey as a man might take out his latch-key on the steps of his home. The veiled French-woman creating an air of mystery about herself was inevitably, I was persuaded, a dismissed governess of romantic inclinations. Alas, of the grandees one saw nothing but their servants, or the dragomans of their embassies, come to purchase tickets for masters who travelled via the Sublime Porte from Kabul to St Peters-burg in pursuit of their deep game, balancing, double-crossing, playing by means of assassination and bribery for the stakes of Egypt, of Persia, of India itself—whilst all it seemed that I was fit for was to sit kicking my heels with a novel in my hand.

Every person I saw increased my discontent. All that they had in common was that they were more enviably placed than myself. I had neither the self-sufficiency abroad of the traveller, nor the wish to return home of the Cockney; on nodding terms, in London, with the type of fellow who calls cousins with half the nobility of England, and who lodges with Sir Philip Currie at his summer embassy at Therapia—I heard that Wilfrid Blunt and Pom McDonnell both passed through in these weeks—I was not able to put myself in the way of meeting such personages in Con-stantinople. I was obliged to learn as my lesson that there is a difference between nodding to fellows of that kind on account of having shared a bench with them at school, and knowing them because one shares with them a proliferation of connexions who meet and re-meet in the embassies or chancelleries or palaces of the world. It was not a lesson which increased my contentment. Above the society of the Cercle d'Orient, I was below that of the embassy, and found myself a great deal alone.

I fell to comparing myself with those I saw. I began to question my clothes, hair, face, by minute examination in the glass before descending to dine alone in the hotel. Should I not tie again my white tie?—clip my moustache a trifle on the left side?—part my hair in the centre?—grow a beard to add force to my chin? As is the case with women, my want of self-confidence was supplied by ever-increasing vanity.

Occasionally loneliness drove me to Rachel's rooms. I would change my clothes for others I thought she would find more agreeable, I would practise a soft manner before entering her door; but alas! when I found that she was not the wife I had pictured—or the child I had remembered—disappointment drove me to speak to her so irritably that our interview was sure to end in slammed doors and sal volatile. Where did this accursed stiffness of mine spring from, that seemed to serve only to separate me from all the world? Splendid isolation indeed! And what was Rachel writing?—scribbling away upon a velvet cloth under a shaded lamp, shawled shoulders bent over her task. It made me uneasy. I considered forbidding her writing. Suppose we both died of fever, let us say, and a stranger reading her journal found comments which exposed me to ridicule. For nothing is half so comical, to the low mind, as a fellow who has not consummated his marriage—not that the least blame could attach to me in the matter, for I have proved my manhood in the arms of a score of professional women of pleasure, but I could not be certain that I appeared in Rachel's writings quite as I wished to appear before posterity. But to tell the truth I wanted the firmness now to confiscate her pens and paper. I thought with envy of what Mrs Watkins had related, that Turkish women are never taught to write, lest they correspond with an unapproved suitor.

My confidence was undermined. Like the garrison of an invested citadel, I had to make a sortie if I was not to lose all self-respect. There persisted in my mind an uncomfortable feeling that I had shown the white feather over acquiring a slave-girl.

Having found and furnished the house—having most ingeniously discovered a source of slaves—having ventured so far, for want of spirit I had turned tail. I remember that at school I had rescued my reputation for pluck, both in my own eyes and in my schoolfellows', by the following circumstance : I had said idly to a friend one day as we walked through the Great Park that nothing could be simpler than to knock over one of the Queen's pheasants with a catapult for one's mess tea (birds abounded in the park at that time, it being difficult I believe to persuade the Queen to allow sport to be enjoyed where the Consort had fired his last shot—a monument marked the spot—and where his bones reposed). My companion opined that I could not achieve the feat; and as long as I did not come up to the scratch, my self-esteem and my reputation declined together. I had made a catapult and lead bullets; I had practiced upon scugs in the street below my window until I was an accurate shot; but still I scouted the execution of the deed.

Finally, able to live with the white feather no longer, I had broken away from a skating party in the park one winter's afternoon, and had stalked and shot a cock pheasant roosting in a spinney. Unfortunately the bird was a runner, and I followed it up with such heat that I ran into the very arms of a keeper on his rounds. The game was up.

Nevertheless, reputation and self-esteem were restored; indeed my capture and flogging, by spreading the fame of the story, improved my heroic status. As was always the case with a flogging, the transgression itself was lost sight of in the excitement surrounding the punishment, and there was a good deal of confusion as to the motives of the beaks in plying the birch. My tutor, who was a sportsman, made a great point of my having shot the bird in February, and gave out the impression that it was for infringing the Game Laws that I was to be flogged; whereas the Headmaster—his post being very much a Court appointment—took a grave view of the pheasant being a royal one, and flogged me I believe for treason. Of course it was the opinion of the Praeposters I cared for, both excellent fellows who stood me a pint of Champagne after the execution; their attitude assured me that my only crime was to have been caught, and for this they voted me fully paid-up by my soldierly bearing at the flogging-block. To accept punishment without flinch or question, with the air of Regulus returning to Carthage, was a great part of a school reputation for heroism—the most-flogged fellow in the school was pointed out with quite as much awe by Lower Boys as was the fellow who had won the Newcastle—and flogging assuredly remains in my mind as a thrilling test of one's pluck, not at all as a corrector of vice.

That is by the way—and serves to show off how absurd is the notion that a flogging does a fellow anything but good!—for the point of my recollection is this, that only by coming up to the scratch in the matter of bagging that bird had I been able to restore my self-respect, and I stood now in the same case with regard to completing what I had undertaken at Emirghian by obtaining a female slave. I must do the deed, or regard myself a shirker.

I landed one morning at Topkhaneh with that somewhat tremulouse sense of occasion which makes the world a stage, and 'oneself' a part to be played before an audience. Rapidly I walked into the maze of Fundukli. Soon I stood at the gates in the khan's windowless wall and felt the scrutiny of eyes upon me through the grille. Some minutes passed, and my excitement began to ebb : perhaps I should not be admitted, and would be free to walk off the stage without loss of face. Even making the attempt had restored my self-esteem. But now the doors yawned, and there was no retreat. I entered. My footsteps rang hollow in the cool shadow of stone. In the sunlit garden the fountain still played and the birds sang, but the arcade was empty of tribesmen. Not quite empty though : in a corner was a fat Turk in a greasy coat at work between two birdcages. We drew near, my guide and I. I saw what work the Turk was at. He was putting out the eyes of the birds with the point of a dagger, as brisk as a London waiter opening oysters, and thrusting them blind into the second cage. He looked up as we passed, knife in one hand and shrieking bird in the other; our eyes had met before, and he knew it. He had been one of the two Turks who had accosted the old traveller on the quay at Bebek the day I had first seen the house at Emirghian. My heart for some reason sank. Followed by my guide, or guard, I walked through the dark passage into the second court. Azeez laid aside the amber mouthpiece of his *kaleon* and rose from his carpet with extravagant phrases of welcome.

'You put out the eyes of your singing birds,' I said as I seated myself, for I could not forget that ruffian all spattered with birds' eyes.

'So, my friend,' said he, 'we help them sing good and live. Sing we feed, not sing—poof, we kill. You saw how in first cage is silence, in second is all singing? Of course!'

'It is a cruel way to make music.'

'Poof! Cruel—what is cruel, what is kind? To Mussulmans all is one. *Mashallah!* God is great! You know Ferduzi? Of course. *Gaki pusht ber zeen, gaki zeen ber pusht.* Means, "Sometimes back carry saddle, sometimes saddle carry your back". One day *nasakchi*, next day is your head chop off. Is all life. *Mashallah!* So my friend,' he went on, bending his fierce visage upon me, 'you come for womans? Of course! I know when you come before. Watkins you play tricks with, eh? With such a dog all the world plays tricks I think. Come! I show you womans.'

The sense of unreality increased as I followed his swaggering cloud of draperies along the colonnade. Under the yellow rose still waited the *felek*, causing a *frisson* of excitement in my blood. We entered the low chamber I recalled, tiled and cool and dimly lit. There awaiting us, foreheads on the ground and broad backs spread, were four or five females—at least, I took them to be female, but each was as totally encased in linen as a grub in its cocoon, and one could see nothing of the creatures whatsoever. Azeez clapped his hands, and these mummified objects arose. He clapped them aagin, and an oblong of white linen rushed towards us to set out coffee and *rahat loukoum* on the divan beside us. Was it a joke played on me? Azeez sucked down his coffee and smoked impassively. Now another bundle of linen had approached us and, kneeling down, began to undo my bootlaces. I could make out nothing about her, but suddenly I was much charmed to hear a quick little chuckle of amusement deep in her wrappings, as her finger unravelled the mysteries of Western footwear, as though somewhere in the midst of the laundry-bundle a child was hidden. Another of the shapes had taken up a mandolin, and had begun to quaver out one of the tuneless ditties which pass for music in the East. When my feet were out of my boots, and eased into Turkish slippers, the creature who had laughed set about the removal of my trowsers, still on her knees at my feet, by the expedient of undoing certain buttons. Fearful for the equanimity

83

of my person under this assault I pushed her hands away from their work. Immediately all was stillness. Two or three of the mummies had, I saw, items of Turkish dress in which they had intended robing me. Removing the pipe from his lips Azeez growled out :

'Speak, say to me what womans you need.'

'Well . . .' How was I to choose when the pigs were all in pokes?

'*Baziger* you need? Dancer? For cook? For storyteller? For rubbing? You say. Or for love?'

'Well . . .'

'Of course !' he roared, 'for love, yes. All good for love,' he assured me, a gesture encompassing his captives, 'you choose !'

Despair seized me. Then, at a further syllable dropped from his lips, the wraps fell from the slaves with the suddenness of statues unveiled at the twitch of a drawstring. They stood in absolute nakedness. I recoiled.

The truth was, that they were utterly repellent to me. Vastly fat, white and fat, but with the impression of a whiteness and fatness procured by drugs; rivers of perspiration dissolving henna and khol in stripes across their persons; in general their expression low and bovine, as though they did not properly comprehend their situation . . . Their vast nudities charged the chamber with oppressive—indeed threatening—feminity, as of naked Amazons, which was the very reverse of our Western notion of the harem, where we imagine lovely and submissive captives ministering to the lolling male. The Turk of course dotes upon corpulence, but an Englishman, bred up to admire a more boyish physique, cannot but feel that marble is the medium in which such feminine amplitude should be represented, and a plinth in the sculpture gallery the proper place for its display.

What was I to do? I wished that the business would conclude itself in some acceptable fashion, as my exploit with the royal cock in the Great Park had done. But a glance at Azeez warned me that he had command of punishments harsher than the Headmaster's birch. Watkins' description of the *felek* came to mind, and I tucked my feet further under me. I wished the whole concern heartily at the Devil . . . and then, on a sudden, for no reason, there revived within me—just as I had hoped—a spirit of adventure. Here sat I in the midst of the Arabian Nights ! It had the

84

makings of a famous lark——! And, after all, what Afghan slaver would dare to lay a finger upon an English gentleman? I bent my gaze more cheerfully upon the enormous captives.

'Tell me, Azeez,' said I, playing for time, 'a Mussulman woman would come to me? To a Christian?'

'I offer you no Mussulman womans,' he retorted.

'I see.' It was a good deal to swallow, the contempt of his tone. 'And as for language,' I said, 'do any of them speak a European tongue?'

'Speak in Frankish all.'

'I see.' That could mean anything. I saw no other way of eliminating any, or all, of the slaves without telling him the truth, that all repelled me, but this I did not quite like to do. The last emotion I felt was pity for the creatures; rather, I felt resentment that I should be put to a stand on their account. Femininity so aggressive upset one's notions of relations with the sex, trampling down all the erections of chivalry. Nothing distinguished one of these vast females from another—until I clutched at the memory of that chuckle which one of them had emitted whilst unlacing my boots. The chuckle settled it. Of course I could not tell which of the odalisques who stood before us on the chequered stone, like white pawns set out on a chessboard, was she who had shown weakness enough to giggle.

'Whichever one unlaced my boots,' I whispered into Azeez's hairy ear.

He clapped his hands. Instantly the creatures prostrated themselves, presenting to us a row of backs like a team of kitchenmaids set to scrub the floor. Then, clutching their linen, they arose and withdrew in single file.

'Maryka!' Azeez spoke beside me.

As though shot, a female stopped in the doorway. My impression—my fear—was that she was appalled. Slowly she turned. Should I smile? Lowered eyes gave nothing away. Was she less immense—less overwhelming—than the others? Or would any one of them alone have seemed, as this Maryka seemed, diminished to manageable proportions as she stood in solitary humility before us?

'You choose well!' cried out Azeez with great joviality, sweeping his moustaches upward, 'See—the moon face, the stag eye, the cypress waist—she has them all, the Jew!'

85

'She is a Jewess?'

'Of course!'

He clapped his hands and the girl went. I was startled—guilty —that I had selected a Jewess. Of course I recognised now the marks of her race, shared indeed with Rachel, in the tints of skin and hair. But surely my choice might have fallen upon a woman of different blood from my wife?

I wondered what would happen next. Azeez was smoking with vast contentment, his beard and robes whitened with sugar from the *rahat loukoum*. Would the girl be brought with her valise, for me to lead away? The larkish aspect of the adventure came uppermost once more in my mind, and I laughed to myself with delight, as I had not laughed for many a month. After all, I could simply let her go—moon face, stag eye and all—when the joke palled.

'So, my friend,' I said to Azeez, 'now to the reckoning. Will the girl wait here until I come to take her away?'

'She will come home to you, Caper Meester.'

'Home?' I was startled. And he knew my name!

'To Emirghian.'

'You know I have a house there? How?' Watkins did not know of the place. Only the landlord and the old traveller knew of it. 'How do you know?'

'Wait and she will come on the third day.'

'And the money?' I asked.

'Of course. For that too we come.' He looked at me. As I opened my mouth to ask how much I should pay, he rose from the divan in a shower of sugar and ended the conversation by bawling out, 'One *lakh* of gold *liras* you pay. In three days. It will be ready. Of course!'

This picturesque sum meant nothing to me, but there was evidently to be no disputing it. I too rose. I was the owner of a slave. Of course (I told myself) I will set her free—and I needed telling, for upon the instant of realising my ownership there slid from a fissure in my mind, the ugly flat head of a snake which I had not known slept in that cracked rock. As yet I but felt it stir in its coils, but its existence, and its waking, shocked me. Moreover I felt myself now linked to Azeez, whom I followed out into the court, and from that connexion came further electric tremors of unease. The East, Byzantium, had hitherto appeared to me like a felucca standing offshore at dusk, a far dim hint of romance against the sunset : now I awoke to find that hint become a slave ship tied up to the wharf, her murderous crew of ideas come ashore into my mind—and, worse, I realised that there were lodgings prepared in my head, as in the slums of any seaport, where those ruffianly ideas would find comfortable quarters.

How the singing of the blind birds sickened me in the outer court! Sunlight—fountain—garden—all were spoiled. Near the gates Azeez stopped. He turned upon me and shouted out with fierceness which no longer seemed mere theatre :

'Friend I beg of you—do not, do not laugh at my beard. You understand this saying? Good. We do not make joke. No, no! Of course!'

He caught me round the shoulders in that ursine embrace, stinking of jasmine and rotten teeth, and swept me along the colonnade. Then my heart stood still. By the mighty doors, his back against the wall, slumped that same ancient whom Watkins had recognised with such dread. Now that the bandages had been taken from his head I recognised two facts : *primo*, that he was eyeless; *secundo*, that he was that same ancient traveller I myself had met upon the ferry.

I exclaimed in horror; and by the sudden sharp upward tilt of that dreadfully wounded face, I believe that he had known my voice. Was it only the cruelty with which his face had been used —the eye sockets yet leaked a horrid ooze—which explained the cruelty of his expression? It seemed to me that upon hearing my voice his lips curled back in a snarl of ferocity and hatred which chilled my blood. Was it possible that he thought me implicated in his betrayal? I turned, to escape my connexion with him if I could, and my horrified gaze fell upon a sight no less disquieting : for there, lounged against a pillar, was that singularly repulsive creature whom I had seen wielding a sledge-hammer at Emirghian. I saw now that his hairless head had looked large because he was a dwarf; I saw too why his gelatinous, white, shapelessness had so repelled me : he was a eunuch.

That he grinned with all appearance of friendliness only made his expression the more malignant. I shrank from him; but in a reaction of panic, conditioned doubtless by an upbringing which compels one to master physical repulsion, I found myself extending my right hand to take his, as if he were a mere misshapen labourer brought to one's especial notice on a friend's estate. Though bewildered, the brute evidently understood the sense of the gesture, grunting in a way which I took to express pleasure. Little did I know at the time what an ally I had secured to myself!

In a moment more I was in the street, alone, the doors of the khan closed upon me. Only when I made off down the dirty street at a rapid pace did I notice that upon my feet were the Turkish slippers which the Jewess—my Jewess!—had exchanged for my stout English boots. Although I felt a kind of horror of them, as though they were fetters fastened upon my by the powers of the underworld into which I had strayed, I could not very well remove them, and expose myself to the ridicule of walking barefoot through the gutters of the town.

VI

The Devil to pay

WHEN I LANDED at Galata and climbed the steps onto the bridge I could not help reflecting that I had at all events connected myself into that busy and multifarious crowd which thronged across the Golden Horn. I had earned my right to move amongst them. I need now fear that no traveller taking his ticket for the Orient Express harboured a secret more bizarre than mine. Even Wilfried Blunt, surely, would have lost some of that damned superior *insouciance* of his had he known that I (whom he thought so green) had bought a slave-girl off an Afghan trader for my *yali* at Emirghian. This much I had achieved; but at a price.

For where was I to lay my hand upon the money? I cursed myself for not having procured a large sum already from Rachel; but the truth was that I had gone to the slavers' khan with no settled intentions beyond restoring my self-esteem, and events had moved a trifle fast for me. Now I had to pay up and look pleasant. It was imperative that I had hold of the blunt within three days. The punishment suffered by the wretched Persian traveller was a plain warning : blindness and the *felek* are not penalties to incur for a lark that goes wrong. The parallel I had drawn between this venture and a schoolboy 'dare' seemed to have led me into deep water. Well, I must pay—or, rather, Rachel must pay, since the law now sees fit to allow women control of their marriage portion, to squander upon the trivialities of a petticoat mind, whilst a husband can remain penniless at their side.

Although I travelled up to Pera determined to demand the necessary without explanation, I no sooner had my hand upon the handle of her door than I realised that it could not be done. A *'lakh* of gold *liras'* was one thing, such sums came by rubbing magic lamps; but translated into plain sovereigns by the dragoman the sum became quite a different pair of sleeves. A hundred or two I could extract from Rachel without question; but my campaign against her had not as yet reached the point at which so large a sum as this could be demanded without my weakening my own strategy, which was to affect high indifference to herself and her fortune alike. Besides, added to the money I had already used in renting and furnishing the house, she was probably not in possession of such funds at Pera. Angry with her on this account I spoke to her more severely than was consistent with asking for money. Nothing so destroys a man's independence— or indeed undermines his very masculinity—so much as being constantly constrained to recollect on which side his bride is buttered. I left her in her usual fainting fit, having told her that I should move to Emirghian for a few days, since she found my presence so deleterious to health.

How then was I to raise the wind? I had nothing to sell. I could only go to the Jews—to those members of the race not already in my household—whom I did not doubt would lend me the sum at 80 or 90 per cent. I recalled then that Watkins had spoken of the Armenians as the Jews of Stamboul; and I further recalled that my landlord at Emirghian was Armenian.

Quocumque modo rem: I was upon the first boat to Emirghian next morning, and an early hour found me applying at my landlord's door. Petros was his name, and I found him strolling on his terrace at the water's edge, having just come from Mass. Coffee was brought, and we sat upon rugs in the shade of his fine walnut tree.

When first negotiating to lease his house I had thought it the zenith of orientalism to sit here upon his carpets in a garden lapped by the Bosphorus, the cries of the *kaikjiis* in my ears and the wooded shore of Asia in my view; now, by comparison with a slaver's khan, this garden, and my host's converse, seemed no less homely than the lawn of Skindle's hotel. He spoke excellent English, having at one time been connected with a London merchant house, and our talk took many turns. His chief business now, he told me, was the export of *tiflik* and chickpeas. I asked him what he knew of the old Persian traveller who had introduced us. At once his face closed, a mask of craft.

'The Persian traveller?' he repeated, his tone casting doubt upon such a description.

'How should he be described?'

'Sir, he was many things.' On pretence of shading his eyes he watched me through his fingers. 'Always a rogue.'

'I have heard he searches for a daughter taken from him by slavers many years ago.'

'Ah. And I have heard he was a blackmailer, sir, and a murderer.'

'How so?' I asked.

There was judicious pulling of his spade-beard for consideration. 'No matter,' he decided upon saying, 'we may forget him. He is now dead. You, sir, are very fortunate.'

I did not disabuse him, but listened to his tale. I learned that it was the Persian's custom to inveigle a stranger into taking some retired house upon the straits—just as he had served me : Indians or Egyptians making his more usual prey—where they would be supplied with 'slaves' from amongst his accomplices and encouraged in unnatural vice of all kinds (I recalled with a thrill of horror his phrase *every kind of pleasure*) until they could conveniently be blackmailed, or plucked, or murdered, according to the case.

'You are sure of this?' I asked.

'He has used my house more than once.'

'The house I am at? And you didn't prevent him?' I exclaimed.

The Armenian spread his hands wide. 'Sir, my tenants were not murdered before each had paid a year's rent in advance. Who am I to complain if vice meets its deserts?'

'You are not merciful.'

'Sir, I am an Armenian. I have received no mercy. My race receives no mercy.'

'Let me tell you,' I assured him, 'that the Persian has not died.' His face shrank and whitened. 'And I have betrayed him to you?' He clutched his beard, and his dark eyes dilated. 'Sir, tell no one.'

'You expect mercy from me?'

'Tell no one, or you die. Leave. Leave at once. Your life is in utmost danger while this man lives,' he told me earnestly.

I was amused to see the fellow's funk. 'If I leave, will you return to me my year's rent?' I asked. 'I thought not. If I've paid, I may as well stop on I suppose.'

'The English are crazy. It is why there are holes in the ground all over the world where their murdered bodies lie.'

'The Persian is not dead,' I confessed to him, 'but a close prisoner, and without his eyes. He will not harm you, never fear.'

'He is a child of the devil. Yes, I mean it so—that is his race—a Yezedee. Have you hired servant or slave at his recommending?'

'Not one. He was seized directly he had shown me your house. His escape is impossible. Come, let us forget him,' I urged the quaking Armenian, for I felt wonderfully cheerful at the escape I had had. Luck was upon my side. Nor would this timid old fellow refuse me a loan, I judged, so long as he believed it possible that I might inform the Persian that his game had been betrayed, and by whom. 'Tell me,' I said, turning to topics that might please him better, 'have you children?'

'Sons, two fine sons, sir,' he replied proudly.

'They live at Constantinople?'

'No they do not,' he told me firmly; and then continued, 'I will tell you how it was. After the bad times of 1876—which by God's grace alone we survived here at Stamboul—after those days, sir, I made up my mind that this was not a land where the children of our race could live at peace. I had seen terrible things. Sir, I did not know that human creatures could act thus. Burnings—burnings—stones—the *yataghan*. I did not know.' He shook his head, a venerable old skull with the flat occiput and lofty cranium of his race, and I saw a tear gleam on his withered cheek. I could not help recalling that pious fraud Gladstone tramping England to divide the country into Atrocitarians and Anti-atrocitarians (with his speeches on the Bulgarian massacres of '76) merely to make a stick to beat Lord Beaconsfield. Nothing so removes an event from the sphere of real compassion as making it an issue in domestic politics. In this poor old man I saw for the first time the tragedy of his race. He was silent, and his hands opened and shut upon his knees. 'And so,' he continued with a sigh, 'and so I sent away my two sons, my two fine sons, out of reach of the Osmanli to Europe. One is in Hamburg living, one also in London. They thrive. But—they do not return. And now, sir, in my old age, do you know I am sorry I sent them away? So it is. I had no faith. I allowed the terror of '76 to shadow my mind with its dark. I said to myself, "What the Osmanli has done he will do again".

I was wrong. He has not. My two fine sons could have lived by the water here and lighted my days.'

'Maybe you were right though,' I said. 'The Turk could surprise you again.'

'No,' he said, 'it will not be so. We are modern. The past is over.'

'Yet last year at Sasun weren't there—disturbances?'

'Hotheads, sir. Political hotheads.'

'Twenty-four villages destroyed? All hotheads?'

'Sir, there is a commission looking into it. Just as if this was Europe. You see? We are modern now in Turkey.'

I saw that he was determined to hold to his view, and said nothing.

'No, no,' he said, 'in our modern city, what can happen? And I will tell you,' he went on, smiling with pleasure in his confidence of Turkey's progress from the barbarisms of the past, 'what I am doing now that I believe this truly. In Haskeui—you know it?—I have had my business house always, my strong khan with gates could be close fast if peoples, crowds, come to attack or burn. Now, sir, I have moved it. See? I have instead a new house built at Pera. No walls, sir. No heavy gates. No, a modern house in modern part of town is where I live now. London, Hamburg, is not more safe—I tell my two sons this, but they do not come.' He cheered up and said, 'Do you know what I have done with old khan in Haskeui, sir?'

'No notion.'

He rocked forward with laughter, and rubbed his hands delightedly. 'I have sold it to a Jew! At a huge price! Huge! For the Jews will never feel safe, sir, no though they lived in the New Jerusalem. Never!'

I judged it propitious to ask at this moment, whilst he made mock of the city's chief moneylenders, for the loan of the sum I required. I did not attempt to elaborate upon my needs, knowing by experience of the race of usurers that by explaining your prospects, your ill-luck etc., etc., you do but damage your credit. I simply asked, and said that the principal would be repaid at three months. He was not surprised; I could see him turning over in his mind, as he smoked, how best to realise the sum from his assets. Then he agreed. The money, he said, would cost me 60 per cent.

'Upon my soul!' I cried, 'for a man just come from his devotions you drive a hard bargain with a fellow Christian!'

He smiled, opening his hands as if frankly. 'If the old Persian was dead, sir,' he said 'I would be quite confident that I should see my money in three months. But he lives——'

It seemed hard lines that I should have to pay for the old fellow's timorousness, but there was no arguing him out of his funk. I arranged that the gold should be sent to my house the day following, when I would be installed there, and left him. I little knew in what plight I would next see that tubby Levantine. Having made sure that my thick-skulled Greek housekeeper, who had only one eye, understood that the house was to be made ready for my residence, I caught the ferryboat to Constantinople.

I was well content. So long as Azeez was paid, I could fancy myself floating in a pleasure-craft whose well-caulked timbers preserved me from that infernal undertow—the *sheitan akindisi* —which had sucked down the old Persian to torture and eyeless incarceration. Melancholy as were his prospects, I could not but rejoice that his fate had saved me from the trap he had laid for me. Whether his own version of his history, or Watkins' version, or the Armenian's, was the truth, I felt myself more secure with the fellow locked up. For my own part I had been inclined to like him, but evidently I had been misled by his gentlemanly bearing which, like his refined features and considerable height, had made me suppose him a man of breeding. Well, Azeez and that dwarfish brute of a eunuch were unlikely to let him give them the slip! So long as I owed no money to the slavers, I counted myself free to enjoy my good fortune.

Whether or no I presented my captive with her freedom— and I would of course, no question—I determined that the delights of the harem would at all events for a week or so be mine to savour. *Every kind of pleasure*, the Persian had promised me. I shivered at what I had avoided at his hands. Like Jason before me, in these very straits, I had contrived for my craft to slip uncrushed between the Cyanean Rocks of ancient Asia on the one hand, and this modern workaday Europe of 1895 upon the other.

On the third day after making my purchase I awoke upon bedding laid on the sand floor of my house at Emirghian. Today the girl would arrive. I did not know what to expect : in the darkness before dawn I could wring from my imagination no picture of the events to come. In place of the future all that recurred to

94

my mind was an early morning long past, in my childhood, when I had woken to awareness that my strongest ambition was achieved; for did I not possess a tool of my very own, a hayfork bought for me the day previous by a doting nursemaid? Yet, for all that my cup seemed full, there were difficulties : true, I owned this pykle, but how was I ever to enjoy it, since I knew that everyone in the house save the nursemaid (who alone wished to share its delights) would take my tool from me the instant they learned of its existence. Behind a door in an outer porch, unenjoyed, it had remained until my father had discovered it. Wrath descended! I was flogged, the nursemaid dismissed without a character, the offending pykle ordered to the tool shed. When I had looked for it there many years later it had not been possible to distinguish my own especial tool, the gift of my nursemaid, from other similar implements in the shed. . . Now I could not help fearing, as I lay listening to the lap of the Bosphorus below my window, that some incontestable power would intervene to deprive me of coming pleasure, as my father had snatched from me my beloved implement. As I dozed, slave-girl and nursemaid and pykle became one, the type of all pleasure, what I had wanted and had never achieved—or had achieved, at least, only with a flogging, as a hunting man may be said to achieve his objective 'with a fall'. I wondered by what means my captive would arrive, and how she would treat me. Made aware of a movement in the room I turned, and discovered the housekeeper standing over me. She had entered in the usual sly manner of Greeks.

'What is it? What do you want?' I demanded, feeling myself quite at her mercy in my nightclothes on the floor.

'Is come for gold.'

My heart thumped. 'But where is——?'

'Woman is taken to her cupboard.'

I struggled to my feet and shoo'd the crone from the room whilst I unlocked the strong box to take from it the wash-leather bag containing the Armenian's gold. With this secreted under a Turkish robe, for dawn is ever a chill hour upon the Bosphorus, I opened the door—and found myself confronting the dead-white and loathsome visage of the eunuch!

I almost cried out. He reached out his hand. Evidently he had pondered this gesture, the extended hand. I forced myself to touch that fell and shrivelled flesh. He smiled—great Heaven! I never saw a more evil expression than that wrinkleless smile. I pushed the bag of gold into his huge hand. He uttered some sounds in his throat and turned away. Was he dumb too, as the Sultan's executioners are said to be dumb? And of this monster I had made a friend! I closed the door and cast myself down upon the rich silks of bolsters and cushions. *Persicos odi, puer, apparatus!* I would gladly have exchanged my situation for that of my father's footman, rising at that hour in his narrow attic to a secure world ruled by a known authority. The eunuch at my door had affected me as the sulphurous mutter of a volcano, which serves to remind those who grow their vines upon its slopes how thin is the earth's crust above the fires of hell. So I lay in craven fear of where my rashness had led me.

The waterfront at Emirghian, however, faces towards the east, and it was not long before the earliest sunlight was penetrating my shutters and charging the room's grey shadows with the colour and warmth of day. When I opened the shutters the spectacle was magnificent, the windless straits reflecting sky and shore, the sun gladdening the scene and washing the flat waterside façade with light; long ripples sucking under quays, or sparkling where the wash of a ten-oared *kaik* sped away from the village. They were rare, those swift craft with five oars a-side, and belonged to embassies or merchant princes. I wondered if my bag of gold was gone aboard that one, to be carried to the treasure chest of whatever financier concealed himself behind Azeez. But what was money! I rang the silver bell eagerly for my breakfast, wondering if perhaps my captive herself would bring it to me. Now that the sun was up, and such a prospect before me, I would not have exchanged places with footman or master of the richest castle in all England.

But the slave did not bring my breakfast. The morning passed, indeed, without her making an appearance at all. I recalled the housekeeper saying that she had been taken to her 'cupboard'; a slip in her English, I had thought, but I now wondered if the phrase 'taken to her cupboard' had some arcane meaning I did not understand. The truth was, I was quite at sea. The floor above my own quarters was silent; when I looked up at her windows from the garden, their shutters remained fast. I strolled about the village, and sat at the café under the plane trees of the *meidan*, and smoked my cigar, and returned to eat my luncheon; but from the harem no sign came.

What was I to do? What did I expect? I had not the smallest notion.

Inaction that afternoon compelled me to consider just what I desired, or needed, from the possession of a female slave. Hitherto I had only cast the most fleeting of glances in such a direction. I must confess that attempts at frank appraisal of my desires suffused my being with shame, and did not in the least clarify my mind. It is a common enough confusion; one only visits a *fille de joie* in such a haze of intoxication as cloaks one's doings even from oneself, after all. Between visits, the base self that makes the visits is forgotten : rightly so, for that brute no more resembles one's drawing-room self than the depraved street women resemble sisters or mothers or wives. I ever emerged from a house of ill-fame glad to forget what had passed. One left behind in those secretive little upstairs rooms the whole sexual life, the whole of carnal knowledge . . . And when the next time comes, there is no decision to be taken apart from the decision to call a hansom and give its driver the address, for once within the brothel door one's body is given up to the debauched females whose skills, and knowledge of the body's desires (not to say its gymnastic capabilities), are a measure of their baseness.

Only thus had I been prepared for the possession of the female slave now established in my upper storey (only thus had I been prepared to take possession of a wife, for the matter of that, and the débâcle at Rome had made me wonder if some weapon was wanting in my armoury). At sunset I sat disconsolately smoking in the water-lapped garden, watching the golden light fade upward on the further shore, watching too the gilded swifts dart hither and yon in the upper air. I never could watch swifts at sunset without a tinge of melancholy, for they recall to me summer dusks when I would lounge at my window at school, and watch the swifts' flight in the belief that the absolute freedom which their wide arcs represented would very soon be mine. How one looked forward to 'freedom'! I thought that it would be a further good added, upon leaving school, to the good things I already enjoyed! I did not realise that I must exchange the whole world that had formed me, and all I had achieved within it, for

an untried article which turned out to be of no use : 'freedom'
. . . In following a swift's flight my eyes glanced over the upper
windows. The shutters were open : I glimpsed a flutter of veils
withdrawn. Had she too been watching the swifts?—and dream-
ing of freedom as once I had dreamed? So poignant was the
thought that I felt my heart go out to her. I almost threw away
my cigar and ran upstairs to release her from bondage. And
then, for the first time, I felt desire.

But what was the procedure?

Supper was brought to me in the garden, many dishes on a
great tray in the Turkish style that I was determined to adopt,
and I pondered how to act. Had I laid in a stock of Champagne
there would have been no facer, but with the thin wine of Turkey
I could not sufficiently cloud my mind to abolish my difficulties in
proceeding. When the surly Greek came out to remove my tray
—and to take the remains I suppose upstairs to the harem—
I screwed myself to the sticking-place.

'Tell her,' I said, 'tell the—woman, tell her to make herself
ready to receive me.'

The die was cast. I sat puffing judiciously on my cigar (which
kept off the anopheles), and looking as much like a pasha as I
could contrive, whilst she gathered up the dishes onto the tray
and carried it indoors. Before long there was an interesting stir
about the house, lights on the stairs, the chink of buckets, hastening feet, the sound of water poured into a tin bath. It seemed
that I had set in train events which I myself was expected to
crown. I confess to waxing exceedingly nervous as I waited. My
agitation recalled nothing so much as the mingled trepidation and
excitement with which I had waited in Upper School for my
coming interview with the Headmaster's birch rod. At last there
was silence above. I could delay no longer. I mounted the
darkened stairway and strode into the harem with only an
instant's hesitation at the door.

My captive sat in the corner of the divan by a window, which
was open, her knees drawn up to her chin, her veils stirred by the
air from the Bosphorus, the line of face and body beneath them
gilded with the last light from the sky. Her attitude was that of
a bird which has tired itself with vain flutters at a window, and
now sits with bright eye and palpitating heart as its captor
approaches. Nothing could be more opposite to a bawdy-house,

no woman less like those painted hussies who had hitherto emblemised, to me, the sexual act. Desire left me, for this was not an atmosphere in which its brutish appetite had ever been slaked. Here was a pickle! I crossed the room; and since there seemed no right point at which to stop I fetched up at the window, half out of it indeed, craning over the garden and snuffing up the scent of the magnolia as though such pastimes were my only delight.

Evidently I could not remain in this posture for ever. At last I pulled in my head, rather sheepishly, and prepared a stern glance for her. But she had gone, flown to the other end of the room where only the trembling stuff of her veils betrayed her in the dusk. I held out my hand, an involuntary gesture whose warmth must I fancy have reached her, for she returned on whispering feet into the twilight and took up an infinitely submissive pose before me. I placed my hands upon her shoulders, as one human being comforts another, and waited for her to lift her head. When she did, although the eyes darkened with kohl did not meet mine, the plain round face, moonlike indeed, was calm. I impelled her towards the divan; her arm stiffened in alarm and her dark eyelashes fluttered. When I sat down upon the divan myself and patted the cushion beside me, in a moment she too took her place, folding up her limbs stealthily as if to secrete their vulnerability. My confidence grew, feeding on her alarm.

'So,' said I—but my voice came out so hoarse with the excitement I had undergone that I had to clear my throat and fire off again—'So, first, tell me something of your history, won't you, so that I may learn a little about you.'

'My 'istory?' The voice issuing from the veils wavered uncertainly, low, rather guttural, not unpleasing. 'The 'istory of my life?'

'Yes, just so,' I assured her, 'I should like to hear it.'

It was as though I had given her the signal to commence reciting a part. 'I was born,' she began rapidly, 'into a family of poor fur merchants in the small town of Kuchuk Derbend, not far from the borders of Rumelia and Thrace. Those days were 'ard for our peoples, for the tax-gatherers of the empire had squeezed what gold there was from the peasants, and in some seasons of late frost and bad 'arvest many and many were starved. I will describe for you the life of those days so far off . . .'

So she did. Her voice, like a wax candle I had succeeded in lighting, soon burned steadily. The story was evidently rehearsed —this perhaps was the skill she had learned at the slavers' khan —and I listened with the interest one feels in hearing a folk-tale recited. Into her narrative were combined so many of the expected Eastern ingredients that I soon ceased to regard it as a literal account of her life, and enjoyed it for the flavour and colour of the Balkans which invaded my mind as she told her tale. As an infant she had been caught up in the war of 1875 in Bosnia Herzegovina; her father had no sooner escaped this conflict and travelled in a haycart with his family to set up anew at Tatar Barzardjik than the Bulgarian freedom movement had broken into insurrection. Then had come the massacres at Batak. Fleeing these, she and her family had been enmeshed in the Russo-Turkish war and shut up within Plevna for the horrors of its siege. Made a prisoner by the Muscovites, though only a child, she had been carried with their army to threaten Constantinople from San Stefano. Her parents had perished at Plevna—I wondered if their skeletons had comprised a handful or two of the shipload of bonemeal imported as fertiliser by my father-in-law from that unfortunate town—and she had been adopted, part mascot and part slave, by a Georgian prince with the Russian cavalry. In this household she had remained (it was how she had learned English) until, implicated in the disturbances at Sofia in '86, her master or protector had found himself upon the losing side, and had been seized at the Tsar's orders. At this point her tale plunged into such a maze of Balkan intrigue that I cannot now recall how she had come to be travelling disguised as a male with a Tash-kent merchant's caravan between the Black Sea and the Caspian when Circassian raiders had fallen upon them and carried her off for a slave. Only her new master's decision to turn his hand-some captive into a eunuch revealed, when the knife was already sharpened, that the operation was impossible. Thence by sale and barter she had come at last into the hands of Azeez.

Her story paused. I came to myself as if from a dream. All the tribes and nations of Asia had passed through the room while she spoke, and all the most desperate and bloody deeds of the last twenty years had been re-enacted in my sight. I looked at where she sat, but could make out nothing of her features, only the faint luminosity of veils in the darkness. Although I did not believe that her narrative was the veracious history of her life, I was at the same time convinced by the artistic truth of the story she had told; and I identified her sufficiently with the heroine of that story to regard her as a truly romantic personage, her plight an expression of Asia old as its stones and deserts. . . . This was not the lascivious encounter I had expected from owning a slave, but it was baptism into the climate of the East, it was immersion in that ancient and sanguinary river of Asiatic history, it was a decking-out of myself in Eastern dress which I had not looked for as a consequence of my purchase.

'Thank you,' I said, making a bow towards her glimmering outline, 'you have told me a wonderful tale.'

'It is enough?' she asked, her voice uncertain again now that her words were unrehearsed.

'Enough,' I told her. 'It is late, time to sleep.'

Again I had cued her to perform. She rose immediately and fluttered to and fro, taking bedding from the cupboards under the divans and laying it upon the floor with quilts and shawls. In my mind, as I watched her, were all the camps and tents and bivouacs and palaces in which she, or her heroine-narrator, had laid herself down to sleep. And beside what men——? Warriors, cut-throats, ruffians of the deepest dye, as well as a prince from Tiflis, had proved their manhood in that breach. I felt myself summoned to her as a traveller in old times might be summoned to satisfy the Queen of the land he sojourned in. Her gauzy figure had subsided amongst her preparations and, movement and rustling being now succeeded by silence, I supposed that she had undressed. I crossed the yielding sand-softness of the Persian rugs and stood above the mattresses laid on them. And then, alas, I thought of my father.

Instantly there swam before my eyes, in place of the *luxe* of these Cashmere shawls and the *volupté* of those silken cushions, my father's cold white sheets on the deal boards of his dressing-room. Cold and chill they were as that high severe idea of Virginity he embraced. I stood irresolute, unmanned. Mistaking my irresolution, the slave arose like a white flame in the dark and began to strip me. When I too was unclothed she sank away from me. I tried to conjure away the paternal dressing-room, to make my eyes see this Eastern voluptuousness which was real. In vain. What is seen by the mind's eye is believed in by the instinct which governs desire; of this truth my jacent person was proof. As though penetrating a physical membrane I lowered myself onto the floor where the two images, real and illusory, fought for mastery, as the lion of desire is ever destined to fight with the unicorn of virginity.

That I did not know how much of Maryka's tale was her own history, and how much was art, made it difficult to determine her true character. She was familiar with the customs of Europe—had she learned, for instance, to eat in masculine company from the Anglicised Russians of her story?—whilst retaining the natural habits of the peasantry of the Levant. She had for example the trick of squatting on her haunches, as comfortable apparently in that pose as upon a feather-bed, and I know of no spectacle more gypsy-like—nomadic—Asiatic—than a woman balanced upon her hams eating her mess of food from a hand curled into that curious spoon-like manner of holding the fingers. At first I instinctively turned away when I saw uppermost in her the squat peasant of her origins, assuming as I did that such a creature was repellent. But I soon made a discovery which surprised me : that natural behaviour is attractive. To behave naturally, as Maryka did, makes all actions partake of one another, flow into one another, so that the body which can be seen relaxed naturally can also be imagined in natural action, the one suggestive of the other. In each action is the potentiality of all actions. Barriers disappear.

And so, that second night, I found that my arms encompassed the girl who had chuckled, the Scheherazade who had told tales, the peasant who had eaten squatted upon her hams, the slave who had bathed and dressed me—in short I held in my arms a whole woman, and possessed myself of all her attributes, instead of undergoing the mere contact between genitalia which was all I had known of sexual life before. I was astonished.

She was not beautiful, in face or in figure, but I began to think her so. Her voice beguiled me, her accent I found ravishing. She had many further stories to tell, and in the heat of the afternoon, the shutters closed and the watery sounds of the Bosphorus cooling the air like a fountain—*placida pellacia ponti*—I lay smoking upon a divan in a long Turkish shirt of embroidered linen whilst she sat cross-legged before me hands and feet tucked

102

out of sight, spinning her yarns which captivated me. I studied her. By sight and by touch I possessed her, the sable hair, the open-pored and rather sallow Jewish skin upon which gold looks so well, the large and weighty swell of breasts castled with nipples which were almost magenta, sturdy hips—so this is a woman, I found myself reflecting as I took her to pieces and put her together in my own mind. Neither whore, nor heiress to be seduced into marriage, nor wife, but a woman, the great mystery. There came an easing of pressure as though tight screws in my head were loosened by a turn or two.

Alas! the simplicity of our intercourse did not endure. I was obliged after three days of this life to return to Constantinople —lest Rachel send to find me—and even on the ferryboat my simple vision clouded over. Like rags and tatters of cloud, extraneous notions blew into my mind and blotted out my clear sky and my sun.

I mean that I began to consider what a man should want, or could desire, or might contrive, in the circumstance of having a female slave shut up in his house. At first I had thought myself no end of a dog for my own exploits, and had smoked my cigar with my feet on the boat's rail and my hat tipped over my eyes. But as the steamer came in view of that sombre campanile, the erection of the Egyptian Caliph, rising amid its secret groves, I could not help speculating on the rumoured lusts gratified by that potentate. On either hand, now that the subject had taken hold of my mind, I saw *yalis* and palaces which suggested to me, as the ferry steamed past their glimpsed delights, all the depravities of Europe and Asia. With the marble landing-stairs at Beylerbei came thoughts of Rome's decadence, and Tiberius on Capri; as Cheragan floated by I imagined the sad monster said to be confined in its dungeons; the walls and towers of Yildiz whispered of abominations which made the blood pulse in my veins; by the time my ferry had swung into the Golden Horn under the very eyes of the Seraglio, I had begun to think my idyll with Maryka a very green piece of innocence—indeed wasn't the notion of an 'idyll' with a slave-girl thoroughly risible in the first place? How contemptuous the true libertine would be!—why, I was contemptuous myself!

I had been somewhat hurt, too, by the indifference with which

Maryka had viewed my departure. It had obliged me to recollect our real relationship, owner and slave. Since it was so, since I had the power, was there not some quirkish desire or half-formed fancy I could wreak upon her? As I rode up to Pera in the funicular I tried if I couldn't dredge up from memory an unquenched ardour or two, so as not to be put quite to shame in the lizard eye of caliph or pasha or slave.

Rachel was not in. Exceedingly irritated, I demanded of Nanny —sewing as usual under the lamp—where she was gone. To the harem! I was enraged, and promised myself I would put a stop to these indelicate excursions the moment she returned. She had run off with Mrs Watkins of course, absurd woman, nosing about the harems of Stamboul on the pretext of the Abolitionist. I changed my clothes for evening dress and went down to dine alone.

A bottle of Champagne improved my temper. When I had drunk it, and had done eating, I tipped back my chair and congratulated myself that my situation was unquestionably the most interesting of anyone in the dining-room. That Cockney matron amongst her daughters, what would she have responded had she known my position? I pictured her mittened hands flying up to her bonnet, her mouth a perfect O of horror, her daughters casting fascinated glances upon me—I could have laughed aloud. But a thought returned to me : would not even a Cockney grocer, like the paterfamilias finishing his mutton across the room, have sniggered at the innocence of my dalliance with Maryka? House on the Bosphorus, slave-girl all snug—and there sits this rare muff listening to her stories with his mouth open, and thinking it a privilege to sleep in her arms! A regular greenhorn! I sent the waiter scuttling for brandy and sat frowning round the room as though the Cockney cur had really laughed at me. And I fell once more to trying if I couldn't drum up some fancy—desire— need—which could be exacted from my slave.

Nemo repente fuit turpissimus, says Juvenal. In my head was only shadow, and shapes I couldn't grasp. On I sat over my brandy. What did I desire? I do not know why it came into my head, but I found myself thinking of that unspeakable brute Wilde, whose abominations had been sentenced a month or two previous (we had been out of England, thank the Lord, so that I had not been obliged to keep the newspapers from polluting

104

Rachel with their filth during the creature's trials, as had been every respectable husband in the land). The first persons I had seen at our hotel in Monte Carlo, where we had arrived on our wedding tour in March, were Wilde and his catamite Douglas. Well, I had run across the fellow once or twice at crushes in Town, where I confess his greasy Irish manner had misled me into thinking him a gentleman, as well as an amusing enough dog, so I resolved to make myself known to him at Monte. You never saw a fellow condescend as did that sleek toad! Didn't introduce me to Lord Alfred—didn't wait whilst I presented Rachel—off in a cloud of his confounded Turkish cigarette smoke and the scent of patchouli—leaving me looking devilish flat to Rachel. However, two months later when I opened my paper and saw him sentenced to two years hard labour I knew which of us had the last laugh. That the beast was a cad as well as a degenerate had saved Rachel from the contamination of knowing him. But he and his beastliness had stayed in my mind—one of the creature's worst crimes was that he must have made half the upper class of England recollect events which they had turned their back upon, in a manner of speaking—and he came into it now with his filth, until I crushed out my cigar and strode upstairs to take my mind from such abominations by blowing up Rachel for her absence earlier.

But she was not in her rooms, had not returned. What could she be about? Not——? No, unthinkable. Pera besides, unlike Continental watering-places and spas, does not abound with that despicable dago type 'the ladies' man'. Unsteady on my pins I soused down rather heavily in a chair—full upon Nanny's infernal sewing! I snatched up the whole bag of tricks to hurl it away when out of a blue satin pouch fell cascades of *mousseline de soie*. I picked them up. Undergarments! Rachel's undergarments! Quick as thought, out of the clinging softness, ideas formed themselves like genii arising from a lamp. Excitement. Jealousy. She should not escape me! There came to my mind a desire I could gratify. I stuffed the feminine underthings into my pocket. More, I looked rapidly through Rachel's drawers for what I sought. Then I stumbled to bed with my booty.

I would have left Pera next morning without disturbing Rachel had she not tapped on my sitting-room door whilst I was breakfasting. I pulled a velvet dressing robe over my shirt-sleeves and opened the door to her. *En déshabille*, her hair loose and heavy and raven dark around her ivory face, she made a most taking picture, similar enough to that which I had been gazing upon these past days to arouse my concupiscence.

'Archie,' she said, 'the house at this place on the Bosphorus, is it prepared yet?'

'No, no,' I said, 'that's to say, yes—or no, not prepared, most uncomfortable, a mere bivouac as yet, impossible for ladies. The drains,' I added wildly, 'are most unsatisfactory, unsafe indeed, dangerous for anyone in low health. I have to go down there to meet with the plumber today as it happens. I shall stay several days, a week probably. Certainly a week.'

She looked somewhat surprised at my vehemence, but drew a letter from the folds of her peignoir. 'As to the plumbing,' she said, 'of course I must leave all that to you to judge. I am sorry it is taking up so much of your time. But here is a letter from Papa. He thinks now of reaching us earlier.'

I took the letter and read it. But I could not remove my mind from Rachel, who had seated herself upon the arm of a chair at the window. About her draperies there was an Eastern hint, and within them, against the light, the swell of her full figure was revealed. At wrist and neck and ankle showed skin of the same tint as Maryka's, pearly where the light fell, alabaster in the shadows; from my fresh intimacy with the slave's body I could transpose knowledge which filled in details of my wife's adumbrated shape against the light. Would she too not have those same magenta-brown nipples whose erection I could yet feel against my lips from yesterday? She found me staring. I buried my nose in the letter.

'Yes, yes,' said I, making a bustle with the paper and speaking testily, 'well, if he comes we shall have to make the best of it. I don't know what the child Ben will do. Indeed I can't conceive of what your father will do, or why he is coming.'

'He will have business here you may be sure. Papa has business everywhere,' she added, just as if that were enviable or admirable! 'I know you couldn't,' she went on quickly, seeing me ready to protest, 'I don't mean that. It's just that Papa—oh, Papa finds Grimsby quite as wonderful as Constantinople if he has work to take him there. A connexion with the place. I mean that he doesn't have to depend upon sights and spectacles as I do.' She sat contemplating the skyline of Stamboul with a melancholy air. 'Travelling and travelling, and only seeing the surface of things . . .'

'I hear from Nanny that you were again at the—the—ladies' quarters with Mrs Watkins yesterday,' I pointed out, beginning to be stern.

'Yes,' she said meekly; and then animation flooded her voice, 'It is so droll, you can't conceive! Everyone contrives to have a perfectly delightful time except Mrs Watkins—yet she alone is intent upon putting an end to what she alone is not enjoying! There is a girl, a slave, who speaks French, and she and I have such chats. I have heard all her history. Oh I so wish you could see it all!'

'Hardly likely,' I said drily, and was about to censure the indecency of her intercourse with such females when she said:

'By the by Archie—Nanny says you came to my rooms last evening; you didn't happen to pick up her sewing did you? She has mislaid it; a sort of pouch full of articles she was mending.'

'A pouch? A pouch?' I huffed, a good deal discomposed.

'There must have been a thief broke in, for Nanny finds several things gone. Never mind.'

'Never mind?' I cried out, hiding my discomposure with a fit of anger, 'Really, Rachel! You must take more care! Oh, I'm aware the money is yours, and no doubt you will simply replace what you have lost, but the principle is altogether a wrong one, and you'll find I won't tolerate your spendthrift ways.'

'There was nothing taken that signifies,' she said, 'nothing I will even trouble to replace. Some undergarments and two old dresses I have had for ever so many years—oh, and a rag doll I kept out of mere foolishness. I daresay the chambermaid took them.'

'But the principle of property——'

'Let us not think of it again, Archie,' she appealed to me.

I appeared to relent, the danger of discovery past. 'Speaking of money,' I said, 'I shouldn't wonder if all this digging about in the drains at Emirghian don't end with me being presented with an account as long as my arm. But it must be done. I couldn't be responsible for your papa's health else, nor the little boy's either. Have we money enough at the bankers?'

'How much do you suppose you will need?'

'It's not I that needs it Rachel—not I! It's for the sake of your father, hang it all!'

'What will the bill amount to?'

'Oh! Who can say?' I made a show of calculating, jotted a few figures down on the cloth covering my breakfast table. Then I named the sum I had paid for Maryka.

'For the drains?' said she. 'But, Archie, what is the house worth? It must be a palace!'

'Really!' I exclaimed, resorting again to anger as a dodge to conceal the truth, 'Really, Rachel! You know nothing whatever about the matter and I'll take it as a favour if you won't meddle in what don't concern you! Do you fancy I am trying to steal from you? Is that your idea of it now? Eh? Accuse me of running off with your under—your sewing, that's to say, sewing and dresses and dolls and I don't know what besides! And now I'm to be told to my face that I set out to rob your pocket, if you please! Why, let me tell you, I live like a begger I do, like a beggar, when most fellows in my shoes would insist on a house in Town as their side of the bargain, so they would, and Comet-claret at two guineas the bottle every night of their lives!'

I continued after this style until Rachel took herself off and left me free to secrete in my Gladstone bag what items I had removed from her drawers. With these I slipped away to Galata and the ferry station. I had at any rate broached the subject of the quantity of tin I should require within three months to repay the Armenian his loan. Then I settled down to enjoy my voyage and the pleasures I planned at the end of it. With a half-dozen of Champagne poked into Rachel's underclothes in the bag beside me I felt well able to meet the Sybarite's gaze of palace or *yali*, caliph or sultana, as the ferry clove the waters of the Bosphorus under their jaded eye.

Before dawn next morning I walked—tottered—from my harem in order to sleep alone for what little remained of the night. ἆσέ με δαίμονος αἶσα κακὴ καὶ ἀθέσφατος οἶνος. So weak that I could scarce stand erect, filled with disgust too, I lay down all dirty as I was on a divan and covered my nakedness with a shawl. Even with eyes closed and ears stopped, even burrowed into the bolsters, my mind was a slate the chalk screeched on, slate I couldn't wipe clean. Never, never again—was all the sponge I could use upon that slate. On that promise I slept.

I awoke to the light of day at my shutters. I explored my self for damage as one might test out one's limbs, coming to one's senses in a mine-shaft, for breaks. I sat up gingerly. Never again, of course—but so long as that was understood, all seemed to be well. Only think what I had done——!

Alas, to think of it was a mistake. My body, to the brain's pious horror, expressed its firm interest. Was there then—asked the brain, that superior article left with one's galoshes at the brothel door—was there to be no escape from the creature I had loosed upstairs? Must I like Actaeon be devoured by my own hounds? —But in truth I was already impatient to experience the hounds' sharp teeth tearing my flesh! Before I had finished my breakfast my head was busy with a hundred more schemes of venery. The brain had soon given up its cant ejaculations and had turned, like a Scotch attorney, to serving the stronger cause.

I need not describe how that day passed. As my physical capabilities required ever more mechanical assistance, so the elaboration of my contrivances increased. By evening the village had been ransacked for apparatus, carpentry-work had been undertaken, fragments of a dozen fantasies littered the house; but in the midst of the filth and the rope-ends, the woodshavings and scraps of *mousseline de soie*, the splintered canes, the limbs of a rag-doll, the swing looped over a beam—in the midst of exhaustion and self-disgust, I yet recognised the futility of saying 'Never again'. I would go on. I would go on building ever more elaborate card-houses out of my lusts, as each last erection was knocked flat by a puff of satiety, or of common sense . . . It is how the ludicrous pyramids of de Sade's fantasy came to be constructed, that piling of Pelion upon Ossa in the hope that the tip of so prodigious an erection would at last penetrate to Heaven. Yes, I was doomed to go on. Who will not experiment, if he has in his pocket the keys of an alchemist's laboratory, and in his head the half-remembered receipt for the elixir of life?

The early evening I spent dozing in my own quarters, unable to look upon the slave's face except with disgust, until my desire for her body should again revive. How different from that first evening was this. And what fudge it seemed, that I should have sat listening to a slave's history!—as though the mutton chop upon one's plate was to postpone being eaten by reciting nursery rhymes.

As the sun sank I felt better able to encounter the light outside, and went down to my quay. On the water between myself and Asia craft came and went in the marvellous radiance, *kirlangich* skimming by, feluccas and the high-prowed Arabian dhows, merchantmen plodding up the middle channel under fulginous smoke clouds. What a lively company they made! I looked about my kingdom with satisfaction—and saw what made my heart beat uncomfortably quick. In the creek between my house and my neighbours' lay a long dark boat, its stern hooded, its prow grating the slimy water-stair. Still the dwelling above it (in whose garden I could not forget that I had first seen the eunuch) retained its gloomy and deserted air. I shivered. Thank Heaven I owed the devils no money. I walked to the water's edge.

The Devil's Current swept by with the noise of an animal that licks its lips—*strepitumque Acherontis avari*—so full, so overfull, like a flood on the very point of breaking its bounds. What devastation if it did! I peered down into the rapidly darkening water. What gloomy mysteries and treacheries these depths had devoured! I looked—I gasped in horror; for in an undulous cloud of tendril and membrane, like blinded souls doomed to wander, was slowly pulsing by upon the current a ghostly horde unending—a horde of jellyfish, in thousands beyond counting.

Perhaps I should have attended to the presages—the hooded boat at the water-stair, the avatars of the Devil's Current swimming by—presages to send a half-delightful shiver through the heart; yet the straits and the enchanting scene before me exerted so lively a fascination that I caused carpets to be brought out so that I could eat my dinner *al fresco* as the light failed. After I had dined I would retire once more into the fantasies of the *anderun*. Or so I determined; in the event I fell asleep before my dinner was brought to me.

When I awoke it was dark—a darkness so impenetrable, moonless, unlighted by any gleam of lamp or star, that I could make out only the loom of the house in front of me, and hear only the chuckle of the waves. Had I been wakened? I carried into waking from sleep a notion that I had been aroused by a tapping, a shuffling, which had warned me to wake. Now I heard nothing but the lap of water fretting the quay. In getting upon my feet I stepped into the large brass tray on which my meal had been carried out to me whilst I slept, and I clattered and cursed loudly amongst dishes and sauces until I was free of them. I found my way over the flagstones to the house, and entered by the half door, a contrivance like a stable door, which had been left open. I felt my way to the wall and so mounted the stairs. Tomorrow I would give orders that lamps were to be kept lighted—indeed why were there no lamps burning tonight? Was it late—my attempts to live at Emirghian by the mad Turkish clock, with midday at sunset, had ended in my utter confusion—or could an intruder have extinguished the lights? The door of my own room I found to be open, and I moved more confidently through its darkness towards the spot upon the floor where my bedding should have been spread for me. I put down my hand. There was the bedding, but what was this? A handful of feathers? More, surely the stuffing of a bolster, of a mattress, of cushions . . . And this? My fingers discovered the torn edges of silk. The bed had been cut in ribbons. Then the door closed quietly.

In a second my mind made the connexion between door closing and slashed bedding: and in that second I heard the soft shuffle of someone who was in the room with me. How dark it was! I moved with breathless fear away from the bed. It had been attacked murderously with a knife by one who thought no doubt that I was in it. Now she waited for me—for of course I was persuaded that this was the slave's work—with cold steel in her hand. Evidently she saw no better in the dark than I did, for I heard her feet slide forward as carefully as a blind man's as she came towards me. I had gained the wall, and round it I moved with the greatest caution. At last my fingers met the panel of the door and could creep over it to the handle. I grasped it, flung back the door and darted onto the landing. Rushing downstairs, my feet jumbling the treads as in a nightmare, I slipped and fell, struck the wall where the stairway turned, collapsed on the cold flags of the hall. Pain jabbed my leg. Ankle? Knee? Already the shuffling, sliding step of my pursuer was upon the upper stair. I crawled towards that half door onto the waterfront, opened the bottom half and dragged myself outside. In a stone corner, close to the water, I crouched waiting. Could I not contrive, despite her knife and my injury, to trip or wrestle her into the Bosphorus?

Through my mind as through its waters wavered those myriad blind jellyfish I had seen at dusk. Then came another thought, another hope : the house next door across the creek, the eunuch, would he not aid me? Rapidly I found the supper tray. I chose a heavy brass dish and hurled it with all my strength across the inlet. By good fortune my third sauceboat struck a window. Glass shattered. A dog woke.

But now another sound drew all my attention : the creak of the half door as it opened, the inexorable shuffle of those soft slow steps of my pursuer. I crawled back as near the water's edge as I dared. Still the footsteps came on, still from the dwarf's house came no light, no sound but the grumbling of a dog. Then from my own house sprang out a sudden tongue of light. I looked up. There in her window, lamp in hand, stood the slave-girl gazing down. Who then hunted me? Terror of the unknown clutched my heart. The dwarf? Who? In the faintly falling rays of the slave's lamp I made out first a sliding, shuffling foot which protruded from the deep shadow of the wall, then a shrouded figure, then the gleam of steel. Then I saw the head. Dear God—it was the blinded Persian! Horror transfixed me. That he was eyeless— those leaking sockets fixed upon me—gave for some reason utter hopelessness to flight. That he was blind and yet had found me! —would find me, as the Armenian had warned, wherever I hid. I screamed up in despair to that figure with its calm lamp in the window high above. In vain : unmoving, unpitying, she gazed down. Now the long blade of the knife settled its aim upon me like the snake's unwinking eye.

I now became aware that outside the mesmeric field of the Persian's attack there had erupted certain rough-tongued and avid sounds. Following upon them there crossed the terrace at a rush a black beast's shadow. Large and heavy as a black bull it charged, its onslaught felling the Persian. The two were plunged in the utter dark of the shadow of the house. I could see nothing. But I heard. If you have watched wolves fed, you will have heard the sounds—except the scream, which you will not have heard unless you have witnessed a man eaten alive. Despite my damaged leg I crossed the space to the house with the speed of terror and bolted the half door behind me. I collapsed against it. But what was that stir above—an opened door—the creak of a stair? The slave would come now, seizing her chance. Where could I hide?

I fled into the downstairs room where was stored the European furniture bought against my family's arrival. I limped to and fro pushing gimcrack chairs and sofas against the door. Then, rather as a shipwrecked sea captain might drag himself from the whelming waters onto one fragment of his foundered ship, I dragged myself up from the floor onto a European bed. There I lay in utter prostration. Modern Western furniture piled against the door seemed a flimsy barricade against the terrors of the East which I had unloosed on its further side. But I could do no more. Soon I passed into unconsciousness, or sleep.

I came to my senses—would that I had not—in the grey luminosity before dawn, aware of the flapping of a shutter in the breeze which ruffles the Bosphorus at that hour. Though fear still slopped about in my head, I limped to the aperture and reached out for the shutter. Then I saw the head. A rotten and dripping fruit, it hung by its hair from the branches of the magnolia, the blinded head of the Persian swinging above a puddle of its blood. To its ghastly wax-whiteness the magnolia leaves lent a greenish tinge. The lips had been devoured. I slammed the shutter. I crawled back upon the bed, and fell into a kind of swooning nightmare.

It was full day when I was brought to myself once more by the pain of my knee. That I could endure. But I lay a while waiting till the talons of nightmare should release me, as they do with such reluctance when one wakes, so that I could sort the chimerical fears from those perils that must be faced. I sat up. I rose. I did not open the shutters, half fearing to discover that the magnolia's ghastly burden was no chimera vanished with the night. I dismantled the barricade of furniture against the door and climbed slowly upstairs, relieved to find my knee serviceable. The house was silent, the hour, I judged, about ten o'clock. I rang the silver bell which summoned breakfast; by the response to that I would gauge the temper of the household this morning.

The tray was carried in by the one-eyed Greek who seemed neither more nor less surly than was usual. I told her to clear away the feathers and my ripped bedding. This done, I had a further test for the reality of the night's terrors : I told her to open the shutters. This too she did, and quitted the room with her armful of débris. Surely had there been a severed head suspended in the tree she would have shown surprise or shock?

With increasing confidence I poured coffee and began to eat the bread and *yaourt* the woman had brought. Then commenced from without the heavy, measured blows of a hammer. I put down my cup. It was the same flat beat I had heard before, the first time I ever stood in this house. I went to the window knowing what I would see. Above the wall of the court across the creek, in the dwarf's vast hands, the sledge-hammer rose and fell. As before, the object into which his blows smashed was hid from me; as before, the huge dark hound watched with the listlessness of a satiated appetite. In the indifferent brutality of the dwarf's work, too, I discerned that his greed or lust had been already satisfied, and that he was engaged in the mere destruction of evidence . . . I looked down at the magnolia tree. Yes, its grim fruit had been gathered. Below the tree the paving had been scoured clean.

It is extraordinary how far the removal of evidence goes towards restoring the *status quo* before the event. No corpse, no murder. All that remained of the night's work was a painful knee, and the pain of that, too, had sensibly diminished by the time I had eaten and bathed and dressed myself in a good English suit once more. It seemed that I was to escape evil consequences. I dared hope that the night could be forgotten. One action more remained to be performed. Having told the Greek slattern that she was to inform the slave to be prepared to receive me, I limped upstairs and entered her quarters.

She stood in the centre of the room, veiled submissively, head bowed, her hands and feet concealed from me. Perhaps in response to her inanition I felt neither lust nor loathing. Impassively as she had recited her life's history, or had undergone what I had inflicted upon her, or had watched the Persian's attempt on my life—with indifferent impassivity she awaited my will now.

'You are to go,' I said. 'You are free.'

She did not stir, nor respond in the least.

'You are a slave no longer,' I told her, 'I release you.'

I turned and left the room. I left the house immediately and went to the village quay to discover the times of the ferries—indeed to discover what hour of the day it was, for confusion between the Mussulman's clock and the European's had so upset

114

my ideas that I scarcely knew whether the sun rose in the east or west. I now set my watch by European time, and determined to keep it so (if, that is, I kept the watch; for two of my timepieces had already levanted since my arrival in the East.)

I was not altogether sure that I would not be accosted—even arrested, for crimes had surely been committed—and I walked somewhat nervously across the dust of the *meidan* to the coffee shop, aware of that shrinking sensation between the shoulder blades which I hadn't experienced since breaking bounds from school. However, no one took the smallest notice of me. I sipped my sweet coffee peaceably until the ferry's funnel could be seen gliding swiftly behind the plane trees as the boat approached the quay.

Nevertheless, I was only relieved of all anxiety when I found myself safe upon the upper deck, the ferry under way, my game leg stretched onto the seat opposite and a cigar alight between my teeth. I had left a good deal that was unpleasant behind me.

The Persian undoubtedly was dead, slain by the circumstances of life at Constantinople as certainly as a Cockney who persists in ignoring the traffic will sooner or later be knocked down by an omnibus at the Marble Arch. Had he imagined myself to be the cause of his capture, since it had been immediately on quitting my company that he had been seized by Azeez's ruffians? Possibly. Or possibly (if either Watkins' or the Armenian's account of his pursuits was correct) I represented to a diseased brain a piece of uncompleted business. Doubtless he had been brought a prisoner to Emirghian in the hooded boat I had seen at the stair, perhaps to be put to death there, and had contrived to escape and make his way into my house. That house he was familiar with, having used it before as a place of execution, if the Armenian had spoken the truth. Awakened by my sauceboat, the eunuch had set his hound on the Persian's trail—I shivered, and exchanged my seat for one in the sun.

Two things I could count upon, *primo*, that the Persian was dead and, *secundo*, that I had set free the slave. Circumstances must therefore return to the *status quo* before I involved myself in this aspect of Byzantine life—to innocence. Why, it was as simple as deciding to abandon the Turk's confused horology, and by resetting one's watch to revert to the settled noons of Greenwich.

VII

In which Freedom proves a Benefit hard to confer

I HAD THOUGHT at first that I would make little of my damaged knee, for I did not want to dwell upon how I had come by the injury, nor did I see how it could be turned to my advantage. It seemed essentially an undignified affliction, best ignored.

But when I saw the sympathy which it unlocked in Rachel's bosom I changed my mind. At last, as an invalid, I might be accorded the respect proper to a husband. I gave out that I had slipped into the accursed trench dug by plumbers renovating the drains to make the house habitable for her father. Had I been knocked from my charger whilst defending her name from calumny in the lists, I could not have been more sympathetically received. Her own chaise longue was given up to me and placed just so, neither too near her writing table nor too far off, with a view over the steeply descending rosy roofs of Pera to the Inner Bridge across the Golden Horn, and to the skyline of Stamboul where it swelled into the magnificence of Soleyman's mosque. Upon this sofa, amongst a thousand shawls and plump cushions, I reclined.

Strange to tell, I too soon began to regard my injury as one suffered in a noble cause. The beef tea, the medical man's visits, the cool hand upon my brow and the glass of fizz at eleven—all these I accepted as no more than my deserts. If I wished to talk, Rachel was at hand and ready to lay down pen and book in order to sit beside me and listen; if I seemed to doze, the blind was drawn and she tiptoed from the room.

I had never before understood that injury or illness elicits affection—or is made the occasion to show affection—because neither my parents nor the grim female charged with our health at school had ever displayed for the invalid other than cold disapproval, reinforced by draughts of punishing physic. But

116

Rachel showed love. Perhaps because I had not in my heart felt deserving of her affection, I had always before turned aside to evade the responsibility of recognising it. Perhaps the somewhat awkward sense of my own dignity in danger, which had cumbered our relationship since we ceased to be children—or, rather, since I had left off childishness—perhaps that stiffness in me was softened by my position as an invalid. For my sense of fitness told me that the orotund phraseology and pompous sentiments of my intercourse with my wife did not come so well from the lips of a horizontal spouse. I believe she would have laughed at me. As a result, we were happier together than we had ever been before in our marriage.

It did not suit Nanny. 'You'll bring on one of your attacks will be the end of it,' she warned whenever Rachel lifted a hand to help me in some way. 'We'll have you in the hystericals again at the finish like them at Rome.'

'Nonsense, Nanny,' Rachel would reply, 'do you know, I believe I am stronger than I have been for months? I think I could pick you up, Archie, and put you in bed should you want it.'

'Don't go trying your foolishness pray,' said Nanny wagging her grey head over her needle, and muttering to herself about 'grown men acting the little boy, and grown women acting the giddy goat'.

Rachel and I would catch one another's eye. By whoever's wish Nanny played the duenna, we now agreed for the first time in confounding her. Some evenings we contrived to employ all the lamps so that she would be unable to see her work, and must either waddle with massive disapproval into her bedroom, or fall asleep. As Nanny slept one evening in her chair, Rachel whispered to me :

'I believe she is harder to be free of than ever Lady Mary was. I never knew how you contrived it, Archie, to dispose of Lady Mary when we took tea in those dear rooms in Berkeley Street.'

She had never mentioned those occasions before. I myself had put my courtship out of my mind as being somewhat undignified, the means employed even not quite gentlemanlike. To turn the talk I said, 'You didn't regret her absence as I recall'.

'Indeed no! Indeed I didn't. Even when——' She stopped.

'Even when what? Pray go on.'

'Nothing. No matter. You wouldn't like it.'

'Rachel it is your duty to inform me of——'

'Oh very well, Archie. Even when the anonymous letter reached my father, informing him of what had been happening at Berkeley Street—that is what I was going to say. There now! And do you know what Papa said? Did I ever tell you?'

All this was devilish uncomfortable. 'I daresay you did,' I said briefly, casting about for a way to end the conversation. Old Dolfuss was a sharp 'un, and apt to nose out the truth.

'Papa said that he was convinced it was you had written the anonymous letter. There! So that I should be obliged to marry you, he said. Is it not a despicable notion?'

'Rachel, this deuced leg of mine—ow! By Heaven!' I exclaimed in ringing tones to waken Nanny, 'is my injury to be quite neglected? It is but 40 years since poor devils died in thousands across the straits at Scutari from injuries not a whit worse than mine!'

Rachel employed herself busily with the pen. When I enquired what she was scribbling she was at first unwilling to share her secret—covered over the paper when I stole up behind her—locked away the manuscript sheets into her letter case—turned aside my questions.

'You will only laugh at me if I tell you,' she said, 'and it is a mere pastime, I haven't the least notion of publishing.'

'So it is to be a book,' I concluded, 'an account of our travels no doubt. Well, there can be little harm in that,' I allowed.

'It did start as a journal,' she rejoined, 'I commenced keeping a journal the very day we left England you know. But it became so tedious—why, I was yawning over it myself before ever we reached Monte. And at Rome I abandoned it.'

I shuffled my feet. 'Yes, Rome of course has been so much described,' I hazarded. Rome! From the tenderness of our new intimacy I looked back with horror to my attempt upon Rachel at Rome; especially since I had learned from my three first days' experience with Maryka that even a sexual relationship need not be quite brutal.

She sighed. 'At Rome I abandoned my illusion,' she said, 'and faced the facts.' I said nothing. She went on, 'The fact is, a mere girlish account of our travels isn't of the least interest. It was at Rome I thought of fiction.'

'What?' I cried out, horrified, 'fiction? Upon my soul, you don't mean to tell me you would serve up an account of those events in the guise of a sixpenny novel?'

'Which events, Archie?'

'At Rome. When I—you—I mean to say, events in general don't you know. Events in our lives and so forth. Lord no, it won't do, you know, Rachel. *Roman à clef* and that style of thing, why, people twig to you in a jiffy.' That she was laughing added greatly to my confusion.

'Oh Archie, how absurd you are!' she cried, 'no, no, not that at all, no one would be interested to read of that! No, no; at Rome I began to look about me, that's all, for what was interesting enough to serve as basis for a story, rather than recording the mere flat surface of things and then moping over how dull it was. At home you see I never minded being dull, for I always supposed that dullness would all end when I was married. But . . . So I resolved to look into people for what I could use, do you see.' She laughed. 'It is amazing how the most tedious people become tolerable if one watches them with a view to taking their likeness!'

'Whom are you speaking of?' I asked suspiciously.

'Oh, people who are tiresome,' she said. 'Really, I believe I am proof against the most trying persons now I set down their traits in my book. Nobody bores me, nobody frightens me. I won't be provoked, I simply listen, you see, and run home to my novel with their likeness.'

'And this—novel,' I enquired, 'what is its theme?'

She laughed gaily. 'Oh Archie, it hasn't a theme you goose! Such stuff as that I leave to Mr George Moore. It's just a tale, it's going to be.'

'And who is to be in it?'

'Characters Archie! Have you never read a book?'

'I shall be in it I suppose.'

'Not a bit! Nothing about you!'

'Why not?' I asked, somewhat piqued at this slight, 'Not romantic enough for a novel, eh? That's what you think I suppose.'

'I have done the great part of one already,' she said, ignoring this. 'What has so captured my interest has been visiting the women in their harems. You can't conceive of the stories I have heard!'

119

I was now persuaded that mere prejudice objected to the word 'harem' on a lady's lips—though in Rachel's copy of *Roget's Thesaurus* (as in the English mind) I had found the word classified under 'Impurity' and made a synonym for 'brothel'—so I made no objection to her language.

'Of course,' she finished, insincerely as I thought, 'I haven't the least notion of publishing.'

It was ludicrous to suppose that any publisher would purchase what she wrote, but the occupation kept her from mischief. I wager that poor Watkins wished his lady a similar occupation, or wished her at the Devil, for her meddling in the arrangements of harems was, as I understood, beginning to cause him uneasiness. He and his wife came to take tea with us whilst I was still nursing my injury, and he muttered to me that Azeez had sent for him to the khan to demand that he 'closed his wife's mouth'. I looked across the room at her. Her huge face was thrust close to Rachel's whilst her mouth opened and shut relentlessly. Short of Azeez's own extreme methods I did not see how the orifice could be stopped up.

'I don't want to pick no crow with Azeez, I don't,' he said unhappily, 'remember that poor old Persian we saw do you? Saw what they done to him? My God man. Of course he was a fanatic anti-slavery man, granted, no lengths he wouldn't go to, no lengths. I'm not like that, am I?' he appealed, 'not fanatic like, no.'

'But your good lady is,' I pointed out.

'Just so, just so,' he admitted, twisting his hands miserably, 'she is, yes. Mad fanatic, mad. But she hasn't met Azeez, that's where it is, Mr Caper. Hasn't seen what that Moloch done to them who crossed him. I tell you, man,' he squeaked out, his long narow head wagging to and fro, 'talks about slave merchants, she does, as if they was the gang of kiddies rings her door bell in Bangor and runs off before she can catch them.'

'What are you menfolk plotting?' bellowed Mrs Watkins at us.

'Nothing, dear.' He jerked his head away from mine.

'Telling you of his plan was he?' she enquired of me, sailing down upon us like a clipper before the wind in her formidable rig of bombazine and jet, 'this plan he has got into his head, foolish man, to purchase a slave?'

Poor Watkins made levelling gestures with his hands, to suggest that his wife's words must be expunged from the record—and kept from the ears of Azeez. 'Quite given up that idea, you know I have, dear,' he claimed, 'mad it was.'

'Pray remember that I am still considering it,' his wife warned him magisterially. 'I may very well take up a collection and purchase an elderly female. Imagine the sensation, dear Mrs Caper!'

'You would be famous,' Rachel allowed.

'Might you not expose yourself to some danger?' I suggested, owing Watkins my support thus far at least. 'The slavers are more or less desperate fellows I take it.'

She opened her mouth and laughter fell out of it like the brass clamour from the mouth of a dinner-bell. 'What a romantic the dear man is! Mr Caper, you are living in the Arabian Nights,' she scoffed, 'you picture slavers as villains with eye-patches and cutlasses do you? Not a bit of it! Men of business, Mr Caper, I do assure you. Respectable shipping concerns you'll find. Swagger offices. Not a scimitar or a bowstring to be seen I am afraid.'

I bowed my head to her superior knowledge. Watkins however bleated out, 'My dear, if you would only consider the danger——'

'That will do,' she said firmly, with a tap of her fan on his arm, 'Let it never be said that I put self first when the cries of my poor enslaved sisters were as the lamentations of Israel in the ear of Moses. Alas, you have not seen the wretched females, Mr Caper, nor has your heart been seared by the weakness and weeping of captive women. We have suffered all this, have we not, my dear?' said she to Rachel.

'I have seen them certainly,' Rachel replied, 'only I am not so sure they even wish to be turned loose.'

'Our task, my dear, is to educate them up until they do.'

'You say "educate",' Rachel rejoined, 'you mean make them think like Englishwomen. That is what puzzles me, you see. Is it helpful, really, to make Turkish slaves and their mistresses think like Englishwomen? Oh I know it's helpful to the button-makers, for the more they resemble Englishwomen the more buttons they require, but——'

'My dear, you are too young to form an opinion in the matter,' rasped out Mrs Watkins. 'Next you will be questioning our duty in disseminating the Word of God amongst the Heathen!'

'Well I do wonder, yes,' retorted Rachel.

'But then of course, my dear,' said Mrs Watkins with a smile of ice, 'you will pardon me mentioning it, but you are not quite Christian are you? Nor British neither. So I think you must accept what a Christian Englishwoman tells you,' she said with crushing majesty.

I did not altogether care to have such a nobody as this teach my wife her place, and started to say something sharp when the woman held up her hand like a traffic policeman and began to read off a scrap of paper she had discovered in her vast bag: ' "There has never in the world's history been anything so great as the British Empire as an instrument for the good of humanity." That, my dear Mrs Caper, is what we British believe. I am quoting the words of our Prime Minister's new Under Secretary, a Mr Curzon.'

'I'll tell you what it is, Mrs Watkins,' I said, forbearing to tell her that George Curzon's real notion of the thing was that George Curzon was the greatest instrument for the good of humanity the world had ever seen, 'I'll tell you what it is, it's because you and the Empire are as up-to-the-minute as the fresh paint on a battleship that you suppose the rest of the world goes the same way. You suppose the slave-traders at Topkhaneh have kept abreast of the times, do you? Commercial gents in frock coats you fancy them, do you? Bills of lading to hand, taxes paid on the nail? Well I wonder. I do indeed.'

She shook her fan waggishly in my face. 'I see you are a convinced romantic,' she declared, 'I dare say he believes, does he, all the dragomans' tales of headless corpses in the Bosphorus?' she asked Rachel.

'I hope your head don't join 'em, Mrs Watkins,' I said, 'for I shouldn't care to have my point proved in so irreversible fashion as that. Eh Mr Watkins?'

The poor fellow's own head retracted into his high collar in a nervous shrug. 'If you would only be content with selling buttons, my dear,' he besought her, 'buttons and bikes, that's the trick. Put the *zenana* on a pair of wheels, give the good ladies the freedom of the open road, and the safety of buttoned clothing of course, them's the freedoms to give them.' The fervour in his eyes was soon extinguished when his wife said:

'Freedom! Freewheeling you mean. Freewheel to perdition you will, no bother.'

He sucked his moustache. Rachel said :

'Do you know, I have enquired of the slave-girls where we have visited what they would do if their masters set them at liberty. They said——'

'My dear, what poor ignorant creatures say is——'

'What did they say?' I asked, for I had an interest in this.

'One said she would kill her master. Another, most of the others, boasted they would poison their rivals and so become *beuyuk hanum*. So you see? All freedom meant was that they would be free to kill.'

I retired from the conversation. I had set Maryka free. Would she then wish to kill me? (That she would wish to kill Rachel was expecting too much.) I had set her free; but had she taken her freedom and gone? I had no way of discovering save by travelling to Emirghian at the risk of my life.

It was not the slave's freedom from me that concerned me, but my freedom from the slave.

After a wretchedly disturbed night I recognised that I must go to Emirghian at whatever cost. Dangers must be confronted; that is a lesson well taught in our public schools. It was with the feelings of a Regulus on his way to Carthage—of a Curtius preparing to leap into the gulf—that I took ship from Galata.

When I reached the house it was as usual to find it shuttered, its silence penetrated only by the liquid sounds of the Bosphorus, its darkness pierced only by gleams of water-light trembling on the ceilings. There was no doubt that it exercised a powerful attraction—the magic lamp awaiting the merest rub for its *geni* to appear and perform whatever is desired. Whatever is desired . . . I had not thought that I would again feel its temptation, but I did. To bring the house to life I rang my silver bell. The curmudgeonly Greek materialised.

'Is the house empty? Is the woman gone?' I asked.

She showed toothless gums and cackled at me. 'She stays!' she said.

It was as I had feared.

'Tell her to make ready to receive me.'

I was not free of the succubus. Upstairs waited that slave body which I owned as I owned my own. The notion of power aroused that half-drunken appetite called desire. My foot was already upon the stair. Death at her hands I must face, for I could not keep myself from the life—the life of the beast—which her slave body promised. I entered her room.

There she stood in her usual attitude of submission. She would let me die by the Persian's knife, but she would not kill me. She was too indifferent to make an assassin. My apprehension of danger—of punishment at her hands for crimes committed—passed, and with it passed also desire. She must go.

'You must go,' I told her. 'You are free, I have set you free.'

She raised her cold moon face to look at me and said—nothing. But her legs seemed as obstinately planted on my rugs as oak trees.

'Nevertheless you must go,' I repeated, just as if she had articulated her objections. 'This house must be empty, do you understand? You are to be gone in one hour. Here, I will give you money, here is ten francs in gold. Or five,' I corrected myself, tossing the golden coins down.

The money lay where it had fallen. She laughed—the one melting attribute she had was her chuckle—and said, 'I stay. To make me go is two ways : or sell me, or kill me.'

'You are to be gone in an hour,' I cried, and turned on my heel and left her.

I had already taken the foil from a bottle of Champagne, my hands shaking, when I changed my mind and shouted down to the Greek to make coffee. Champagne had conjured out of my mind desires I had not known possessed it, out of my body deeds I had not known I could commit. I did not know what further discoveries might not insinuate themselves into my head by way of my gullet if once again I sat in this house, where I had a despot's powers, and intoxicated myself. By the power of owning I feared myself enslaved. It was true that a corner of my nature —like a corner of our civilisation, the Greece and Rome so prized by those who had educated me—rested upon slavery; but that exceeding sweetness I had relished at school in the relations of fagmaster to fag, and had since sought for in all my intercourse, I found out now to be the horrid sweetness of corruption. At school it had been the taste of sugar plums; but a grown appetite does not satisfy itself with sugar plums. I feared the despot's temptations.

So long as my slave, my creature, remained in the house, there was temptation. I turned the Champagne bottle in my hand as the suicide revolves his loaded pistol. In these days just passed at Pera with Rachel I had glimpsed the possibilities of a different relation, a new tenderness : I had learned in this same house from Maryka, before I had promiscuously trampled our relationship into the mire, to value the tender feelings which spring from full intercourse between the whole of a man and the whole of a woman . . . Lacking the confidence which entrusts itself to innocence as a fledgling to its wings, I had allowed myself—had forced myself—to corrupt the sensibility Maryka had shown me. But it was not to return to that mire that I was tempted.

I was tempted to something worse. No one becomes his very worst all at once, says Juvenal. I felt again the serpent's coils sliding upon themselves as the reptile stirred in its hole in my mind. 'Or sell me, or kill me,' the slave had said. I did not know how to set about selling her. The attempt would plunge me once again into that Devil's Current of Stamboul from which I had thought to buy my own freedom by giving to Maryka hers.

But to kill her would be simple. A simple and fitting end. It is perhaps not even a crime in Turkey to make away with a slave. I should have nothing to fear. It would take courage; but there is no other way to overcome one's difficulties than by confronting them. I recalled the exhilaration of knocking down that cock pheasant in the dark wood. I recalled too what researches in the Classics had revealed to me of the necrophiliac tastes of Heliogabalus. My hand was upon the Champagne bottle. To untwist the wire would be to release the *geni*. At that instant the Greek sloven entered with coffee. I rose angrily—or was it thankfully? —and stalked past her. From the landing I shouted up the stairs :

'Be gone before I come again, or it will be the worse for you !'

I left the house and flung myself onto the next ferryboat like a fugitive. I felt a most urgent need to regain Pera. I feared to be too late, I feared what tentacles might not have reached up from the *sheitan akindisi* to overturn the frail craft which Rachel and I in these last days had shared, like a honeymoon gondola upon the filthy canals of Venice. My ferry was a slow one, dodging from shore to shore, and with the villainous Turks who embarked at each village there embarked also the murderous ideas I had fled from. I would kill her. Death was the proper

125

climax to what she had endured; killing the proper climax to what I had inflicted : by punishment the slate is wiped clean. Her body would be taken by the Bosphorus. The Devil's Current would scrub my steps. The longer Death dwelled in my head the more it was at home there.

Yet as the accursed dawdling ferryboat at last neared Constantinople, and I saw the embassies and villas and gardens decorating the green slopes of Pera, the talons of these monstrous Eumenides released me. Here was the life I knew. I leaned upon the rail and watched the never-failing glory of domes and palaces and minarets draw softly near. Flocks of *yelkovan* skimmed amongst the shipping, so close to the water that they looked like wind-scuds darkening its surface, till the flock turned and the sunflash caught their rapid wings. To skim over the Bosphorus without wetting a wing—I wished I could. To see only the face of Stamboul that I saw now, smiling at the sun—for the future I would. I lit a cigar.

I thought of the sea caves of the Euxine where the *yelkovan* nest, close to the Cyanean Rocks, the Symplegades of the ancients. It had been my mother's view—part of her attempt to Christianise pagan mythology—that Jason's dash between the Clashing Rocks (which allow only no-time in which to pass safely) signified Man's need to step outside Time, and temporal possessions, if he is to pass quick (that is, alive) upon his Journey. The parallel she drew from Scripture was with the rich man who must pass through the needle's eye. As the ferry entered the bravery of flags and shipping in the Golden Horn I trusted that I was past the Symplegades; and hoped that they had clashed fast behind me before letting pass that possession from which it seemed I could not free myself, my slave.

Agitating news greeted me at the hotel. A letter had arrived from Rachel's father, sent from the Piraeus, announcing that he would be at Constantinople within the week. 'How are the drains?' Rachel enquired. 'Will the house be prepared in time?'

'Drains? Drains? Upon my soul I don't know, I don't indeed,' I cried. 'Rachel I have had no luncheon, the dining-room I don't doubt is closed, try if you cannot get something sent up—a fowl, half a dozen chops, whatever snack they have to hand.'

'Very well, Archie. And a bottle of Champagne?'

'No!' I shouted. 'No, no, I mean to say, a pint of sherry will do capitally,' I added in modified tones.

With my repast upon the table in Rachel's sitting-room, and herself opposite to me whilst I ate, I enquired what connexion her father had with Constantinople, that she knew of.

'Oh——!' She sighed, and twisted her rings—'Oh, there is nowhere in the world that Papa has not connexions. No grubby port that's to say, or shabby waterfront—not between the Channel and the China Sea I believe, that he hasn't an agent or two carrying on business for him.' She rose, and walked up and down with that lilting stride her long skirt emphasised. She never walked with the little steps of a fussy woman. 'Those are his connexions —my connexions too,' she said a trifle bitterly, 'men with greasy collars to their coats turning their hats round and round in their hands, standing there waiting to have a word in Papa's ear as he steps off the train or the boat. Those are his connexions.' She stopped, leaned a hand on my chair-back. 'Do you know, Archie,' she said 'they have always frightened me a little, Papa's connexions.'

I shifted in my seat. 'I don't see how the sort of fellows you describe could harm you,' I said. Her hand left my chair, as though it was a bird I had shoo'd from its perch, and she continued to pace the room. She had needed comfort, but some cursed stiffness in me kept me from supplying her want. I helped myself to a couple more chops.

'I could always see it so plain that they weren't fond of him these men,' she explained, 'that's what frightened me : that he lived amongst people who had no affection. I could see it. I could see it in the way they would smile at me; no love, just sly. Sly to please Papa because they'd profit from pleasing Papa. I wondered if he knew—knew there was no affection.'

She was silent. 'And did he know?' I asked, eating my chop.

She nodded. 'More frightening was that he didn't miss it. He said so. It hadn't any value. He told me that. Affection led to confusion he said, and confusion to bankruptcy. True. "And I have you to love," he'd say.' She clamped her right hand on her left arm as she spoke, not a gesture of love but of possession.

'Come now,' I said, drinking my sherry, 'he was a regular trump when he played with us as children.'

'Ah, with children!' She swept off about the room again,

127

impatient of her father's virtues. 'Yes, he played with children,' she said harshly.

'You're deuced hard on him,' I said as I cut into the cold fowl.

'Not so hard as he is.'

'He hard upon you? Come now!'

'Hard. No, not upon me particularly. Just hard. And cold. No friends you see. No friends, no qualms: he can cut any man's throat. That is true. He has achieved that. There is no one in the world whose throat he would scruple to cut.'

'Except yours, surely.'

'Except mine,' she agreed, bowing her head as though this were an additional burden. 'For me he would cut throats. I mean literally he would. Yes, for me, Papa would kill,' she said, watching me eating. I found that my appetite had gone. I laid down knife and fork.

'And the boy?—Ben; how does he come upon the scene?' I asked.

She shrugged. 'A nephew. But you know, I had never heard even that Papa had a brother until Ben was produced. Isn't it strange, don't you think, a family where relations can appear so mysteriously? Is that not strange to you?'

'It would surprise me no end in my family,' I allowed.

She turned away, wounded. 'Yes, maybe that is all it is,' she said, 'that we are Jews. I think in all Jewish families there was a blow fell upon some part of the relations, oh, in each generation some blow which fell somewhere. A massacre, an expulsion—we scatter like the bits after an explosion. That is what Ben is I expect. A bit from some explosion.'

I always found it a trifle awkward when Rachel spoke of her Jewishness, which she did in a particular elegiac manner, as though reciting a blank verse tragedy imperfectly translated from the Yiddish. I had never made up my mind as to whether she looked upon her race as a grievance or an honour; and nor I believe had she. But in the context of Stamboul I found it a good deal easier to have a measure of insight into a family such as hers, or into a fellow such as Dolfuss; for here was the entrepôt where the races of the East met and traded, a mule-load of lamb-skins from Ispahan one year being the basis for a caravan of Brusa silk to Grand Cairo the next, and thus could a commercial fortune be founded upon the mere astuteness which was evident in Dolfuss. There were a thousand fellows just like him to be found in the bazaar, all the better for not being Anglified the way Dolfuss was, for it was his frock coat and silk hat which gave him his look of a half-bred Jew tradesman. This attempt to appear respectable to the English made him risible to them in a way that the desperate-looking Levantines of the bazar most certainly were not.

Although anxious that my affairs should bear investigation by the time Dolfuss reached us—even without Rachel's warning of his cut-throat potentiality I had recognised that Stamboul was his opportunity to show his disapproval of me with impunity in a manner which would bring him to a rope's end in England—I was yet more alarmed at what might be the dangers of visiting Emirghian to find that Maryka was still in possession. In consequence I did nothing. One evening, in the sitting-room we shared after dining together in quite a Darby-and-Joan style, Rachel looked up from her reading and said :

'Tell me, Archie, shall we remove directly to the house on the Bosphorus when Papa comes?'

'Directly? The house? I can't say. I must go again. I will have to run down there.' I buried my nose in a gazeteer.

'And staff, Archie; have you engaged domestics?'

'No. Some. Yes.'

'Then there was the question of payment for the plumbing work. A sum you mentioned.'

'Yes, yes there was that,' I said hopefully. 'Our circular note upon the bank will cover it I take it?'

'Well, no, that's just it,' said she, a shade put out, 'you see when I sent off the letter you drafted requesting funds, all the bankers wrote in reply was that Papa was travelling out and would himself bring what money was required.'

I clapped shut the gazeteer, furious. 'The bankers wrote that? Damned impudence ! By Heaven that's cool ! What, are we to run to your father each time we buy a pound of cheese?'

'Hardly a pound of cheese, Archie,' she pointed out timidly.

I was silent. If news of the sum I required had reached Dolfuss I would have some explaining to do. I did not fancy making such explanations to such a man amid the bowstrings and scimitars of Stamboul. Lofty contempt for the Jew pedlar was all very well in Mayfair, where there are policemen to protect an English gentleman, but you could holler very loud in the Bosphorus before you'd call up a London policeman.

I did not know what to do. After much furious cogitation I hit upon an ingenious plan, as I thought, to make the house at Emirghian respectable : I hired such a great many other servants for the place that the presence of one slave would go unremarked in the uproar. This I did through the dragoman of the hotel, as dishonest a rascal as ever trod the pavements. When I had enumerated the domestics I required he ran his grubby finger down the list I gave him.

'For these peoples, Excellency,' he said, 'hire servants you want, or slaves?'

I was taken aback. 'Servants of course, you fool!' I shouted at him. 'But do you mean to tell me,' I went on, curiosity overcoming me, 'you mean to tell me, that obtaining slaves is so simple a matter?'

'More simple than find servants, Excellency, but costs a more,' the fellow said.

'How much does a slave cost then?'

'Girl-slave? You mean young girl-slave, very pretty?'

'For example. How much?'

'I find you one most cheap, Excellency, not worry, one girl who know all tricks you English mans love. Or boy you want? Boy most——'

I silenced the cur with a blow in the mouth before his vileness insulted me further, and left him to find servants as best he could. It was nonetheless exceedingly provoking to discover at this late hour that I could have acquired a slave, like a newspaper, by asking at the hotel desk. But the discovery came too late. I could now do nothing but wait upon events, and trust to Providence to extricate me from the scrape, as that Power had so often done before.

VIII

The Stamboul Mob pays off Some Scores

THE DAY AND hour of Dolfuss' expected arrival found us waiting at the hotel for word that his ship had passed Seraglio Point.
Rachel had wished to wait upon the quay, but I did not; because
of this difference we were in separate rooms at the hotel, already
divided by a parent whose steamer stood as yet some miles off in
the sea of Marmara.

I had taken her animadversion upon her father as an indication
that she and I now thought alike about him, since we shared an
opinion of his character : not so, for his approach across the
eastern Mediterranean seemed to melt her heart as if he were the
rising sun, and her rational opinion of him a mere rime of frost
which his coming dissolved. It annoyed me of course; that blood
is thicker than water cannot fail to irritate a spouse.

She would have waited for the old Jew on the Galata quay
since first light. I refused to leave the hotel until the steamer
had moored. As we drove down to Galata in the hired carriage
at last, news having come of the ship's arrival, Rachel was provoked enough to speak sharply.

'Now I dare say we shall miss him in the crowd! I really cannot
see why we could not have waited upon the quay, for all the
difference it could make to you.'

'It is a matter of principle, Rachel, which of course you do not
understand.'

'Oh, it is to be a principle that we should slight Papa is it?'

'Pray do not aggravate me, Rachel.'

We arrived at Galata staring out of opposite sides of the carriage. As I could not see the sea from my side I was obliged to
turn my head and gaze past her in as lofty a style as I could
contrive. Now I saw the brilliant scene. There at its buoy lay
the steamer, a smoking colossus amid the thousand darting *kaiks*

and cockleshells which swarmed about its iron flanks. From the masthead fluttered the flag of Dolfuss' Line. I was struck suddenly by what a grand thing it is to own ships; I could conceive of nothing which would so justify an individual's self-esteem, as to be the possessor of that magnificent iron vessel lying off the Golden Horn. My opinion of Dolfuss modified accordingly.

As we watched, an individual passed through a cluster of ship's officers at the vessel's rail and descended the ladder towards the launch, leading a child by the hand. They stepped aboard, the launch cast off and swung its stem towards us, growing inexorably larger as it approached. The child stood upon the deckhouse roof, steadied by old Dolfuss' arm, and looked eagerly and brightly this way and that at the sights pointed out to him. Although our carriage must have been visible from the launch, we were not amongst the objects selected for attention. Nonetheless I was relieved that he had a child with him, a human touch in this display of the power of possessions.

Already attendant upon the quay when we reached the waterside were jostling a half dozen unsavoury creatures, Jews and Mussulmans, Christians too, who formed a reception committee of ducked heads and grins and dry-washing hands. Whilst I kept aloof—these were the wretches exactly which Rachel had depicted as her father's connexions—she mingled her way through them. Indeed she competed with them to embrace her father. The whole entourage then followed Dolfuss into the Customs' House, he as impassive amongst them as his iron ship amongst the *kaiks*. Unwilling to be greeted as part of such a rabble I had missed my chance of receiving any greeting at all. Evidently he was not going to seek me out, so I took myself stiffly round to the Customs' House exit, and there waited for him to emerge.

Fortunately, when he reappeared at the head of his toadies, the little boy Ben (with whom I had struck up a friendship in England on account of his pretty nursemaid) ran forward and caught my hand. I was thus able to greet Dolfuss in an off-hand style despite his command of the terrain, and walk to the carriage hand in hand with the boy. A man, especially a hard man, is nowhere more exposed than in his connexion with a child, and I could see that Dolfuss had a good deal rather that Ben had ignored me.

'Is your nursemaid come, Ben?' I asked, looking about for the girl whose attractions I had felt strongly in England.

'I think she is,' he said, screwing up his eyes, 'she's saying good-bye to a sailor in my bedroom. Are we going in a train now? Is this Turkey? Have you got a house here?'

I spent as much of the next days as possible in Ben's company. For one thing the child provided a kind of buffer state between myself and Dolfuss, in whose company I was not anxious to be much alone. Added to his defects of appearance—the drooping eyelid, the lips so large and wet that they could scarce be looked at without a shudder—he adopted towards me a manner which was somewhere between a cringe and a sneer, like that of a tailor to whom one owes a long bill. Nor did I spend more time than was unavoidable with Rachel, whose evident partiality for her papa I found most aggravating. She had as good as stated her opinion to me that the old Jew was as vulger as he was heartless, and capable of any outrage in furtherance of profit: now she hung upon his arm, and lighted his cigar, and took walks with him as if he were the finest gentleman in the land. Her 'health' took a decided upward turn, too, for she undertook excursions to Scutari and to the Sweet Waters of Europe which had been quite beyond her strength, or the strength Nanny had allowed to her, in my company. I had persuaded them that they should not sail up the Bosphorus, but look about the environs of Constantinople until the Emirghian house was made ready; for I still delayed our departure thither day by day for fear of falling into a scorpions' nest.

A further reason for preferring Ben's company above that of Rachel and her father was that with Ben I was in company with his nursemaid, Zara. Under the excuse of acting as their *kavass* to protect and guide them, I walked them to one or other of the many cemeteries of the city each day, the nearest equivalent to a park that Constantinople could supply. Here Ben and I would bowl his hoop surreptitiously amongst the tombs, or whip tops on a flat gravestone, or play at hide-and-seek amongst the cypresses; and Zara would sit like any prim nursemaid in the Kensington Gardens with her two harum-scarum charges. It diverted me to find that the girl—though a Muslim born, and evidently familiar with the language and habits of the Turk—

133

made a great to-do about the contaminations and dangers of the streets and of the natives. She had in her opinion so thoroughly thrown off the taint of her origins that she had nothing but contempt for them. Like master, like maid : as the Jew pedlar in his frock coat aped the English gentleman, so his nursemaid (if nursemaid the dark-eyed fascinator was) aped the starch of the English nanny.

She was not, however, so starched that she did not return my kisses when she could be persuaded into a game of hide-and-seek. But she would not let Ben out of her sight for above two moments together. At first I thought that she made this her excuse for resisting the further amorous suggestions I made to her when I had her pressed against a cypress, but the resolution with which she dodged her head about to keep Ben in view, and the earnestness with which she feared offending Dolfuss on this point, persuaded me that she had a more compelling reason than mere virtue for guarding her charge. In light of what was to befall, her alarm was well justified.

At the time I remarked as a curious fact that if other children were about, native children of Ben's age or thereabouts, he melted into the pack like a fish returned to its shoal. Was that what Dolfuss and Zara feared?—his loss of the new identity they had contrived for him, as for themselves, in England? Or did they fear kidnap? More than once Zara would break away from my embraces and run towards a cluster of children in real alarm : then one's eyes would pick out Ben, and of course in his English clothes how could one have lost sight of him? Nevertheless it would happen again. And take away his linen breeches, and his smocked shirt and his English shoes, dirty his face and wrap a scrap of cloth round him, and Ben would have passed off as a street-arab in any town in the Levant. There was the rub for old Dolfuss : he had provided whatever money could provide to divide Ben from his origins—as he had provided himself with a top hat, and as Zara had cast aside the *yashmak*—but God's laws of blood and breeding, of race and rank, decreed otherwise, and broke down his puny divisions as the tide levels a child's walls of sand. One could not but laugh at them, secure oneself in what I have seen recently (and rightly) called 'a consciousness of unassailable primacy'.

It was just this ragamuffin side of Ben that grew upon my

134

affections. He was so bright and cheery, he ran so quick and laughed so clear. Because he had no reserve I found that I could dispense with mine; I could dismantle that whole awkward armour of gravitas which I had acquired (to the destruction of my natural cheerfulness) with adolescence and education. At first in our games together I had carried myself about like a fragile ornament, and ran and jumped in profound fear of tumbling down. But once I had fallen a time or two I found Ben thought no more of it than of his own spills. Perpendicularity did not seem to be as essential to dignity as I had imagined. I was soon rolling about amongst the tombstones for the sheer fun of the thing. This was an extraordinary freedom Ben taught me—I might liken it to the exhilaration I had felt the night I had been knocked down at Topkhaneh and had begged my way home— or indeed to having learned from Maryka that the attempt to retain one's dignity in bed occasioned as much confusion as an attempt to retain one's trowsers. What larks I had with Ben. Under my own clothes I found a child too, if not a street-Arab : had it always been allowed expression, and not confined too close by all those notions learned at school, would simple games ever since have served to satisfy my appetites? Were the debauches of Heliogabalus made necessary by the gravitas required of Rome's public men? The games Ben and I played were those I recalled from my own childhood with Rachel, a past I had thought as irrecoverably lost to me as innocence itself. But perhaps (I began to think) innocence is recoverable. I remembered with greater kindliness my poor father's attempts to recover his Virginity by stretching out upon the bare boards with Froude's *Remains*.

Dolfuss was determined to cut the most conspicuous dash. A carriage was hired, and a pair of enormously fat horses to pull it, and in this flamboyant equipage we were jolted about the town to view the sights and curiosities. What we were to notice was decided for us by Dolfuss upon his own system : that is, if a place was open to the public it could not be worth visiting, but if influence, if bribes, if *firmans* or *tezkarés* were required, then he would go to all lengths to gain entry. By this method we saw the inner courts and gardens of the Seraglio (by *irade* of the Sultan) in company of an Imperial aide-de-camp—a rogue with the furtive air of a Yildiz spy who entertained us to coffee in one of the hundred kiosks of the place—where we grew bored quite as rapidly as we would have done in the outer courts where the public is admitted. It was a cold, sullen, dead-and-alive sort of place which seemed more prison than palace. Never mind : it was a privilege, and for privilege Dolfuss was ever hungry. On quitting those shabby courtyards and ponderous gate-arches to regain our carriage, I saw Dolfuss slip off and bustle into what appeared to be the mouth of a cavern. I followed him. To my surprise I entered a church—at least I found myself in the lofty brick shell of a church of high antiquity, beneath a fine dome whose windows lit mosaics and gilt Greek inscriptions; but the edifice was in use as an armoury. In place of a congregation were stacked thousand upon thousand of rifles and long bayonets. It was these weapons that Dolfuss had come to see. There he stood, coolly calculating quantities and examining their manufacture, whilst the light from the high dome fell indifferently upon Christian mosaic, upon Saracen steel, upon Hebrew merchant—an allegory of the city's history, thought I as I looked on. Then I heard Ben's interested voice. He had followed us, and was gazing at ancient swords and armour heaped pell-mell in the side aisle. What a treasure-trove for the antiquary—if such existed in Turkey—was heaped here in rusty disorder : upon the great iron key of a captured city was hung the sword of Scanderbeg : an armlet of Tamerlane hung on a pike-handle : whole suits of armour leaned in the shadows like warriors resting from battles 500 years old. How curious to warehouse these weapons with modern arms; as though in the East the past is not over but lives on in the shadows, not separated from the present by any dialectic of history, or by progress . . . Yes, in Constantinople the Dark Age survives, it is true—of that I had been made aware by my entanglement with the slavers. That these ancient weapons were not in a museum but in an armoury confirmed the fact. I tried to decipher the faded ink on decayed labels whilst Ben revelled in his find.

'I might be a Turkish soldier if they're allowed to have swords to kill people,' he called to me. 'Are they do you think?'

'I believe it's encouraged,' I replied. 'So long as the *bashi-bozuk* is well mounted for flight, and the enemy unarmed and elderly. Who would you fight, Ben?'

'People. Enemies. *That* doesn't matter,' he avowed. He had his hand upon a horrible poignard, a sliver of Damascus steel four or five inches long, and he looked up to see if I objected. I recalled the pykle I had yearned for, and looked away so that he might take the dagger if he wanted.

Soon Dolfuss trotted back to the carriage, frock coat tightly buttoned and silk hat crowded down upon his ears, and away we were trundled by the shining fat horses. He did not explain his purpose in visiting the armoury, and of course I did not ask. Our destination was Santa Sophia, which he mistakenly believed could not be visited by non-Mussulmans without some *laissez-passer* he possessed. The minarets added around the ancient basilica, and the Crescent gleaming upon its dome, led one to expect another trumpery mosque within : the *coup d'oeil* when one entered was therefore the more staggering; that immense dome, large and dusky as the night sky itself, imposed itself immediately upon the mind as a great wonder. Its vast solemnity, moreover, dwarfed the thin gabbling chant of *mullahs* and the tinselly bunting carrying texts from the Koran; its Christian magnificence outshone its present misuse as the sun outshines a tallow dip. The grandeur of the place made one proud to be a Christian, rather as two or three capital ships of the Royal Navy, with a foreign port under their guns, make one proud to be an Englishman. Lord knows what a Jew makes of it. I pointed out to Rachel that in order to align themselves with Mecca the natives had been obliged to square up their carpets and themselves not upon the axis of the great building's nave, but facing into a corner, which contrived to give their devotions the usual hugger-mugger air of a jumble sale. She didn't appear to see the humour of it.

She had allowed the influence of her father to divide her from myself. Either his example encouraged her to exaggerate her own Jewish traits, or else his mere proximity emphasised them, but the two of them together were as unmistakeably Hebrew as anything upon the music-hall stage, and very plainly hostile to myself. I suppose it is very like the Israelite's notion of fair play, to act the bully's part as soon as he finds himself in a majority. I had also, as it happened, been most vexed by a letter Rachel had shown me, from some jackanapes publisher, offering to buy her novel! I tried to make her see it as a piece of impudence—laughed heartily at the ludicrous figure she would cut when the thing failed—even forbade her to reply—but I was not sure, with her father to back up her rebellion, that she would obey me. I was much displeased.

We had driven out one day ostensibly to view the Okmeidan—a park in which the Sultans practised with bow and spear upon live men as butts—and on the way back passed through the village of Haskeui, a Jew ghetto which was evidently our real objective. By the Jew cemetery Dolfuss halted the carriage and seemed to expect that I should descend with them. I remained in the carriage. The graveyard was infinitely dreary, a treeless Golgotha stubbled over with tombstones, and when they returned I made some remark or other to Ben, signifying that a Jews' cemetery didn't make half such a jolly playground as did a Mussulman's, which Rachel took amiss. She tightened her lip, and just touched the shine of her hair with her fingertips in a way she had when piqued, and very soon remarked with every accent of sweetness :

'Papa dear, Archie has needed to spend an amazing amount upon the drains of this house he has taken on the Bosphorus. What was the figure, Archie?'

'Oh I don't recall. A hundred or two I believe.'

'Come, Archie! A hundred or two?' And the minx named to her father the sum Maryka had cost me. 'I told him,' she went on, 'I told him, Papa, that you would have plenty of money and would give him whatever he requires at once. So that he may throw it down the drains,' she finished wickedly.

'Drains? Drains?' the old Jew shrieked out, 'such a sum for drains? My life! Come now, that's all fudge, ain't it Archie? You think again, hey? It don't cost such a sum as that if you was to buy the house all complete, hey?'

'Then I daresay I have misunderstood the figures,' I returned with hauteur. 'I confess I lack a counting-house education.'

'That's more the ticket! You have another dab at reckoning up your figures, eh, Archie, and see if you don't come up with a set that's nearer what'll wash, hey?'

To so base an insinuation I condescended no reply, but stared icily at the passing scene. I had remembered somewhat ruefully that it was in this very quarter of Haskeui that my Armenian landlord, now my creditor for this vast sum, had owned the stronghold that he had sold to a Jew before his move to Pera. How was I to find the blunt to satisfy his greed? It was of course that cursed Married Women's Property Act was to blame for my predicament, an Act which had stood on the statute book a mere dozen years; before that time I should have had Rachel's fortune, such as it was, entirely in my own hand, and could have discharged my debts in a gentlemanly fashion. It is hard to see how a husband's authority is to be maintained, or indeed how society is to be held together at all, if a man is to account to his wife for every masculine expense.

It was evident that to display his wealth was one of Dolfuss' chief purposes in coming to Constantinople. Round the bazaars he stumped purchasing no end of finery; when he had been there a week he sparkled with jewellery like the first prize at a shooting-booth, and Rachel's person too began to glitter like a Cockney wife at Cremorne. The stones at least were real ones.

The three of us were crossing the outer bridge one day, returning with a pile of rugs from the Grand Bazar, the carriage almost stationary in the press of traffic, when I fully realised—almost envied—the extent of Dolfuss' gratification in basking thus behind his fat horses, in his shiny silk hat, amongst the swarming crowd fighting for its living and for its foothold upon the bridge across the Golden Horn. His delight in his situation was palpable. I could imagine that he was in process of fulfilling a vow made by his younger self as he had struggled across this bridge with a packet of goods upon his back to sell—the same vow which might be in process of being sworn at this moment in the heart of many a young hopeful forced to jump aside to save his merchandise from our Juggernaut wheels : a vow that he would one day drive across this bridge behind shiny horses, a fat coachman striking out with a whip, as ours did, at the backs of the poor devils about us. There was an element of the heroic in his success. Impelled by a kindlier feeling for the old Hebrew I said :

'Wonderful thing to sit in your carriage, is it not, your ships moored off the Golden Horn, what?'

'You think so do you, young fellow? Aye well—it is so. It is indeed.' He sat expansively, his little legs apart, plump as a barrel. He laid a hand on my arm. 'Know what I was at when I was your age? Currants, sir. I was in the currant line I was, not so very far off from where we're sat here.'

'In Constantinople, Papa?'

'No, my girl, Smyrna it was, Smyrna . . . You know in those times what the Christians of Smyrna was particular to have?' he asked. 'Do you? Long sticks, that's what, long sticks to poke at the Jews with, the Jews what's the street pedlars of Smyrna. Yes, yes, every Christian had his stick for that. Comical, ain't it?'

He laughed, but one didn't know whether to join him or not; typical of the quandary in which the Jew delights to place one.

'Smyrna's not where I come from, you understand,' he went on, with his usual anxiety to let no one into the secret of his history, 'but Smyrna's where the currants took me.'

'And you rode upon the currant to England?' I ventured.

He laughed, banging his fat little fist up and down on my arm. 'My life, no! I hopped out of currants quick as blinking soon as ever I twigged the war would come. That was the game brought me to England, war was.'

'What war?' asked Rachel.

'Why, the Crimea bless you! There was money to be made out of that scrap there was! A pile of money! You had a cargo lying here in the straits, animal feed it could be, and half rotten at that—bought for a song and stuffed in a Greek brig—with that cargo you'd be stood on the quay at Topkhaneh there and you'd have the blessed Commissariats of all the armies in the war a-bidding against one another so you would! French, English, Russian—up, up, up they'd bid you! Rare sport, rare sport!'

'Scarcely very patriotic,' I said stiffly.

'But I warn't very English,' he retorted with glee, his black little eyes sparking. 'Nor very Russian nor very French,' he went on, 'so I warn't on no side but my own. And I'll tell you what it is, my side was the only side what won a victory!'

'By "your side" you mean the . . . ?' I shrank from naming them to him.

'The Jews,' Rachel supplied.

'I mean the merchants,' he said, 'it's only merchants ever win wars, that's the truth. Yes, I come out of that little war middling rich. You want to know how to make money, Archie?' he suddenly demanded, turning his face on me with an earnest scrutiny.

I was taken aback. 'Money? Well, it would depend upon the means of making it,' I said. I could hardly picture myself in currants at Smyrna.

He had caught hold of my arm but now he dropped it. 'Then you don't,' he said shortly. 'Them who cares for the means, don't want to make money. But I'll tell you all the same, though you'll

140

not profit by it. You look out sharp for where there's a-going to be a war: that's how. War means big purchases made quick, and war means shortage; and them two particulars is the soul of trade, sir, the very heart and soul of it. Why am I come to Stamboul you ask? To see the sights? Bless you no!—To look for the seeds of war, sir, that's why I'm come. Looked in the Turk's armoury, didn't I? Counted up his Mausers and his Martini-Peabodys. You saw me. And I've peeked in his gun foundry too I have, oh yes.'

'Why Turkey?' I asked; 'Who would trouble to fight the Turk?'

'The Balkans, boy, the Balkans! Never take your eye off the Balkans——! There's Stambuloff murdered in Sofia——! There's Milan upset the new constitution in Servia——! Aye, you can ever rely upon the Balkans to keep the pot a-boiling. And that's aside from the reckoning up there'll be when the Sick Man of Europe slings his hook at last,' he added gleefully.

'I think you'll find that the British Government will settle all matters of that kind,' I told him coldly. 'There's not many dogs can bark in the Levant without asking our good leave.'

He laughed in my face in an offensive manner. As the carriage moved forward again he pointed at the Turkish ironclads at their moorings. 'Six of them fellows the Turk's got,' he said, 'fine ships you say, hey?'

I grudgingly agreed. I was irritated by those imposing battleships, under whose guns one was obliged to live, and hoped that what was rumoured was true—that Sir Philip Currie only awaited an excuse to order the British Fleet to Constantinople.

Dolfuss leaned close and said, 'Boilers rusted clean out. Daren't take them lumps of iron into the Marmara even. How do I know?' He laid his forefinger against his hook nose and sniggered. 'Two torpedo-boat destroyers fresh as paint he's got though,' he went on, 'two Nordenfeldt submariners, 30 or more torpedo boats and no end of gunboats. Now then. What use is all that information you ask. Well I'll tell you, sir, since you can't guess——'

'It's as plain as the nose on your face,' said I, 'if you know the details of his strength and armament you put yourself in a position to supply his wants from your stock when he's arming for war.'

'So! There! He's a deal sharper than we thought he was, Rachel,' said he, leaning back and fingering that large olfactory

141

organ to which I had referred. 'So, Archie, why don't you make yourself active about it, hey? Set yourself up to supply the Turk. I'll lend you money a-plenty, lend you boats, lend you the lot——hey?'

I smiled, and bent upon him a look sufficiently expressive. How degenerate would an Englishman have to be before he would arm a possible enemy of England's?—for so the Turk must be considered, if he persists in squealing at our annexation of Egypt. But of course such notions, dependant upon pride of race, would be ludicrous in a Jew. Having at last reached the Galata end of the bridge, our carriage moved more briskly.

Nonetheless it was tantalising to have the offer of funds unlimited to play the blackguard to one's country, when no tin was forthcoming for my pressing personal needs.

Pride of race—moral superiority—unassailable primacy—I confess that the moment came in the next week or two when I could almost regret my indoctrination with élitist principles which made it so deuced hard to step down off a high horse I couldn't afford to keep in oats. Such a quad as that is like the horses of Diomedes, and ends by consuming one.

Was it the effect of residence abroad?—was it the result of the flexibility I had begun to learn from Ben and Maryka?—whatever the cause, I found myself disposed to question what I had thought was the settled order of existence. I wondered if fellows like Dolfuss, who had no high horse to fall from, didn't have the best of it after all. Hard he was, cold as steel, a man actuated by profit and loss; but he was a buccaneer too, he had played high and plunged deep, and when I saw the ruck he had risen from, upon the bridge at Galata, it seemed to me that there was a romance—a freedom—about his career which I had not perceived in England, where convention dictated my view of his kind. Looking about Stamboul in his company one derived the impression that for all their grandiloquence the empires that had ruled Constantinople had lasted but a short span; whereas a fellow like Dolfuss, who beat less loud a drum, had a knack of surviving down the centuries which imperialists grow too stiff in neck and knees to learn. There's many a town in Asia whose name has reverted to what it was before ever the Romans conquered it. Asia teaches one that a Roman was not the summit and crown of all things, as he thought; from this lesson it may be inferred that no more is an Englishman the end of all things either.

This was the direction in which my ideas were working. Then the violence began, which changed again my opinion of Dolfuss —and indeed altered my opinions in general.

I had come round a good deal towards the old Israelite—that he had not softened his view of myself rather improved my estimate of his character than the reverse—and we were returning in the carriage together from an excursion upon the Stamboul shore of the Golden Horn (Dolfuss employing his sharp eyes upon the Turk's naval dockyards) whilst we talked of the city's history. He had I believe a respect for the superior merit of a mind educated in the Classics (though of course he sneered at an attribute with no market value) and he used to catechise me upon Byzantium's past, crowing over me if I forgot a date, yet listening with the intentness of the self-taught, and the reverence of the uneducated, whilst I expounded a theory.

But those musty theories I unpacked for him!—the detritus of my schooling—the half-forgotten influences of a classical education which had formed my outlook upon the modern world— what pinchbeck they turned out to be! They were like portmanteaux in the attic, long valued though never looked into, which I unpacked at last to disclose not the splendid blaze of a proconsular uniform, but a mere set of reach-me-downs with the moth in them. This wardrobe of toga and χιτων never had been made to fit; only, my mind had nothing else to wear. Certainly I knew the arguments used in favour of an education in the Classics —but those very arguments, advocating independence of judgement, I knew by rote, as I know the scraps of Classical quotations which box up my views as a draper's assistant boxes up genteel fashions. What superior fitness to rule the world does this confer? Is a parrot, caught and taught half a dozen words of human speech, then the fittest bird to rule his wild brethren?—I think not; but certain it is that such a bird must rule or starve, for his education has deprived him of the capability to earn a living by means unbefitting his view of his own dignity.

Once questioned, the intentions of our educators are a puzzle to make out. I have a notion that in the eighteenth century, with fine gentlemen of the stamp of my Lord Chesterfield, the 'man of taste' in the Classic mould was brought to pretty fair perfection.

143

Now, however, another strain has been grafted upon the *beau ideal* of an English gentleman : the brawn of the Viking is to be added to the fair form of the Greek, the horns of Valhalla are to be heard upon Olympus; we are asked to admire as the summit of all human excellence the sentiments of Mr Alfred Austin enshrined in the appearance of Lord Ribblesdale. But the graft don't take. *Defuit una symmetria prisca.* Austin hasn't a word to say to Ribblesdale. So it is that each product of our system of education is a being at war with himself, ἢ θηρίον ἢ θεός, barbarian fights Greek within each one of us. With the revival of racial pride apparent in the Hyperborean maunderings of William Morris it seems that the Viking strain gains a preponderance. Our young men are now bred up to dart pell-mell into a scrap the way the poor devil at Majuba Hill dashes upon his death bawling out *'Floreat Etona!'* in Lady Butler's picture which half the Eton fellows have upon their wall. Why, the Viking in myself feels the glory of it ! But the Greek in me feels its foolishness; for whilst a handful of young fellows rushing to their deaths on the spears of the blackamoors is one thing, a war against a European foe would be quite another, by Jingo. If you breed up a whole generation which is eager to take part in the Charge of the Light Brigade, it will end by performing the Charge of the Gadarene Swine.

With my head full of such stuff as this—and with pretty much the feeling that I approached a crisis in discovering what identity I possessed beneath my reach-me-down *subligatulum*—I had not noticed that our carriage too had arrived at something of a crisis. Events in the streets through which we were passing, or attempting to pass, now broke in upon my reflexions. I looked out.

We had driven as suddenly into trouble as a rowboat runs into a squall, and in the midst of a crowd we rocked and bobbed as its pressures surged to and fro. What was up I could not see, and the ruffianly-looking rogues who composed the crowd paid us no attention as yet. But willy-nilly our carriage was so tipped and lifted by the mob that I was obliged to lay hold of its sides for fear of being tumbled out. I looked at Dolfuss and saw the sweat of terror stand upon his sallow face. Now the horses squealed, catching fright and plunging, and the scoundrels all around turned their attentions upon us like wreckers who see a galleon fall into their hands. I confess I have felt more comfortable. A jeer was

144

set up. Filthy hands reached into the carriage and plucked at us. A murderous set of whiskers was thrust into my face along with a gust of foul breath. 'Jew! Jew!' the fellow shrieked out. Good God! Was I to be paid out for my *mésalliance* in so brutal a fashion as this? Torn in pieces in mistake for a Hebrew! I struggled to see what was happening. Was it a fire? But I saw only the mob jammed between the house-fronts, and heard only its muttering, a strange low growl it was, like a brewer's barrel trundled upon flagstones. Then up leaped a scream with a horrible shrillness which ripped all else in half.

Screams—screams—shooting up like spears they tore into one's heart.

In response that growl of the mob became a roar it swelled so. For an instant the tumult was enormous, rising to engulf the agony of those screams as a bear might reach up to pull down a bird which was escaping his claws. No less sudden—no less menacing —came silence.

Flying faces streamed past. Quickly, on a rush of feet as light as a rainstorm, the mob was scattering. Down alleys it drained off the street like stormwater down gutters.

Soon the way ahead lay clear, and our horses sidled forward, snorting and craning at certain grim relics of the mob's work. I looked. It was as though a butcher's cart had upset. As our wheels rumbled over the stained and stinking cobbles, whose interstices were quite filled with blood, I made out that the victim—for I counted but one head amongst the stumps and fragments—had worn a uniform of black. It was a policeman who had perished so horribly. I turned to Dolfuss.

The pallor of his face was bedewed with sweat. Though his lips worked, no sound came from them. He gestured at the coachman, who was attempting to master his own terror by beating his horses, and when his voice came, it was a shriek :

'*Gidelim! Chapuk! Gidelim!*'

Away lurched the carriage behind clattering hooves. I saw the gaunt shadows of dogs gathering in doorways and alley-mouths as we dashed by. Dolfuss' hand gripped my arm like pincers.

'Armenians!' he croaked. 'Armenian rabble, no Jews, not a Jew amongst them. Was there? No, no!' The creature was so abject in his terror, quite shrunken and fallen in about the face. 'Now the *zaptieh* will kill all they find. You saw he was *zaptieh*,

145

policeman, the Armenians killed? *Chapuk!*' he screeched out at the charioteer, who was already hurtling headlong through the steep streets which re-echoed to our horses and wheels. As we issued out of the labyrinth at last onto the Inner Bridge, the wretch beside me took comfort. He leaned back, and set his silk hat upon his head again, if furtively ('A hat! A hat!' was, I recalled, what fanatic mobs used to call out when they sighted a *feringhi* and pulled him in pieces). I confess that the improved opinion I had formed of Dolfuss was quite dissipated by the weak nerves he had displayed. Perhaps a fellow need not rush upon his death with quite the Norseman's enthusiasm of the poor devil at Majuba, but the Jew's cowardice was disgusting.

We found Pera, and the hotel, quite unruffled by disturbance. Rachel showed little interest in the story her father blurted out in the entrance foyer where we came upon her taking tea.

'Oh dear,' she said, straightening the collar of his coat for him, 'a street accident was it? Poor man.'

'It was murder,' I said coolly whilst her father gibbered, 'lynch-mob tore a policeman in pieces. No doubt of it.'

'Troubles, troubles!' moaned Dolfuss, banging his forehead with his hand. 'Armenians make troubles and poor Jews must pay! I shall be ruined, ruined!'

'For a fellow who got his start by one war, and hopes to prosper from another,' I said contemptuously, 'you show little stomach for combat yourself.'

Rachel threw me an angry look. 'I think you had best go up and calm yourself, Papa,' she told him. 'Archie will order some tea sent up.'

'My girl you do not understand! There will be killing, burning, ruin!'

'Yes, Papa, no doubt there will. But you are perfectly safe, you are in Pera, in a good hotel. Now pray do as I ask.'

If old Dolfuss thought Constantinople less secure against riot than it really was, Rachel had no notion of its dangers. Her faith in the up-to-date fittings of the Pera Palace Hotel was touching. But she had not seen the fragments scattered about the cobblestones, or heard our carriage wheels splash through blood. There she sat sipping tea from a glass and eating very small sandwiches, waiting, so she said, for Mrs Watkins to arrive.

This prospect I could not endure. Ben was upstairs, but Nanny

146

(suspicious of my excursions with Zara and the boy, and possessed of that keenness of nose in scenting out improper dalliance which is found only in elderly virgins) sat grimly by the tub nowadays whilst Zara bathed Ben, and picketted the bedroom doors as though her life depended on it. I was excited by the scenes I had witnessed. In default of gratifying myself with Zara I determined to stroll to the club and see if any of the fellows knew anything of the affair of the lynched *zaptieh*. I fancied myself rather cutting out the old Turkey hands with my eye-witness account of the business.

It was evident as soon as I entered the club that I was not the first bearer of news to disturb its somnolence. There was a knot of assorted foreigners waving their arms about in an excitable fashion in the lobby, but one took very little to do with the aliens as a general rule, so I passed on to the billiard room, which the British had adopted as their meeting ground. Here were three or four men straggled round the high wall-benches overlooking the green baize whilst a subaltern from an Indian regiment practised cannons. A desultory discussion was going forward.

'Heard the news have you, Caper?' asked a youngish fellow, a cotton merchant. Before I could reply he had rattled on, 'Riot no less, dozen dead I'm assured, policemen——'

'As a matter of fact I——'

'Peelers fired first,' interrupted the subaltern, 'know for a fact, opened fire on the crowd silly asses. Only one end to that.'

'As a matter of fact I was in the——'

'Crowd? Damned rabble you mean,' broke in an elderly merchant smoking a cigar. 'Police only trying to do their duty. Arrested one or two firebrands from the Armenian Committee I'm told, confounded rag tag and bobtail sets upon 'em——'

'Fellow told me,' said the soldier, 'half these chappies make up the mob here, you know what they are? Students! *Softas* they call them. Would you believe it? Fancy Varsity fellows kicking up such a damned row!'

'As a matter of fact'—I at last managed to finish—'I was there and saw it all.' Having hollowed out a silence for myself I lit a cigar. Then I went on, 'Yes, ugly sort of crowd, over in Stamboul. Thought they were going to have me out of the carriage at one moment. Then they tore up a policeman and decamped.'

'Not a bit of it,' said the cotton man, 'dozen or more constables dead, shot they were, shot dead by these Armenian beggars.'

'The Jews had beaten a child to death, that's what I heard,' piped up a spindly little fellow in eye-glasses.

'You fire on a crowd,' the young soldier told us, 'you get what you deserve. Rule with us in India is this : one, never let——'

'Too damned soft by half nowadays you fellows,' broke in the old merchant as he puffed on his cigar, 'I've always said it. In the Congo the regular rule was, you bowl a couple of niggers over where all can see, and if that don't answer you pour in a volley. I recall a tight spot I was——'

'Don't need to tell me about riots,' chimed in the cotton-wallah, 'seen 'em in dozens, here, Smyrna, Cairo, all over the shop. I remember once I was in Alexandria soon after the bombardment, '88 must have been, or '89 . . .'

So the British community reacted to the affair, drowning out their only chance of an eye-witness account with their flood of reminiscence. Each had his professional connexion with the East, which they knew I had not, and in consequence they were set upon belittling any information I might possess. When I had the chance I asked the old merchant :

'Armenians you'd say are behind it, would you?'

'It don't matter what I say,' he replied, puffing out his yellow moustache, 'the powers that be will say it's the Armenians put the crowd up to it, you may count upon that.'

'Not the Jews?' I pressed him.

'Well,' he said, and wagged his grizzled head, 'I wouldn't care to be a Jew in Stamboul tonight, you may put it that way. The Armenians are made the scapegoats, yes, but your Jew always collects a sideswipe or two, don't he, if he can manage it. Your old Jew eats babies, you see, has to do it for his religion—well-known fact in the Muslim community that is. Don't make him popular when the mob's got its blood up.'

'Once the mob's up nothing's sacred, not property nor nothing,' said the fellow in cotton huffily.

'Not money-lender's property anyhow,' rejoined the older man, 'that's the nub of it. Armenians and Jews both, its their pawn-broking propensity lays 'em open to dislike by the improvident. Moment he sees there's a row on in the street, that's the moment your idle Turk sees his chance of evening the score. Cuts himself a cudgel and visits his moneylender! There's sense in that, eh?'

I stood up. I was still restless, and these fellows seemed so dead-and-alive in the way they looked at things. 'I think I'll take a turn and see if there's anything to be seen,' I said.

'Have a care,' the old man advised from his seat, 'Johnny Turk in an ugly mood can bowl pretty quick you'll find, and the streets hereabouts are a bumping pitch to play him on.'

The subaltern, Briggs by name, put his cue in the rack. 'I'll come along too if these poor devils of Armenians are going to get it in the neck again,' he said. As we strolled through the club doors he added, 'I wonder where's the best spot to watch the fun?'

The streets of Pera were empty in the last of the light from the west: quiet, too, with a kind of expectancy. The rumour of massacre, like the rumour of plague, gives mystery and tone to an Oriental city. Our footsteps, and my companion's cheery voice, echoed against the shuttered houses and closed shop-fronts of the Grande Rue, here largely stone-built in consequence of the fire of the '70s. We debated what direction to take, and decided upon a right-handed sweep past the French Embassy towards Taksim.

As we tramped along Briggs told me one or two tales of punitive expeditions he had taken part in against the Pathan, great larks by his account of them, which got my blood properly up, and made me keen to see a bit of action before the night was out. I thought we might have to cross the Golden Horn and go in search of our sport in Stamboul, for though we thought we heard a tumult once or twice, and cut along as quick as we could, an hour passed without us having a bit of luck. How it came about, and quite where we were, I do not know, but we swung round a corner at our best pace, Briggs yarning away about the Khyber, and ran ourselves slap amongst the crowd we sought.

They were very quiet. They were orderly, too, assembled like troops before an assault. Our nearest neighbours looked at us curiously, but made no move or outcry against us: this too seemed a surprisingly disciplined reaction from a mob. We were able to stand back in the shadow of a doorway and watch. The stillness and discipline of the scene was sinister and chilling to the blood.

I had heard the rattle of wheels, and now I made out that it was a handcart being pushed through the crowd. Flares burning here and there showed me that the cart was heaped with heavy sticks, cudgels like the Irishman's shillelah, with which the crowd was arming itself, dark thin hands reaching into the flare-light to snatch up a weapon and secrete it in the dirty folds of their robes. Briggs nudged me and pushed a heavy cold object into my hand.

'Billiard ball,' he whispered, 'pinched them from the club. First-rate weapon in a rough-house.'

He demonstrated how he would use it to weight a blow with his fist, and I confess I drew comfort from handling my own ball. 'What's up do you think?' I asked him.

'Hanged if I know. Fun of some sort, depend upon it.' He grinned.

The crowd, still orderly, had begun to divide. Each section followed a leader, a fellow in a turban and cloak. Here and there I saw a *zaptieh* pull on a similar cloak over his uniform, and wind a turban rapidly round his head, at which a dozen or so of the crowd would attach themselves to him. I was about to ask Briggs if he understood this ruse when there broke out the kind of subdued clamour you hear from a crowd's throat when first they catch sight of what they've come for. I couldn't make out what had set them off.

'Come on!' whispered Briggs, and set off at a rapid pace to skirt the crowd, which was now spilling out of the square we had found it in, and growing a little rougher in temper. I ran to catch Briggs up. 'Don't run at any price!' he hissed at me, 'these fellows will set upon anything they think is bolting!'

Amid some stragglers we hastened along the street until we came upon a larger square. Here three or four substantial stone-built houses stood behind railings and gardens, pleasant quiet-seeming houses in the modern style of architecture. The wide lamplit square they fronted upon was empty: the crowd was packed in the narrow streets behind them, where it tossed and jostled in the glare cast by torches. Our détour had led us into confronting the crowd, a position I did not find quite comfortable. I suggested to Briggs that we withdrew.

'Too late!' said he with grim enjoyment, jerking his thumb over his shoulder. I looked.

Into the square behind us there trotted a troop of cavalry. We—and the merchants' houses—were trapped.

'Police,' I said, indicating the horsemen.

'Turks!' he retorted, as if to cancel any relief we might feel that law and order was at hand. 'Look sharp,' he said, 'for I think we'll do better with the crowd.'

As we set off to rejoin the crowd a sudden ringing shout went up from the square. I stopped dead, certain that we were its cause. When I turned, however, I saw that a policeman had ridden through the garden of one of the residences and now waited below its dark windows. The proclamation had issued from him. No answer came from the house, no light, no sign of life The *bimbashi* in his elaborate uniform, his steed trampling gravel, then shouted up a short speech at the façade above him.

'Can you make it out?' I asked Briggs.

He shook his curly head, for he wore no hat. ' "Weapons," I could hear—something about weapons, couldn't twig the rest. Look though, the fun's starting, they're going to search the house.'

A detachment of police in their black uniforms had dismounted and were tramping to the door of the house nearest us. Now the bimbashi leaned down from his horse and rapped upon the door with the handle of his fly-whisk.

'Searching the house for weapons do you suppose?' I suggested.

'Armenians!' he said, 'I'll wager they're Armenians' houses these. I daresay the police think they're storing arms for this Armenian rising the Turk thinks is coming off every time some poor devil from the Caucasus turns over in his bed.'

'And the mob at the back doors?' From where we stood we had a plain view of both the front and the back of the house.

He shrugged. The *bimbashi's* knocking had drawn no response. At a signal, the police attacked the door with rifle-butts. That sudden irruption of noise, that barbarous sound of property broken down, was a shock tearing through the square as lightning warns of storm. The game was afoot, the night now committed to violence. Then Briggs clutched my arm.

'Look!'

A back door of the house had opened from within. At first nothing issued from it. But the entry of the *zaptieh* by the demolished front door evidently decided those who were within to act. Into the lamplight issued two of the triangular, heavily-muffled shapes which denote women in Muslim lands. They waited upon the short flight of steps which curved down into the street. Then a heavy bulky figure clasping two valises emerged, and all three crept like thieves down the steps. They were very evidently taken aback, on rounding the curve in the steps, to find themselves confronted by a crowd.

The mob was horribly silent. Flares smoked over their heads. One was aware of the concentration of their gaze upon these refugees, and the very weight of that stare seemed to drive the fugitives physically backwards. Too late. Lights now blazed forth from the windows of the house they had left. The door by which they had hoped to creep to safety now opened wide, and in its frame, outlined against the lit interior, stood the *bimbashi* swinging his fly-whisk. The fugitives could neither advance nor withdraw. Through everyone present there thrilled an extraordinary low moan, compounded half of agony and half of hunger. I became aware that an outrage was about to be committed. So did the victims. It was a question now of how it was to be precipitated. Any movement would have done it : for that reason the three figures stood still as death. Alas for them, the catch of one of the valises was imperfect, or perhaps the valise had been overfilled, or closed too hurriedly in flight; for whatever reason, it now opened and debouched its contents onto the road. *Gold!*

The man stared down stupidly at the open valise for the moment it took for the front rank of the mob to reach him. I did not see him or his women again. A thicket of clubs rose and fell above the crowd's vortex, then the violent centres of action spread rapidly this way and that, murder no doubt turning to fighting over the spoils of murder, until the street was a perfect mêlée. Of noise I was not aware : it was as though I had screamed so loudly inside my own skull that I had excluded sound from without. Now I was aware of Briggs' hand upon my arm, and his lips moving at me.

'What?'

'Come on,' he yelled, 'I have an idea !'

I followed him as he walked off toward the police horses held by a couple of men in the square. He strolled close by the horses and soon gained the further of the three large houses. Here the lamps cast a mild quiet light. One would not have guessed what was taking place so close at hand. Nor did I know what Briggs was at, studying the two unlighted houses so coolly.

'More of the beggars in these two I'll be bound,' he said, 'wonder if we couldn't get 'em out, eh?'

I confess I had assumed that we would make the best pace we could to safety ourselves. But of course if Briggs was game to stop on so was I. I kept a grip on the billiard ball in my trowser pocket to keep my spirits up and looked the houses over. Then Briggs pointed. Close to the fence in the garden of the house nearest us I saw a shrub quiver. Someone was hiding there. We stole along the iron railings. When he sprang over them I followed. We leaped almost upon our quarry's back, a stout old party much wrapped up in shawls who was burrowing his way under a bush as though he didn't mean stopping till he struck tin. He was a good deal alarmed. Briggs held him upon the ground, squawking like a chicken the fox has laid hold of, and whispered to him urgently:

'Alone? No women, no children? House empty is it?'

He revived a good deal at hearing English spoken, and began upon a rigmarole about 'Two fine sons', but the moment it was clear they were not in the house, Briggs cut him short with:

'Here's what we're going to do: we'll hoist him over the railings and then you, Caper, you stop and see he don't run off while I just step along and borrow a couple of police horses. All right? All clear? Come on then, heave him over.'

The preposterousness of the plan—to gallop off with our prize upon the police horses—suddenly put me into uncommon good humour with Briggs, indeed with the whole adventure. I laughed aloud at the fun of the thing.

'Right ho,' said Briggs when we had the old fellow bundled over the railing, and he and I stood in the shadow of a tree, 'you'll want to look sharp when I come up with the nags, push him up on mine I should, and I'll chuck you the reins of yours. We won't have a lot of time for style.'

He sauntered off, clasping his fingers around the billiard ball in his jacket pocket. The old man was shaking like a leaf at my side, thinking no doubt that he had fallen into the hands of mad-men, and clawing away at my arm. I ignored his gabbling at the time; by the light of retrospect I see that he had probably cottoned to my identity.

In a couple of moments I heard the scuffle of horses' hooves, and a man's cry which ended abruptly. Then came a tremendous clatter of horses dashing towards us; two loose animals bolted past first, and then I made out Briggs pounding along crouched down in his saddle, crowding on all sail possible and leading another animal by its reins. I moved out into the street.

I had not seen the approach of seven or eight ragged Turks from behind me. Now I did. They began to run at us, a couple of them with clubs and one with a flare, and it was a question whether Briggs got to us first. I looked down at the fellow we were rescuing. By the light of the flare I recognised his face in its smother of scarves. It was that of my Armenian landlord from Emirghian. This was his house in Pera. I saw that he knew me. The horses were upon us, and I grasped him by the waist and hurled him upwards towards Briggs' approaching arms. I had then to move like lightning to catch the loose horse whose rein was flung at me, and I was occupied with snatching it up, and flinging myself at the saddle, before I saw what had happened.

Briggs had failed to catch the Armenian. He was on the ground. Briggs' horse bestrode him, whilst a Turk desperado aimed blows of his club at the fallen figure of the stout merchant. Briggs leaned down from his rearing horse and struck the Turk— I heard the smash of the billiard ball upon his skull like a spoon on a breakfast egg—who dropped instantly.

'Pick him up!' sang out Briggs at me, 'I'll hold these devils off!'

Could I? I spurred up to Briggs. Was it possible? I do not believe that I considered the money I owed the fallen Armenian. Then we both heard the clatter of horses' hooves approaching. The police were mounted and after us.

'Have to push on I'm afraid,' said Briggs coolly. 'Best separate.'

He raised his hand and was off. A dreadful cry was wrung from the Armenian, but whether because he was abandoned, or because Briggs' horse struck him in departing, or because he felt the first blow of his murderers' clubs, I did not stop to enquire. I wasted no time in following Briggs, and did not look back. Given its head my horse picked another street from the one Briggs had taken, and was very soon laying its legs to the ground at a very hot pace which I found I could do little to slacken. We were through the stragglers of the mob like a charge of ball-shot through a midge-swarm, and making such very good time over the cobbles and round the corners of those precipitous alleys that I gave up all notion of steering, clung on for dear life and hoped we didn't pitch upon a street which ended in a flight of stairs. I believe my mount knew his way as a cabbie knows London, for in the end his gallop slacked off of its own accord and I was able to sit up and take notice of where we were : when I realised to my horror the brute's reason for easing up. He was approaching home. The police barracks, with a couple of *zaptieh* uniforms at the gate, were 30 yards off and closing fast. I took the only course that occurred to me and dropped off the animal's back. He kept on through the barrack gates and I picked myself out of the softish muck of a Constantinople street, my head swimming a good deal, and sprinted for the mouth of the nearest alleyway as straight as I could with a brain which had a sudden tendency to steer me in circles.

I was safe, but without a notion of my whereabouts. However, knowing that I had not crossed the Golden Horn, I was able to judge the fall of the ground towards the straits and make a cast which must in the end hit off the Grande Rue. This I did; and a longish walk (through streets which were deserted) brought me to the hotel.

The public rooms were crowded with persons in a state of agitation and alarm, the Cook's *Wagon Lit* bureau under siege from any number of Cockneys with the stuffing quite knocked out of them, all squeaking out complaints at the clerk and trying to look big. Quite by contrast with my earlier ambition to make a show in such people's eyes, I found I was not at all anxious to be importuned by the parcel of weeping matrons who came gaping and questioning as I strode through the crowd to the stairway, much dishevelled and dirtied by my adventure. I ran upstairs and entered Rachel's sitting-room. She gave out a little scream, instantly stifled by her hand to her mouth, and poised forward on her toes as though to run towards me. Perhaps she took her cue from Nanny and her papa, who were also present, for she did not execute the action.

'Where have you been?' she asked, her voice frayed, 'you have alarmed us most dreadfully.'

'And dirt all over you, not fit to be seen,' added Nanny.

I looked at them. The old Hebrew, wedged into a chair,

appeared to have shrunk to half his size, fingers scrabbling at the chaircover, black sunken eyes burning in a grey face, his lips livid as meat. He had not a jewel nor a morsel of gold about him. When I took him in, wretchedly degenerate as was the figure he cut, I thought for the first time of the fate of the Armenian we had left upon the ground under the Turks' shillelahs. The elation of rapid action, which had carried me until now, faltered as I recalled the way the old fellow had cried out as we left him. Hitherto I had treated our failure to rescue him as if he were a goal we had muffed at polo—it was just the style of Briggs' yarns of scrapping with the Pathan round Peshawar—but now I saw in old Dolfuss' terror how the game looked from the quarry's point of view. I sat down on a sofa.

'Have you dined?' I asked.

'Packed? Yes, I'm packed,' said Dolfuss in an eager tone, 'I can leave. But where do I go, hey? What have you arranged for me?'

Rachel said, 'Yes, we have dined Archie. I will order some supper for you directly. Will you take it in your own room? Then we need not disturb Papa and Nanny,' she added, speaking of them with considerable disdain.

All Dolfuss' pugnacity was gone: he looked from one to the other of us as if to hear his fate. 'Very well,' said I, and left them.

In a very few moments the door of my bedroom flew open and in darted Rachel to throw herself upon me. I caught her in my arms, wondering at her desperation, in truth not certain whether she was attacking me or seeking my protection. Having thrown off my dirty and torn clothing preparatory to taking a bath, I was all but naked. I heard her sob against my chest, and felt her nails drive into my back.

'Thank heaven you are safe!' she murmured intensely. 'I'm so ashamed of his behaviour, so ashamed——!'

Excitement—action—alarm—every emotion I had undergone now coalesced under the influence of the body throbbing against mine. As the outcome of a chemical combination may be unexpectedly unlike its constituents, sexual desire surprised me as the outcome of my adventure. But the fact made itself felt between us. My problem lay in the realisation of my need. I waited for Rachel to make some move to divest herself of her clothes. She sobbed still, and her hands remained upon my back, but her

156

gasps were less convulsive and her grip slackened. The awkwardness was, that she did not seem to understand what I desired. Nor could I make myself plainer without using words or actions which no gentleman can use with propriety to a lady. I was quite at a stand.

'There, there,' I confined myself to muttering, patting her cautiously on the lower back, 'come, come.'

'I am so ashamed of him,' she repeated. 'Oh how can a man be such a horrid coward?'

What was I to do to achieve my need? I had no more notion of how to undress her than I had of how to open an oyster without a knife. At Rome I had of course lain in wait until she was in bed before attempting to claim my rights. I knew that a lady's vital zone was as well defended by tapes and buttons as ever was a princess's tower kept impregnable by brambles and men-at-arms in a fairy story.

'I say, stop bothering your head about your papa won't you,' I began, dreading to make a fool of myself by starting at the wrong end, 'just step into the dressing-room won't you, and make yourself more . . . and I'll wait for you here, eh?'

'Yes, of course. I am sorry to be so stupid, Archie,' she said, relinquishing her hold upon me and walking off demurely into the dressing-room.

I rapidly turned out the light and climbed into my bed in its dark corner. Some minutes passed. Then the dressing-room door opened.

'Oh!' She was surprised at the darkness. 'Archie? Where are you gone?'

By the light from the door behind her I saw that she was not unclothed : I grasped immediately that she had not understood me, had thought herself sent to the dressing-room only to recover herself. I sank silently and swiftly under the coverlet as a captain might scuttle his ship in the moment of defeat. I heard her withdraw, and the door of her own rooms close behind her. She must have assumed that I had gone to take my bath. In myself a sensation of foolishness and inadequacy replaced desire. When I thought of Maryka's unfastened draperies how I anathematised taped body linen and hook-and-eye stays, and wished Mrs Watkins at the devil for spreading the curse of the button to the *zenana*.

When I was bathed and dressed, and seated before an admirable little supper in my dressing-room (a plain roast of the kind Rachel knew I approved, with no kickshaws), there came a timid rap at my door which, upon my calling 'Come in', opened enough for Rachel herself to steal shamefacedly in. She came and stood in front of the table, hands folded, in quite the Eastern style of contrition.

'I am so sorry, Archie,' she said, 'for my display of foolishness over Papa. He cannot help his nature. Pray forgive me.'

'Quite understood, little to forgive,' I mumbled.

'He is so excited and upset—quite unnerved. As if we were not perfectly secure!'

'My dear Rachel,' I told her, ' "security" is all fudge! You've not witnessed what a pack of Turks can accomplish when they set upon an elderly moneylender. I have, and I don't doubt your father has too.'

As I ate I told her of my adventures that evening. Instead of her interest growing as my tale developed, her attention soon wandered and was at last withdrawn. Her hands began to play with the tassels of the cushions.

'Mr Briggs seems quite the heroic type,' she said when I ended my story. I saw that she did not believe a word of it. She stood up to leave. 'Archie, since Papa is anxious to leave Constantinople I think we must remove to this house at Emirghian tomorrow.'

Her tone was commanding, all contrition gone. I had lost my advantage by relating a true adventure which she dismissed as a fiction. Like Mrs Watkins she disbelieved in the capacity of Stamboul to alarm her. It is a feminine characteristic to believe that soap and electric light repel barbarism before them. However, I was now thrown back upon my resources, for I had no notion of what state my household at Emirghian now stood. I thought rapidly whilst drinking off a glass of the fizz Rachel had ordered with my supper.

'I cannot allow anyone under my protection to travel to Emirghian till I discover whether the disturbances have affected it,' I said. 'Where there are moneylenders, there are apt to be fellows looking for them with cudgels, and——'

'Archie,' she said irritably, 'pray don't speak of Papa as a moneylender. He has no business he need be ashamed of at Constantinople—he has no need to be alarmed at the mob. May I

158

take it then that you will go to Emirghian in the morning and prepare for our removal there?'

I filled my mouth with roast mutton to evade replying, and she left me. There was no doubt that her father's company in these weeks—and possibly the effect too of the correspondence which I suspected her of continuing with the publisher who had taken her novel—had developed Rachel's independence of character. There seemed to be no question now of her retiring to her sofa with the *sal volatile*. Rather, I recognised in the positive and forthright line she chose, that independence of spirit which had ever made her the leader in our childhood games, and myself the follower; or her the pursuer and me the pursued.

When she was gone I assessed my position. My landlord's demise—and surely he could not have survived those ruffians' clubs?—released me from debt. He had been a widower, both his sons lived abroad : I could say with pretty fair certainty that the debt was liquidated. So there remained only the question of Maryka . . . In the euphoric state of release from debt, by however horrible a tragedy to my creditor, I felt persuaded that this question too would resolve itself by some stroke of good fortune.

IX

A Kidnap, a Murder, and a Desperate Venture

'ARCHIE,' SAID RACHEL to me next morning, when she found me eating my breakfast in the dining-room, 'Archie, if you are decided upon going down to this house on the Bosphorus this morning, why don't you take Ben with you? It is become so dull for him here if Papa forbids him to walk about, and he would be perfectly safe with you on the ferry would he not?'

'Perfectly,' I agreed, reaching for another couple of eggs from the dish. I had scanned the idea rapidly and seen no drawbacks. Ben wouldn't know a slave-girl from a housemaid. 'Your father is agreeable I take it?'

'Papa thinks it best,' she replied evasively. 'So when shall they be ready?'

'They?'

'Zara will go with you of course.'

'Of course.' Foolishly I jumped at Zara's company before I realised the catch. She had sharp eyes and knew the East. Well, she would have to be kept out of the house unless Maryka had departed. I told Rachel at what hour I would start for the ferry station, and turned by attention to making a respectable breakfast. Had I known how long it was to be before I next had my legs under the mahogany, I would not have contented myself with the light repast I made.

I took a turn down to the club first thing, intending to discover the end of Briggs' adventure, as well as the news in general. The streets were in their usual cluttered and noisy disarray; no abnormality was evident on the surface of Pera life, nor indeed in the club. Briggs was not there, but the elderly merchant was settled in a cane chair reading *The Levant Herald*. I gave him an account of our adventures, to which he said, 'Hm, Hm,' without taking his eyes off his paper, so strong was his determination to learn nothing from a stranger to the Orient. When I had done he laid his mottled hands on his chair-arms and said:

'Not much I can reveal just yet, I'm afraid. Hear a good deal —a great deal. You been in the East as long as I have, young fellow, you'll find it don't pay to go stirring out of the club much. Young Briggs there charging about. Don't do a mite of good.'

'Have you heard any news of the riots?'

'Course.'

'Well?'

'Oh,' he said, cranking his tortoise neck round to squint up at me sarcastically, 'want to hear now? Ready to listen are you? Finished a-lecturing me about doings in the town I known 40 years and more have you?' When I looked like walking off he shouted out quick, 'Yes I'll tell you! His Imperial Majesty's government is hard at it putting down an insurrection, that's what's happening. Financed and armed by the Armenian Committee it is, who's been stoked up to make mischief by the French and British ambassadors: that's what's happening in Constantinople young fellow. And if you'll just hand me one of those cigars of yours instead of puffing smoke all over me, I'll tell you for why.'

I gave him a cigar. He didn't thank me. When it was alight he spat out a shred of leaf and said, 'Fact number one: arms found on Armenian gangs, pistols and such, all of British make. Self-same arms found stored up in rich Armenians' houses. Here in Pera. Fact too, for the *zaptieh* found 'em out last night.'

'And you think Sir Philip Currie——'

'Think? I know it. Sits out there at Therapia hatching plots don't he? You know who he's got stopping there now do you? Pom McDonnell that's who, private secretary to My Lord Salisbury. That's where he gets his orders—Hatfield! Never takes no advice from anyone as knows the length of Johnny Turk's foot, oh no! Not grand enough we aren't! Quarrelled with the Sultan's government he has, never sees no Mussulmans now, finds it disagreeable, I daresay. Too busy getting up riding parties to the Forest of Belgrade with the Prime Minister's lackeys—in hopes of a peerage no doubt—to see an old Turkey hand who'd put him straight.'

Clearly once the old fellow had climbed upon this hobby horse

—that the embassy don't pay him particular enough attention, an amazingly commonplace steed amongst persons of the inferior class resident abroad—nothing further was to be learned from him. His own source of information was a Turkish waiter evidently planted in the club by Yildiz to spy upon foreigners and to disseminate government propaganda.

On my way back to the hotel to collect Zara and Ben I intended obtaining some *metallik* for the boat tickets, and looked out for a *saraff*'s booth. All were boarded and nailed, their Jew owners fled. Evidently they shared Dolfuss' view that a crowd on the rampage doesn't pause to enquire into the distinction between one usurer and another. It did not signify, for I was able to buy *metallik* from the hotel dragoman (who revenged himself for the teeth I had loosened in his jaw by charging me at a heavy rate for change); and Ben and Zara and I were soon embarked upon a ferry which I, by practice at reading the ferries' flags denoting speed and itinerary, believed to be a direct boat for Emirghian.

Until the boat was under way I made a point of keeping Ben close by our seats on the open foredeck, for old Dolfuss' nervousness had affected me sufficiently for me to recognise that some attack might possibly be made upon us. Once on the Bosphorus however I considered that we were perfectly safe, and encouraged Ben to run off and look about the boat, for Zara's proximity had already aroused my amorous tendencies.

Whilst Ben was by I could do nothing. He stood at the rail watching the activity of the shipping we threaded amongst, graceful feluccas, sturdy grain ships from the Danube, all the colour and vivacity of ship and water and quay. I could see the child's dark eyes fixed steadily and seriously upon the scene he watched, his teeth chewing on his knuckle, his very soul, you would judge, drawn out through his eyes towards that foreign shore. Not foreign to him, I felt certain : no, it was at the rainy window of a vast cold English mansion, as I had once seen him, that his looks had the sorrowfulness of an exile's. As our ferry steamed on past Dolmabagcheh, and the shore was no longer commercial quays but gardens and marble kiosks, his interest waned. With Zara's hand inserted in the pocket of my trowsers I wished the little fellow at the devil instead of scraping away at the rail with the sliver of a dagger he had removed from the armoury we had visited. He saw me looking fierce at him and strolled off, slipping the dagger up his sleeve for fear, I suppose, that it would be taken from him. At a distance from us he occupied himself in watching the shipping, and in particular a ten-oared *kaik* which had appeared off the ferry's quarter, and which kept pace with us. No doubt I should have paid this vessel some attention, but my interest was entirely taken up with Zara.

I proposed to myself to complete my conquest of Zara when we reached Emirghian, so long as Ben could be occupied with a meal downstairs and Maryka had vacated the upper floor. Why she was so amenable I could not make out; but what can ever be the explanation of a woman's sexual laxity (except the hope of financial gain) since it is agreed that the female mind is un-sullied by lust, as is the female flesh agreed to be incapable of lust's gratification? Zara could not hope to gain power over me, for she knew that I (if accused) would deny any connexion with her, whilst her mere accusation would be enough to procure her instant dismissal without a character . . . I determined that I would watch Zara closely whilst she undressed, so that I would not again be baffled so utterly by the fortifications defending Rachel's virtue . . . I wished too that I had obliged Maryka to instruct me in how to undress her, instead of forcing her to suffer Rachel's clothes to be torn and beaten from her back.

As soon as we had disembarked at Emirghian I told Zara to remain close to the quay whilst I went quickly to the house to discover whether it was fit for their reception. I did not know what to expect. As I drew near my heart sank; there was no use pretending that the cacophony I had heard from a distance, and had thought must emanate from a women's *hammam*, or from an encampment of gipsies at the least, did not in fact issue from my house. A shrill hubbub spilled from the windows and ascended skyward—shrieks, singing, music—I stood aghast, my hand on the gate, looking up at the board walls and outbuilt windows which seemed to vibrate with this caterwauling. As to what had happened there was little doubt : the servants engaged by the rascally drago-man had run wild. What could I do? I walked away from the gate unresolved and took a turn under the planes.

And then a brilliant notion came to me : I would rent another house. I would abandon this establishment and start again from the scratch. I was at once restored to cheerfulness by the excellence of this plan—what child is not put in spirits by leaving the nursery floor covered with his spilled bricks and broken toys, and simply walking away?—and I fell to considering how best to rent another house with the necessary speed. Best to quit Emirghian and find a *yali* in some other village. Why not Therapia, under the nose of our summer embassy, and make a bid to enter the respectable society of the Bosphorus? I could easily tell Rachel that Emirghian was unsafe for her father. Resolved to travel at once to Therapia, perhaps to ask at the embassy itself if a house could be engaged immediately, I turned my steps back towards the quay. My love-making would have to be postponed, I thought, until opportunity presented at Therapia.

But it was not to be. The first indication I received of something awry was the soft-slippered concourse, the fluttering of rags and robes, as the idle, the children and the beggars loafed or ran or limped across the *meidan*. It was as though the square had been tipped, and its human contents slid towards the waterfront. I too went with the crowd until I reached its convergence at the water's brink. Just offshore was a rowboat from which leaned a Turk, apparently fishing. I recognised him as the ticket collector of the ferry station. He had a grappling hook upon a chain which was wound round his wrist, and with this he was trying to fish up some heavy object. In a moment he succeeded. An object streaming water broke the surface and was hauled into the boat. It was a body. It was a female body in European clothes. It was Zara.

Thrown from the boat onto the quay the body fell with the wet smack of an armful of seaweed. Zara lay upon her back. That she was dead, and had died violently, I saw from the open, staring, horrified eye. The rivulets running from her clothes and hair, so busily forming a pool, so busily trickling in the dust, were darker and thicker than mere water. I could not think, only stare. No one went near her.

Where was Ben? That question unlocked my brain. The ticket collector understood a word or two of French. I pushed to the water's edge and shouted at him :

'Where is the boy?'

He stood hands upon hips in the rocking boat and I could tell by the slide of his eyes away from mine that he was watched, and would not answer me. But who, in the crowd around me, was watching him?

'Is the boy dead?' I shouted out.

'Not is dead. Is gone—' a quick vague gesture suggested removal by boat—'gone with friend.'

I stared out at the glitter of the straits with desperate intentness. In the usual bustle of vessels large and small what could I hope for as a clue? Only this: disappearing rapidly towards Constantinople could be discerned the flash of blades in the sunlight, blades of oars driving the swift slim hooded shape of the ten-oared *kaik*. Ben had been kidnapped.

And Zara had been murdered. Of the crowd dispersing, having gazed sufficiently long at her corpse in the bovine manner of their kind, there must have been those who had seen the deed done. But from the evasiveness of the ticket collector I understood that whoever had committed the crime was potent enough, or the agent of someone sufficiently potent, to make him invisible in the eyes of a poor Turk. Had I not already grasped this fact I would have learned it from the mumblings of the greybeards who still contemplated the cadaver. '*Mashallah*' they agreed with one another, shaking their heads sagely, 'It is the will of God'.

I had done nothing because I did not know what to do. I guessed that if I associated myself with Zara's remains I should find myself enmeshed in the toils of the police—would very like be accused of her murder for the sheer temerity of objecting to murder—and would thus be obstructed in the pursuit of my only clue to Ben's captors, the ten-oared *kaik* as yet in flight upon the waters. The ticket collector had now stepped out of the rowboat and stood cleaning his hands upon a scrap of cloth, his back to the corpse, as though he had done all he intended doing.

'Can I hire a fast boat?' I asked him.

Again came the look of extreme nervousness. 'No boat. No boat follow. Now go. Go quick, or trouble come to you, too. Go!'

With his hands he made an urgent gesture pushing me from him, his eyes lowered as though fearing to meet the gaze of whoever watched him. I turned to see who it might be. There were only the ancients leaning bearded chins upon their sticks, the vast turbans of old Turkey weighing down their heads, as they studied the effects of God's will upon Zara.

I was obliged to abandon her body. Twenty-four hours earlier

I might have sent for the police, believing that justice would best be served by explaining to them the whole matter and leaving the hunt in their hands. But the work I had seen the *zaptieh* engaged upon last night had altered my view. An Englishman (unless of course he belongs to the criminal classes) must witness events which prove the corruption of the police before he will believe in it. If Zara's killers were powerful, as evidently they were, then I must conclude that the Turkish authorities would protect them, and would probably attach the blame of the murder to myself, at any rate until the kidnappers' trail should grow cold. I could not hire a boat at Emirghian, that much was plain. I therefore walked rapidly towards the corner of the square where horses stood for hire, sorry-looking nags of skin and bone, their heads dejected in a cloud of flies, but the speediest conveyance for hire in Emirghian. I demanded the best horse, holding out a twenty-franc piece, twice the hire for such creatures as he had. I saw his eyes leave my face and focus upon a point behind me. I turned. One of the old men from the quay must have followed me with surprising alacrity, for he stood behind me with a blank half-witted stare upon his face. I turned back and asked again,

'*Bana ver atim*—give me a horse.'

'No horse. Is lame.'

The grubby-looking skin and flat insolent eyes of the fellow exasperated me. The horses were fastened by their reins to a rail. I measured the distance to the nearest of them. I was screwing up my courage to act, when there came a shout from the greybeard behind me :

'*Gel!*—Come here !'

I looked back. The black uniforms of the *zaptieh* crawled upon the quay. I leaped for the nearest horse, wrenching its rein from the rail, frightening it into action as I pulled myself into the saddle. In a couple of moments we were clear. Up the track out of Emirghian I drove my steed with as wild a delight in the flying stones and rushing air as if I had stolen the horses of Phaeton. Ah—action after inaction, how wonderfully it settles doubts, solves dilemmas, sets free the very soul !

I knew the track up which we clattered, for I had walked it with the doomed Persian the day he had showed me Emirghian, and I recollected having seen a landing stage hard by the Castle of Rumelia. Here I might inveigle a boat out of a *kaikji* beyond reach of my enemies : at Bebek, the next village, I feared to find the police awaiting me. Accordingly I turned my horse loose on the heights above the castle and began to descend through the cypress woods alone. The nightingales which had sung in these groves were now silent as I hastened down over lichened rock or needle-strewn lawn, thinking of that day which had begun my adventures. It could not be denied that I was enjoying myself vastly. In the midst of action I did not doubt that action would succeed. The trouble is, that one does not pause long enough to make clear to oneself what 'success' would consist in, beyond the attainment of the next objective. To pause is to doubt.

My next objective, the quay close to the castle's fortifications, was now in sight. Against the rough stones of the jetty were tied two rowing boats and a *kaik* on clear green water through which I could see to a great depth from the heights above. In the immemorial attitude of his race—the 'patient resignation' of those who admire Islam—a Turk squatted by the water's edge. Here the current of the straits is at its fiercest, its eddies lashing and licking against the shore, the moving body of water between the twin Castles of Asia and Europe giving the appearance of the majestic flow of a great river, the Ganges at Benares perhaps, or the Thames at Eton.

I accosted the Turk and made him understand that I wished to be taken to Constantinople. Having made such an economy in the hire of my horse at Emirghian I offered him twenty francs, which he accepted, and bade me enter his boat. The *kaik* is an extremely frail craft, fashioned from planks of beechwood shaved thin as paper, and seems at first as though it must upset. As he sculled out into the ripping races and currents of the channel I saw by the fellow's grin that he thought to alarm me, so, since the sun burned down pretty fierce and I was heated with my exertions, I got upon my feet in midstream and calmly peeled off my jacket. The rascal's terror was amusing as he gripped the gunwhale and begged me to sit down. None of those fellows can swim, whereas I have some experience both of skiffs and of keeping afloat in strong currents, gained in my schooldays at Cuckoo Weir. I folded my jacket into a pillow, lighted a cigar, and lay back with my hat over my eyes to enjoy this novel excursion upon the Bosphorus.

167

Along we rushed upon the flood at what seemed a desperate pace, the craft caught and shaken by eddies, held straight by most skilful use of the oars, yellow foam and gurgling vortices threatening our destruction at every moment as we flew among the shipping, the towering cutwater of a steamer now overhead, the wash of a ferry now slapping into our planking—truly this was the flight of the swallow-boat, the *kirlangich*, as these *kaiks* are called. I was assuredly as near to the Devil's Current now as I might ever have yearned to be from the rail of a ferry!—And, indeed, as freely and wonderfully in action as the swifts and swallows I had so often watched from my windows. With the confidence which action imparts—the body assuring the mind— I had no doubt but that I should see my way step by step to a solution of the matter. Just so had I used to feel assured, the moment I had a ball between my legs, of scoring a rouge at the Field Game.

It was off the quay at Topkhaneh that I spotted the ten-oared *kaik*. Its crew were paddling idly to hold the vessel against the current, the stern sheets where passengers are carried empty except for a fellow who was stooped in under the hood, perhaps fastening a rope, so that I could not see him plain. I motioned to my boatman that I wished to be put ashore, and he sculled our craft towards the quay. We were alongside the *kaik* when the creature in the stern straightened up and looked at us. You may imagine my shock when I found myself looking into the dough-white face of the eunuch.

I now knew—if I were right in connecting the *kaik* with Ben's disappearance—into whose hands the lad had fallen. The moment our craft was within reach of the jetty I leaped ashore and set off at a rapid pace across the cannon-packed square, across the tramlines, into the maze of Fundukli. I still had my jacket hung upon my shoulder, so little time had I lost, for I hoped to reach the slavers' khan before the eunuch should have warned them of my approach.

It seems strange to me now, as I sit on a camp chair writing this tale in the mulberry garden of the French Consul at Diarbekr, awaiting God knows what fate at the hands of our Kurdish besiegers, that I did not pause to consider whether or no I was running my head into a noose. But I did not. All action is of the nature of the cavalry charge; questions of direction or sagacity are ignored by the commander who dislikes above all to lose his impetuosity.

It was by now a late hour in the afternoon. The streets through which I passed seemed in a strangely breathless state, the quietness which anticipates the catastrophe, children invisible, a few figures hastening this way or that with robes drawn over their heads, the very dogs slinking by in the shadows. My English boots rang preternaturally loud in the hushed streets. Intent upon my mission as I was, there came to me a premonition of what destruction was to fall upon the town in the coming darkness.

I reached the long blank wall of the khan and thundered upon the door with all the impetus of my dash from Emirghian, and from Zara's murdered body leaking blood and water on the quay. There was no response. If an eye fastened itself to the grille I did not see it. I was in process of thumping upon the door again when it opened abruptly, and my raised fist was seized so that I half fell, and was half dragged, down the steps into the courtyard. I found my arm in the grip of the large grubby Turk, in a fez and a cloth coat, whom I had seen twice before : once when he had seized the ill-fated Persian on the quay at Bebek, and once when he had stood in this courtyard blinding song birds. My jacket had fallen from my shoulder, and when I turned for it I saw that it had been picked up by another fat Turk who was rifling its pockets. It was the shabby Europeanised clothes of the two men which made me most uneasy. These were not the picturesque ruffians of *opéra bouffe*.

Through the first court, where the singing birds were silent, I was directed into the dusky arcade of the second. At the further end of the colonnade I saw burning a taper, such as is kept alight for smokers, and beside it the motionless bulk of Azeez awaiting my approach.

'Azeez,' said I as I walked up, 'one of your confounded fellows is picking my pocket. I wish you'd tell him to leave off and give me my jacket back.'

One finger was all he moved, but my jacket was restored to me. I took this as a favourable omen. Putting the garment on I instantly sat down as a European would, upon the bottom step of the stone stairway ascending to the women's quarters, judging

F*   169

it expedient to emphasise my Englishness. As the Afghan still had not spoken I began :

'Now look here; I don't know why you've taken the child, and I don't know what you've done with him, but I have come to give you a chance to hand him back to me before you find yourself in hot water.'

There was silence. Then Azeez lifted his beard and laughed his roaring kind of laugh. 'Hot water I like! I love it! And who will hot the water?'

'The British Embassy,' I told him.

He wagged his turban from side to side, and the chuckling turned sour. 'I think no,' he said with absolute precision. Then he took a fresh breath, or a sigh, and said, 'I have told you about mettling. Yes I told you. In case your ear no good I showed you. Yes I showed you. People mettle——' He drew his forefinger across his throat, and made a pantomime of lifting his head by its hair, eyes fixed, tongue protruding—I saw again the Persian's head hung in the greenish shade of the magnolia tree. Then he sighed again, combing out his beard with his finger. 'Why Inglistan mettle mettle mettle with all things? Slaving and so? Is not their business. Is not your business!' he suddenly screamed at me with a great froth of fury.

'Very well,' said I, 'supposing slaving ain't my concern. This is kidnapping this is. Very much my business. I take it you hope for money from——' I stopped short of supplying Dolfuss' name, for I did not know how much they knew.

But he supplied it. 'From Dolfuss Meester? Is you, my friend, is you wants money from Dolfuss Meester I think. I know. No, no, is not money we need.'

I was at a loss. 'But—but you kidnapped——'

'No kidnap. You mettle in what you don't know. Is no kidnap!' he roared fortissimo.

'Ain't it though? Taking a child not kidnap? I'm hanged if I know what other name to give it then.'

'Sir—friend—Inglistani—' he leaned forward, his two great hands made into a fist he extended towards me, half threat, half prayer—'what name you give this thing in your Inglistan tongue not matter. Not matter! In old towns, in old countries, old fights go on—you know? Old fights from long ago. We like that. We love it! Is how we live. Is no good fools come shout out in

170

Inglistani these word "Kidnap!", "Murder!", "Slavery!"—is very bad.' He had settled back amongst his cushions as if to demonstrate the comfort which feuds afforded the Oriental. Suddenly he shot forward again, his finger jabbing at me—'Inglistani come mettling in fight—zit!' The finger ripped across his throat once more.

It is irritating to be continually threatened with having one's throat cut, especially when the fellow breathes his foul odour in your face on each occasion, and I rapped out, 'You know perfectly well you can't go about cutting Englishmen's throats, whatever you may choose to do to an old Persian.'

He smiled amongst his bolsters and cushions, and smoked for a moment before replying, 'My friend, you forget I was at Kabul in '79. Plenty of English throats! You know whose throat this hand cut for him that time? Sir Cav——'

'Hold your tongue!' I shouted at the grinning brute, for I did not trust myself in the presence of one of the devils who had massacred a diplomatic mission.

He had looked very black at me for a moment, but he relaxed again. 'Tonight in this town,' he said coldly, 'many people die. Many. If one die, is big crowd killed him. Even Sir Currie believe it, if Inglistani die tonight.'

I said, 'There is to be rioting tonight then?'

He leaned enough forward to glance up at the sky, still coloured with sunset above the garden. 'Run quick,' he said, 'you run safe to Pera before killing begin.'

I had to consider his words. I had seen the Stamboul mob: his was a threat I could understand. Moreover his claim that the taking of Ben was not kidnap for ransom but a move in some deeper and more ancient game—a ploy in a Byzantine feud—was plausible. It would explain Ben in a way that other speculations about his origins did not.

'Is Ben here?' I asked.

Doubtless Azeez read the uncertainty in my voice aright, for he did not trouble to conceal his satisfaction. 'Come,' he said, rising with a single athletic movement of his large frame, 'Come, I show you'.

I followed him. The khan was enormous, far larger than I had realised. It was in another part of the building altogether—no longer a fortified stone palace of a bygone age but a large wooden house abutting onto the khan's furthest courtyard—that Azeez took me into a room furnished in the modern Turkish style and indicated that I was to look through a pierced lattice. This I did. I saw below me a large room, galleried behind lattices such as the one I peered through, and on the floor of the room I counted six children. It took me a moment more to identify Ben, so similar were the little boys. In age they were too close to be the children of one mother; but not of course too close to be the offspring of a single father. They were seated on cushions around the matronly figure of a woman who appeared to be turning the pages of a picture book whilst another, younger, woman was picking up scattered and overturned toys from the floor. What made me realise that Ben was neither unhappy, nor imprisoned in the sense of the word implied by 'kidnap', was that he was not attending to the book, or upon his best behaviour, but was pulling faces at one of his neighbours whilst at the same time kicking another boy's ankle. He was behaving as a child does with familiar companions in a house he trusts : in a manner, in short, that Ben had no chance of ever behaving in his English 'home'. I turned away from the lattice. I was convinced that Ben, very far from being held kidnap for ransom, had been in some sense restored to his own. This persuaded me of the truth of Azeez's contention, that I saw but one move in an ancient game. Still, I could scarcely approve, so I searched for something else to condemn.

'And the nursemaid, Zara,' I said, 'is it nothing that she was murdered?'

He opened the palms of his hands, and I thought that he too would murmur *Mashallah* as the old hypocrites on the quay had done. But he said :

'This too you do not understand, you Inglistani. It is necessary she die. She bring shame. Her brother put her to death with stone. *Mashallah.*'

Her brother! The feud then was all within a family, if the brother of Dolfuss' nursemaid worked for Azeez's employer. I understood Azeez's explanation, understood the old men muttering on the quay : it was God's will working through the hand of man to execute an apostate that I had seen. For her sins against the Mussulman's honour—for the freedom of her intercourse with the *giauor*—she had been put to death with a stone by her brother. That, and nothing less, was the meaning of *Mashallah*. To call it

172

murder, as I had done, was the impertinence of a foreigner—the impertinence of the foreigner who had called the capture of Ben 'kidnap'—the same impertinence which interfered with slavery —the intemperate arrogance of race or class or creed which finds itself in the ascendant.

All this passed rapidly through my mind as Azeez preceded me down a narrow flight of stairs which ended in a low door. We were alone. With a knife—even without—I might have sprung upon him and killed him and escaped. I thought of it because I had come—reluctantly—to accept Azeez's integrity, and I would not have wished him dead. He opened the door and said,

'Run quick! You will be save I hope. I know! But your friend no——' He shook his head.

'What friend?'

'Watkin. He mettle.'

'Poor fellow it isn't his fault, it's his wife meddles so.'

'Ah!' He wagged his head and his eye flashed fire. 'Is his fault he has such womans to wife. Should stand on his own leg. Now he pay all blames, all.'

'Tonight he will be murdered?—put to death?' I corrected myself, seeing all the Afghan's killings as no murder but execution.

'Run quick, my friend,' warned Azeez, and pushed me into the street, closing the small door instantly upon me.

I would have been utterly lost had I not heard the clangour of a tram passing in the streets below where I stood. From that bearing I took careful stock of my position, and was able to make out the relationship of the stone khan with the new-built wooden house at whose side door I found myself, for the tall dark spire of the cypress within the courtyard overlooked its roof like a watchtower. Certain that I could find the house again I walked at my best pace to Topkhaneh, and there at the carriage-stand I persuaded the driver of the only vehicle, a two-horse closed carriage, to convey me to the Pera Palace Hotel for three times the ordinary fee. From the universal restlessness it was evident that the night would be violent : even the slap of the waves, even the shivering of the trees, seemed ominous, and the wind that stirred them seemed a sulphurous breath.

At the hotel the impetus of action and excitement still carried me to the head of the stairs. But on the dim, broad, quiet landing I paused. What was I to say to Rachel, to Dolfuss?—how was

I to explain?—how was I to translate, in short, the happenings of the world I had come from (which satisfied their own logic) into terms acceptable amongst the mahogany and plush of this other world? Kidnap—murder—these were the terms one used by electric light, which ousted the putting to death and abduction of smoky flares and swift *kaiks* on the Bosphorus. I lost my momentum. I all but crept along the corridor past Rachel's quarters to my own.

It was fortunate I did. Once in my dressing-room, the first sound I heard through the communicating door was Dolfuss' voice, reedy, ranting, hysterical. His words I could not distinguish, but I heard my own name abused with fearful vigour. I hesitated before putting my head into such a hornet's nest. I wondered. I considered. I put my ear to the door. Through Rachel's reasonable murmur came a flare of old Dolfuss' cracked tones :

'Wait? Wait what for, hey? There's his ransom demand, ain't it? His villainy's as plain as kiss your hand. I'll not wait, my life I'll not, not while I'm stood in a city I knows as well as I know this Stamboul, and can get justice done easy as wink what the Queen herself couldn't get done in England.'

Upon that note a door slammed, and I concluded that he had taken himself off. I wondered if Rachel was alone. It had to be chanced. I opened the door and went in.

She gave out a cry, her hand at her throat. She half rose, and such a confusion of emotions crossed her face that she expressed none of them, but ran towards me with a sob, a scrap of paper in her outstretched hand. She checked her rush before we met, and poked out the paper at me till I took it. I read it, and was nonplussed.

'You don't believe it?' I assumed.

'Why should I not believe that you want money? Only money.'

That was hard to rebut. I examined the paper. 'My signature is a forgery, of course,' I said.

'Then where is he? Where is Ben?'

'He has been taken—it is very complicated. He has been taken by——' I could not find words to explain Azeez, or how I knew him.

'So!' she said, withdrawing from me as though I poisoned the air about me, 'so, it is true then. You are what Papa says of you.'

'Rachel it is not I who has Ben.' Her hand was feeling the wall behind her for the bell-pull. 'Rachel—believe me.'

'Bring him back then. If you are not holding him, find him then. It is you who lost him. You and Zara that whore! I knew she was my father's whore, but I did not believe until this that she was yours.'

'Rachel——'

'Find him! Only find him and bring him back. That is all.'

'Rachel listen to me: your father knows—must know—who has taken the child. He is merely throwing the blame upon me. He knows——'

'Pray leave this room or I will summon help to arrest you.'

I had approached close to her, but now I fell back. I was thrown into confusion, unable to judge probabilities. All that seemed evident was this, that I had been duped by Azeez. This idea gave me a focus. I would return to the khan, where I had been made a fool of. From the door I said:

'You and I are both dupes, Rachel. Yes we are. Your father knows perfectly well who has seized Ben, and he knows why. I do not know why. Yes, I know who has the boy. I have seen him and he is safe. For honour's sake I will go there now—I must now that I know of this calumny against me—I will go, and I will probably not return. Perhaps that is what your father hopes. Remember though. Just remember.'

With that I closed the door. She had listened, and would consider my words. I sat thinking what I had best do. But thinking was worse than useless: I must act, and hope that out of action would emerge a plan, a possible way forward, a chance I could seize and act upon. I sprang up.

I looked round my dressing-room. Since I was here, was there nothing I could take with me to improve my chance of success, or at least of survival, in the ordeal to come? Spats, suits, hats, boots on trees—not one article did I see in this world which would be of the least service in the world I was bound for. All that I possessed was worse than useless. I thought again of Jason's bare dash between the Clashing Rocks, and of my mother's interpretation of his passage. As I was about to leave, my glance fell upon the billiard ball with which Briggs had furnished me, placed now between ivory-backed brushes on my dressing table. This I pocketted less as a weapon than as a symbol—a symbol of the

175

readiness and flexibility of mind, the adaptability, which I had admired in Briggs. These were the essential qualities of the irregular fighting man; and is not 'an irregular fighting man', in the end, what a fellow should aspire to be? If one is to imitate the Classic mould then that, after all, is what the Greek heroes had been; irregular fighting men, not in the least resembling the pedagogic 'Hellenist' who pores over their remains.

My hand was raised to open the passage door when the door from Rachel's sitting-room opened and revealed her. There she stood framed, without entering my territory.

'I cannot believe you,' she said in low tones, 'I cannot believe that you tell the truth now, only now, when you have always told me lies before. Yes you have. Always. Oh I know it is a convention that I must pretend to believe you—a convention of your stupid world which is all to you. So I do pretend. There is nothing but pretence. All there is is what appears to be. Well.'

I would have spoken, but I did not know what to say.

'Of course I am to blame,' she went on sadly, low, 'of course, yes. It was your lies I liked, did you know? Your lies to Lady Mary, your lies to me—so, so smart I thought : the smart world, all lies and deceit and making love upon sofas in a bachelor's chambers in Berkeley Street. That I loved. Yes it was deceit and lies I was in love with. You were ingenious too. And gay, you were gay. The gay deceiver—well, such old tricks work on young hearts.' Here a sob almost broke her voice, but she vanquished the weakness impatiently. 'But now what I hate is you are such a dull liar, so boring, such tedious wearisome lies in long, long words—that is what is too much ! Now you recite rigmaroles about drains when you mean to lie to me about your mistress at Emirghian. Pshaw ! Drains ! If you made up an amusing story of it, even, I would pay for your mistress gladly—if I even could laugh, I would pay for that. Why do you suppose I sit writing, writing? Because I must make up a life, or I expire. There is either you lecturing or there is Nanny, who compares Pera to Birkenhead every time she crosses the Golden Horn.'

Touched by this pathetic sketch I moved towards her; but she stepped back, and recovered the first imperious tone of her diatribe :

'All this is nothing to you, I know. I say it so that you understand that I cannot believe you, I must believe that you are lying

176

until you bring Ben back. Bring him back and I will believe that that ransom note is the calumny you claim it to be. Fail, and you may stop away. One thing,' she added through the closing door, 'be careful, for Papa will send men to kill you.'

The door closed and I was alone. I read again the paper she had given me before putting it into my pocket. 'Pay to me one *lakh* of gold *liras* if you wish for Ben to be keep save—A. V. Caper.' Thus it ran, in a fluent imitation of my hand : that Rachel should swallow down such an illiterate note, and think its syntax mine, was a cruel cut which showed me how ready she was to believe ill of me.

The note surely originated with Azeez—the sum demanded was what I had paid over for Maryka—but why had he then sent me back to the hotel? What was the purpose of the note?—to procure me money, or to procure my death? Or was it after all a serious threat against Ben? Unable to answer these questions I took refuge from them in action, speedily left the hotel, and found myself once more in the expectant streets, dark now, through which I hastened *en route* for Topkhaneh.

The streets were empty still, houses shuttered on the thorough-fares, and in the alleys leading down to the Golden Horn no quarrelling voices or laughter, no singing and no screams, re-sounded from open windows as was usual. Instead was a stillness which seemed heavy with the premonition of violence. Only rarely from those narrow lanes does one enjoy a clear prospect, but close to the Tower of Galata lies a small piazza which allows a view over rooftops to Stamboul. There I paused for a moment. The area is a much Anglicised one, housing most of the British insti-tutions, and I joined a crowd of a dozen or so persons (the first I had seen) who were gazing across the roofs and over the Golden Horn. I too looked out—and was appalled.

The domes of Soleyman's mosque—the domes and minarets of the whole skyline—were lit by flamelight, the ghastly refulgence now and then darkened by drifting smoke-columns which were themselves shot through by explosions of sparks from the burning wooden buildings. The effect was sublime and terrible. The fire itself, the great orange lazy tongues of flame against which stood roofs in sharp outline, seemed confined as yet to an outlying quarter on the west. I heard an Englishman at my elbow remark that the mob had a thousand Armenians shut up in a church at

Kapu, and that doubtless what we watched was their funeral pyre. I was thus staring when I felt my sleeve plucked. I turned sharply, my hand upon the billiard ball in my pocket. There stood the doleful figure of Watkins in his knicker suit, a velocipede leaning against his arm.

'What are you doing here?' I demanded of him, expecting that his assassins might dart upon him at any moment—for I had not forgotten Azeez's sentence of death pronounced against him.

My vehemence took him aback. He sucked his moustache. 'Come out to have a look just,' he said.

'Be off!' I urged him. 'Your life is in danger—I have seen Azeez.'

He stepped back as though I were a madman ranting at him. 'Mrs Watkins is giving a lecture, see,' he explained, 'in the Mechanics Institute just here. Promised me a few minutes at the end she has, so I can put in a word for cycling like.' He clapped his machine upon the saddle, and I saw the fervour enliven his dull eyes as he ran on, 'Only an old Starley Rover, nothing great, but she's fitted up with a Fagan two-speed gear—see here—and those is Eadie coaster hubs I put on her—well, sell a few I hope——'

I broke into this farrago by entreating him to leap upon his roadster and pedal clear of Constantinople without delay. He regarded me dubiously with his hang-dog air, settling the little round cap upon his head. I lost patience with him and set out upon my way again. I doubted if he would heed my warning; the egocentric is scarcely aware enough of the outside world to apprehend danger from it.

Because of the emptiness of the streets I came to Fundukli swiftly and, as it seemed, safely. Those few wayfarers I saw were as alarmed by the sight of me as was I by them, each of us attributing to the other some bold and dangerous motive for being abroad. I found my way without difficulty to the street in which stood the house where Ben was held; but since I had not considered my next move I turned the last corner slowly.

It was well that I did. In the street a crowd was gathered. So narrow are the alleys, so tall the houses, that noise is enclosed and I had not heard the crowd's mutter till I was upon it. Other streets no doubt contained other crowds: the massacre, if such it were, seemed to be a piecemeal affair except where the town

178

was fired. I had shrunk back into the hood of shadow afforded by a porch, from whence I watched. Torches smoked, their yellow glare throwing fantastical shadows upon the decorated house-fronts, so animating windows and balconies that these orifices seemed to flutter like eyes and mouths, and one could fancy that the low murmur filling the street came from the houses' lips and not the crowd's. It was around the door of the house where Ben was held—the main door, not the postern Azeez had pushed me through—that the crowd thronged. They evidently had a purpose.

A wild-looking scoundrel who stood upon the steps of the house knocked heavily on its door with his club. A loose robe, or length of cotton, covered him entirely; the garment had the look of a disguise, and I saw that many others of the crowd were similarly wrapped, only their long black locks, greased and matted, swinging about their faces as they turned their heads to and fro. To my surprise the door was opened to them. The torches pressed forward, the ring of light converged around the door; but there was neither a rush nor a shout. Framed in the doorway stood that same fat Turk who had opened the khan gate to me. Seeing him at the door reminded me that house and khan were connected : whoever wished to escape this crowd's attentions could have left discreetly by the great gate in the blind wall of the khan. There was a parley on the steps. If the crowd entered the house, might I not enter too and snatch back Ben, if I could disguise myself as one of the robed crowd? I could not see whether the fat Turk stepped aside, or was pushed away, but in a moment the leaders were pouring through the open door under their smoking torches. Now a sound broke from their throats which made the hair stand upright upon my head. It was the wailing cry of *mullahs* chanting the Koran. In that crowd must be dervishes, their intentions fanatical.

It is perhaps a race-memory of Saracen steel under the walls of Acre which makes my blood run cold when I hear that broken wail, thin and high, sobbing and sawing upon my nerves. I own that fear of it caused me to defer executing any plan to enter the house. The crowd was all gone in, only gleams of torchlight and the dervishes' accursed chanting leaking out of windows into the dark street. What action could I take?

As I wondered, from a high window came a burst of break-

179

ing glass. I looked up. Out of the sky tumbled a scream, a black tumbling bundle screaming against the stars, falling. The uprush of the street crumpled scream and bundle into silence. I had dashed forward before I thought what I was about. Such horrors as this could not be borne. If it cost me my life, a stand must be made. Without a plan, I made a run for the postern by which I had quitted the house. Just as I reached the door it opened. I confronted as fearsome a spectacle as can be found in this world : the face of a eunuch. Nor was his womanish white visage the worst of it; on that hairless skull was perched an object which caused my heart to stop : it was the tiny tweed cycling cap I had seen an hour since on Watkins' head. I did not gaze upon it for long. His eyes unchanging as stone, the creature struck me between shoulder and neck with a blunt instrument, and I fell senseless into his arms.

X

In the Eunuch's Clutches

I CAME TO myself in a boat, and discovered at once that my wrists were bound. The craft was evidently a large one, for I was under cover and lying upon rugs, and I could hear the creak of oars rowing it through the night. No doubt I was aboard the ten-oared *kaik*. Were my feet bound? In moving them I roused Ben's voice :

'Ow! That's kicking. You've been asleep for ages. You missed getting into the boat and everything. You had to be carried in a—oh I've forgotten—a something chair.'

'A sedan chair?' An excellent way of carrying an unconscious man! Still usual enough in Pera to excite no remark.

'That's right. How do you know, have you been in one before?'

'Never, I've always thought people looked rather foolish in them.'

'Yes, you did.'

That he was safe—that he was not a bundle hurled down from a high window—lightened the oppression of captivity. 'Where are we going, Ben?' I asked.

There was a pause. 'Why didn't you come when we went on this boat before?'

'They went off without me,' I said. 'Ben, where are we going, do you know?'

'Zara fell in.' He laughed uncertainly. 'She fell in wearing all her clothes. When she did I was very—interested', he finished, substituting (as I had known him do before) the word 'interest' for an emotion beyond expressing. 'I didn't cry,' he added.

'Who are the other children in the house where you've been?' I asked.

'Don't know.' He fiddled evasively with something in his sleeve.

181

'It's very late you know,' he went on, 'I should think it's about—nine o'clock? Is it? Have I ever been out as late as this before?'

'Ben,' I whispered urgently, an idea having struck me, 'do you still have your dagger in your sleeve?'

'Yes,' he admitted with suspicion.

I shifted my position so that I could see out of the hooded deckhouse. Against the sky was humped the cloaked and huge-headed eunuch, a simian arm steering the boat. I whispered to Ben, 'Just put your dagger in my hand, can you?'

'It's mine.'

'I know it is,' I said, 'I just need to borrow it for a second.'

'No.'

'Please, Ben, there's a good fellow.'

'I need it.'

'Then will you cut the bits of string round my wrists? Please Ben, then we can go home.'

'No, I can't.' He edged away from me. 'Don't tell I've got my knife,' he said apprehensively.

'You wouldn't have it at all if I hadn't let you pinch it,' I reminded him. Had preoccupation with his accursed knife deafened him to my offer to take him home? 'Please lend it, Ben, then we'll go home.'

'Anyway,' he said, 'anyway, my father doesn't mind me having a knife. Anyway, he'll give me a proper dagger I expect. He says I can put out the birds' eyes when I'm bigger.'

'Your father? Have you seen your father?'

'When Zara fell in the water there was a huge splash! It wet me a bit.' He paused. 'I just cried for a minute.'

It was useless. I sat back. Here was a child contending with each event as he met it, and intent upon allowing to no event the abnormality which might have ruptured all his security. He was learning to survive, an irregular fighting man, under whatever circumstances prevailed. To have gone on questioning him would have been to force abnormality in upon him as deep water presses inward upon the skull until it smashes it. I made a last attempt to trade with him :

'Ben,' I said, 'if you look in my pocket there's a billiard ball I'll lend you if I can borrow your knife.'

'What colour is it?'

'White.'

'I only want a black one.'

He didn't trust adults. He had emerged the loser from too many bargains with them. He crawled carefully over my legs and out of the deckhouse. There he sat hoping to catch the attention of the eunuch, of whom he evidently had no fear.

The eunuch's gaze fell upon him with absolute indifference. The creature was cloaked in a dark wrap, so that the face, whitened as if with flour, shone with the horrid pallor of a Hallowe'en mask made from a hollowed root and hung from a hook in the boat's stern. Is it only by association with a parallel hidden in our own minds that another man's appearance can horrify us?—for the eunuch had showed me kindness, had saved my life indeed; yet his kindness by no means gainsaid my horror and fear of the mutation he represented to my mind. Ben was below the age when such fears come to a man.

I turned from these reflexions to consider my own position. I was quite impotent. I too, like Ben, must wait upon events and hope, if not to profit by chance, then at least to survive. There was a wonderful liberation from care in this. I was wondering how long our voyage would continue when I felt the *kaik* alter course. Soon the creak and splash of the oars ceased, the craft cut silently through calm water until orders rang out and the dipped oars hissed in the sea, checking the boat. In a moment more we touched a quay.

I was half lifted to my feet and propelled onto a wooden jetty. From the set of the current I deduced that we were upon the European shore, possibly near Bebek, in a deep bay whose thickly wooded flanks gave the place a secretive air. It was silent, save for the lap of the water, and the curve of the hills made a high black rim against the star-filled sky. Here before us were lawns, the massy shadows of garden trees, the low pale bulk of a *yali*. Why had they taken no precautions to prevent me from identifying the place? Were they too powerful to fear reprisal? Or did they intend that I should never leave?

Others, apart from the oarsmen, had landed from the forward part of the boat. The swathed figures of women, and some children, straggled ahead of me over dim lawns towards the pale glimmer of the house. As we drew near I was surprised to find a building something after the manner of a villa built in Regency days in England : a low, wide-winged affair under a pitched roof with a deep eave, the windows having venetian shutters which opened back against the walls; wooden-built of course, but new-painted a lively pink, and surrounded by a neat parterre. These details I noted because they formed together too comfortable and familiar a type of dwelling for me to feel much apprehension as to how I should be received within. I might have run down into Berkshire for a Saturday-to-Monday and found just such a trim billet as this. We entered by way of a side yard and servants' door.

The interior was silent. The children had disappeared. I was hustled the length of an ill-lighted passage and pushed through a door. Expecting an English parlour, easy chairs, a cheerful fire, I was surprised—shocked—to find myself in a room entirely in the Eastern style. Evidently the house's gentlemanlike exterior had been misleading. I was amongst tiled walls, and a profusion of rugs and bolsters, and I was startled to find the duty of candlesticks performed by a couple of half-naked blackamoors in the room's corners.

But I was very much more taken aback when I made out who it was who was seated cross-legged upon a divan at the room's centre. For there sat Rachel's father.

Surely it was the old Hebrew himself, and none other? He had upon his head a kind of quilted, box-shaped affair with a gold tassel, he was clothed in a heavily-worked *kaftan* which gleamed with gold thread, and his fingers were crowded with jewels; but this finery made not the least difference to the fellow's furtive and ill-conditioned air of having stolen his clothes, whether frock coat or *kaftan*. He squinted away at me as usual out of his little black eyes, and said not a word, as if the better to enjoy my overturn. He made however a gesture with one finger, upon which a knife of rare sharpness sliced through my bonds in the twinkling of an eye. I had felt the humiliation of standing trussed before the fellow, but I don't know but what I didn't resent more his evident confidence in setting my hands free. At last he removed the amber mouthpiece of a *narguilh* from his purplish lips and spoke.

'Keeping you out of trouble is becoming a nuisance,' he complained. 'Twice now, yes twice, Moostapha here has rescued you from certain death.'

It was not Dolfuss. The voice, though Jewish, was more precise in diction and pitched upon a less whining note. I turned my attention to what he had said. 'Rescued? Twice? There was the Persian fellow after me, I concede—but when else—?'

'Tonight. Tonight, Mr Caper. Do you not know if you had become known to the fanatics at my house they would have put you to death? Of course you do.'

'Who was thrown out of the window?'

He waved a fat flashing hand. 'A maid, a nurse, a servant—an Armenian.'

'Whom you left to——'

'Be calm. Do not protest. Or that, or they burn the house with ten, twelve persons. What would you? Eh, sir? Sir, the Armenians must live with persecution as we do, as we Jews do. It is the tax we must pay for our abilities. This is nothing. It is the question of preserving your life or not that we should look to.' He held up a finger which he crooked. Instantly the eunuch hurried to his side, his dwarf's legs working away like steam-pistons. 'To your shadow here,' said the Jew, 'you should show your gratitude.'

My shadow! I could not deny that the mutilated creature beside him had saved my life. Not by a jot did the fact lessen my loathing for the dwarf, or lessen the horror in which I held his emasculation. My shadow! He was indeed all that was dark to me.

'We had made you a neat arangement,' the pseudo-Dolfuss continued, 'but you did not accept of it. Why is this?'

I was puzzled. 'What arrangement?'

'You never grasped it? You never saw that the money was put into your hand?' He rocked back, seeking his *narguilh* again for comfort. 'Such obtuseness! A *lakh* of gold *lira* we put into your hand——!'

'The ransom?' I tried to follow. 'But I hadn't kidnapped Ben, how could I give him back?'

'No, sir,' he said, wagging his head at such a slow student, 'but you could have taken the money, sir, for promising that the child was safe, eh? It was all the note undertook, to say he was safe. This you could have done, and took the money and cleared off. Now how you going to pay up when the money for the slave-girl's due, eh?'

185

Slowly I said, 'You imagined I would take money in the matter of a kidnapped child?'

I was appalled. There dawned upon my mind the estimate this base creature had of my character. A kidnapper! I!

'Come, sir,' he said, 'the methods you use to extract money from your wife are all according to Cocker are they? Is that it?'

'I don't bargain upon the safety of a child!' I told him. 'Devil take you, you have an odd set of notions indeed if you suppose an English gentleman will stoop to play——'

'Stoop! Stoop is it? It don't serve to try and make a moral stand with me,' he rapped out. 'Recollect that I know—unlike your wife and her father just yet—I know. Oh, "gentleman" is it? You buy a slave you can't pay for, you borrow, you lie and beg and steal, on account of you there's men killed, and girls——'

'What girls?'

'She you called Zara. There now. On account of your carryings-on with her—yes, out in full day in the *champs de morts*, on the boat too—that's what brought her brother to put her to death. There now.'

'Maybe so, but——'

'Oh pray, sir—"but" nothing. You sir, the point you'll stop at, sir, is where your perception won't carry you further.' He tapped the side of his skull with a forefinger. 'Truth is, you didn't understand your opportunity this evening—that's the truth of it. My word but a slow fellow like you don't half have to pay for it! Eh? See where you've fetched up? All the blame for taking the boy, and none of the tin. And now you're thrown back upon our hands . . .' He resumed smoking thoughtfully.

That the fellow should suppose me capable of blackmail had appalled my deepest instincts. Yet it had to be confessed that such a low creature as this, given knowledge of my behaviour only, might infer that I would employ any tool put ready to my hand. He was quite wanting in those instincts which are required to distinguish the ordinary peccadillos of married life from the dastardly crimes of kidnap and blackmail—he lacked the instincts of a gentleman. That he did not perceive such instincts in me—that he took me for a common criminal—cut away the ground from under my feet. Why had he troubled to save my skin, confound the fellow, if he hadn't made out what I was?

'Why am I brought here?' I asked.

'Because Moostapha here has taken a fancy to saving your life whenever you look like throwing it away,' he returned irritably, stopping up his mouth again immediately with his pipe, in the manner of an infant with its comforter.

'And what do you intend doing with Ben now you've abducted him?' I asked further.

'The child you call Ben is not your affair,' he rapped out. Then he softened enough to add, 'But I believe you were fond of him. I will tell you. You know chess? The child was brought to Stamboul as a pawn is moved forward one square to offer a trade. But I did not trade. I took him.' He rubbed his hands. 'I took him! My brother loses.'

'So you are brother to Rachel's father?' I said.

He did not reply, having meant perhaps to reveal nothing I did not already know. Then he admitted, 'We are one family. I am trader here as you see, my brother—yes I call him brother— is merchant in the sound English style, is he not? Ships—the English require a man to own ships if they are to trust him. With his ships full of wool and cotton, and with his son-in-law who is gentleman—why, one day he will be trusted, no? Am I right?'

'Trusted more readily than if he traded in slaves,' I agreed.

'Ah! A gentleman shouldn't buy and sell slaves, is that it?'

'A gentleman shouldn't be a merchant, sir. He may buy and sell a horse occasionally, but that ain't to say he should work at Tattersalls.'

'Such fine distinctions!' he said, raising his hands and letting them fall. 'In trading too, I think. Listen. My brother buys cotton from Egypt where slaves pick it. Brings it to England where——'

'Your brother conducts a decent trading business,' I said.

'No, sir, excuse me, there is no "decent" trading to be separate from "indecent" trading : there is only trading. Ah, maybe trade shows a different face in each country, to oblige different scruples, but its heart and soul remains the same in all the world's markets. You find me the widow and her mite, sir, in any country on God's earth, and I'll show you a trader ready to part them. That's trade, sir. Whatever shows a profit, that's what trade is. Growing fat on famine and war and death, that's trade in every corner of the globe. I wear the clothes you see me in, my brother wears a frock coat and a silk hat; but that ain't to say one of us is "decent" and the other not, for we're both honest traders.'

'Honest!' I ejaculated.

'Honest to ourselves,' he rejoined. 'For a trader can't afford to dupe himself you see, the way a gentleman can. And at bottom there's no other honesty worth the name but that, that a fellow don't dupe himself. Why, I knew my brother had brought out the boy as an article to be bargained upon. Of course I did. I rejoice in that. For why? Because it sets me free to fight honestly —Catch weight, no holds barred. And I get the little fellow back. All right, so I owe my brother a favour now. Maybe I see a way to pay it.'

'Ben is your son is he?'

He stared at me as though his thoughts were far away. 'The future, sir, that's what we have to consider. What do you see as your future, eh? What's to be done with you?'

I had no ready answer. This abominable fellow's low opinion of me seemed to have knocked the stuffing out of my own notions about myself.

'No plan?' he said. 'No plan at all? Well—I may have a use for you, if you have none for yourself.'

He crooked a jewelled finger and the eunuch bent down to listen at his lips. It seemed that I was to be given into his charge. Against all my instincts I must master my revulsion at the creature's exterior and trust to his humanity. I contrived a smile as he wobbled towards me, his tiny legs trotting in a mincing, womanish gait. At that moment I understood the feelings of all the tender virgins of legend given in marriage to crook-backed lechers, for it was, curiously enough, sexual assault that I feared at his hands. My shadow!—I saw in him the awful shadow cast by the two-backed beast.

'Where am I to be taken?'

There was no answer. The Jew looked on, a chess-player who has made his move. I was the piece. Was I to be exchanged for Ben?—the favour he owed his brother?

I could only do as I was directed by my gaoler. We quitted the house as we had entered it and walked towards the water. The moon had risen, and by its light I could discern the wooded shore, the silvered bay. A number of boats clustered at the quay we approached. Should I take my chance now of escaping? I had no doubt the creature padding behind me was armed. As we reached the wooden jetty I half turned to assess my chances of jumping into a boat and making off. I met a pad of cloth reached towards me. Chloroform! With a last impression stamped upon my mind of the monstrous glimmer of that face—bloodless, sexless, its lips gaped wide with hunger—looming upon me like a vampire on a virgin's couch—I knew no more.

XI

The Eye of the Needle

I AWOKE IN the hour which precedes the sunrise, alone on a hillside, and very cold. I heard the lap of water very near, and found that my boots were a very few inches from the small collapsing wavelets of the Bosphorus. Had the straits been tidal, by Jove I should have been carried off!

I was unhurt, unbound, suffering only from cold and from wet, for I had been either soaked through by rain or immersed in the water. I stood up, stamping my feet and swinging my arms like a London cabbie. From my feet extended the green waters of the Bosphorus, at this hour almost empty of shipping and rippled with the dawn wind. Already the light behind me was strengthening, touching the hills across the straits with the day's first colour. But wait! This sun rose in the wrong quarter! Something was very much awry. I stared about me. Then I realised what it was. I had awoken in Asia.

It is remarkable how unsettling is the effect of disorientation of this kind. One's view of a house, no matter how familiar a house, is quite thrown out by awakening in a bedroom not usually slept in. It might seem a trifle, which side of the Bosphorus I found myself upon; but to me all the difference between Europe and Asia was latent in my sense of slipped perspective. The sun rose behind me instead of in my face, the Devil's Current flowed the wrong way, the world was out of joint. If I had been dropped upon a strange planet I could not have experienced a stronger sensation of the unearthly—of recommencing my journey alone, stripped of possessions and unencumbered by a history, from a mere geographic point like a needle-prick in eternity.

Supposing it to be the eunuch who had brought me hither, I wondered if he remained at hand. I doubted if his instructions had been to cast me away on this empty strand: I felt very strongly that his orders had been to put me to death, as the concession my captor had owed his brother for the abduction of the child. Perhaps he had slid my chloroformed body into the straits, and I had swum ashore. Or perhaps my saviour had again given me my life. I looked all about me, and saw no one.

The scene was beautiful, the earth and water yet in shadow, the tall trees on the slopes above me touched with light where the earliest sun threw its beams, the green and rocky sward enamelled with the yellow crocus. It was indeed like a world new-made.

I expected my sense of disorientation to dissolve, thinking it but a momentary effect of my drugged sleep, a transient illusion soon to be replaced by the normal perspectives of the world. Instead, as day declared itself and my castaway plight became plain to me, it was Europe, and familiarity, which receded into unreality like a dream. There was no help to be looked for from that quarter. By whoever's hand I had been saved, I must now help myself, or perish.

I left the water's edge and climbed through meadows until I came upon a cart track skirting the woods which clothed the slopes above. There was nothing for it but to follow this track, so rough that it was evidently a stream-bed in winter, until I came to some recognisable landmark. I knew nothing, and had heard no one tell, of the inhabitants of this Asian shore. Upon the European side, in the villages, one saw in the main only such natives as served the wants of the *yalis*, though I had once or twice seen gangs of ruffianly-looking men come in from the hills, or from the Forest of Belgrade, driving mules loaded with skins and firewood and suchlike. Upon this Asiatic shore I did not doubt that the dwellers in the hills were a wild set of fellows who would think nothing of robbing a traveller, or worse. I set off southward as briskly as the track allowed.

My path climbed and fell, and zig-zagged among clefts and promontories of the shoreline, so that I had walked for an hour or more before achieving a point which commanded a view extensive enough to discover my position. Now at last from an outcrop above the straits, looking north, I made out the broad extent of the Black Sea not a mile from where I stood. I therefore computed that I was about twenty miles from Constantinople.

Not that I was anxious to reach Constantinople, now that I considered the matter. Far from it. Where, for the matter of that,

191

was I to go? I could light upon no spot in the entire world, let alone upon the Bosphorus, where I would be welcome. To counter such gloomy thoughts as these I rose from the ground, where I had sunk down in dejection upon realising how far I was from Constantinople, and began once more to walk rapidly towards that capital which I had no desire to reach. My clothes were still wet, and my exertions in the strengthening sun caused a cloud of vapour to rise from them and hover about me as I walked.

I made an attempt to recover Briggs' carefree spirit—the elation of our adventure together—and pictured myself changing my name, taking ship or caravan eastward from Stamboul, pitching up perhaps as an ensign with a troop of irregular horse in the Deccan, perhaps as Grand Vizier to a potentate of the Coromandel Coast, perhaps as a corpse dragged by its foot from a sandy grave in the Dahna for a jackal's supper . . . From this I fell to recalling those adventures and journeys which Rachel and I had conceived of together as children, in all that vast realm of the imagination which stretches eastward from the shore where I walked as far as the palace of Kubilai Khan beside the Yellow Sea—romance draws a thousand maps upon which the armchair traveller makes his journeys. But I was not in an armchair. Though I was walking through the midst of a map drawn by the imagination, with romance and fancy all about me, yet this journey—this journey I could hardly believe in, which I seemed to be making through realms of fantasy from nowhere to nowhere —this journey was the true reality of my life!

Overcome by the thought I sank down beside a clear pool formed where a stream flowed across the track. Reality—! Cupping the water to my mouth I was revived by Pindar's words, ἄριστον μὲν ὕδωρ. Pindar indeed! The fact of a tag of Pindar coming pat to mind made me dash the water from my lips. What in the world was Pindar to do with the matter?—A mere convention of my upbringing, a mere pretence of education. But where then was I to drink? Truly the wells had been poisoned behind me if the education of a gentleman was to be suspect; there was no source of water left. *There is nothing but pretence*, Rachel had said, *all there is is what appears to be, the conventions of your world which is all to you.* True.

But that world was precisely what had now vanished. Convention, pretence, what appears to be—the woof of my life and its warp too, the whole woven fabric of the world which had been all to me, was flown off like a magic carpet I had travelled upon all my life, but had now tumbled from into this harsh world—the world I had hitherto supposed to be fantasy.

How was it that I came to be so utterly adrift? Was it that I had taken such featherweight stuff aboard as ballast—school rules, scraps of Pindar, society's conventions—in place of stowing in the unshifting weight of the Decalogue; and so in the first rough weather found the vessel unsteerable? What a gentleman counts upon, is meeting with no rough weather. Seamanship—trust, truth, integrity—is not required on a voyage across the millpond of our late nineteenth century. But to a fellow running under bare poles, on the stormy sea where I now found myself, trust—Rachel's trust in me at least—would have counted as a good deal in the way of a port to steer for. She had been right, though, not to trust me. I could not quarrel with that.

For fear that no other water would offer I took a draught of the wayside pool before setting out once more on my journey to Nowhere. I had not walked very far before a very vivid sensation of regret at having drunk so deep of the Hippocrene began to creep upon me. The devil take it! Foul and bitter it had tasted, but I had supposed that spring water in such a land as I now found myself must always taste so. Pretty soon I sat down again, before I tumbled over. The sun on my head seemed to have grown exceeding hot, though my damp clothes still chilled me, for sweat dewed my brow and I scarcely could endure the light upon my eyes. I remained some time at the roadside.

As possessions bang about a cabin in rough weather, and one has not strength to secure them, so thoughts banged to and fro in my head. Thoughts came and went of Dolfuss—of a species of two-headed Dolfuss, for my mind ran the brothers together into one being—and my shame at his estimate of my character. Yes, shame : *fas est et ab hoste doceri* (for tags, you may be sure, banged about in the storm in my head too). I *had* learned from my enemy; I too seemed now to have lost the instinctual touchstone which had hitherto allowed me to distinguish my own behaviour from that of a common criminal. A gentlemanly instinct seemed precious little use to me in my present scrape. Worse than useless indeed; what it did for me was to get me back upon my feet, when I should have been better off resting, and keep

193

me from vomiting up the foul water which I should have been better without. The instincts of a gentleman, in fact, carried on business upon the Asiatic shore of the Bosphorus for all the world as though I had taken too much Champagne at Willis' Rooms, and it was their duty to restrain nature from outraging convention. I believe the gentlemanly instinct, curse it, very near killed me that day.

Under a reeling sun I stumbled on, half blind, half fainting, wholly beat, fit subject for one of Lady Butler's pictures, until I was aware of trodden earth underfoot, of the rough touch of a drystone wall which shored up the roadside (and myself), of men's voices and the creak of wheels. I had reached a village. I was aware of fierce dark faces thrust into mine like the feverish masks which come and go by firelight in the wallpaper pattern of a sickroom. But no hand was held out to me, no comfort offered, no word spoken; instead a hollow square was made for me, such as spectators form around a marathon runner near collapse who is disqualified if touched, and in this hollow square of curious travellers, which dodged one way and t'other to keep its distance from my reeling course, I dragged myself on through dust raised by feet and wheels until I halted unsteadily in the centre of the *meidan*. Against a wall I made out the raised benches, the impassive line of smoking Turks, which denotes a café. Towards its door I faltered, every step doubtful. What I desired was a bed, one of the clean white beds of Europe. A fellow's face loomed out at me as I tottered into the dark interior.

'A bed, a bed,' I whispered hoarsely, repeating the word in every language known to me as if to conjure the article itself into existence.

He studied me for a moment. Then he turned without a word and walked into the back of the low room where he twitched aside a greasy curtain which hung there. Beyond I saw a cell with the humps of one or two recumbent bodies upon its floor. I pushed past the Turk and down into this den. Mats were laid upon the earth floor. Onto one of these I sank. The wall against which I laid my back, of earth like the floor, was rough to the touch with an encrustation of squashed bugs. The air stank foul as a privy.

I would have given much to have been under the sky again; but enslaved to the end by my conventional instinct I had used

194

the last of my strength in driving myself to reach that sanctuary of a sick European, the bed, here in Asia where no beds exist. I had now no strength left to undo the work of instinct and of convention, which had led me into a hole where I should surely die. Inch by inch I took off my coat and my boots and made them into a pillow, and laid myself down upon my stinking mat. I determined to recover my strength and fight my way out.

I must have slept and wakened many times—was aware of jerking awake and of slipping back into unconsciousness—until a more lucid interval of waking allowed me to put together the fragments of myself and to understand that the café through the curtain (whose noise had made part of my nightmare) was quiet and dark. I drew reassurance from this, I know not why, and was soon able to fall asleep again more peaceably. When next I woke it was to see daylight under the greasy curtain. I gathered the strength slowly to pull on my boots and to get upon my legs with my jacket in my hand. Beyond the curtain I found that the proprietor slept across the café door, no doubt to keep his guests from moonlighting. I felt sufficiently restored to myself to stir the fellow awake with the toe of my boot, thus I hoped somewhat retrieving my position in his eyes after my abject state of the evening previous.

'Bring me coffee, bread, cheese, hurry!' I ordered him.

He came to full commercial consciousness immediately, rapidly calculating that I was to be treated with respect, and went off about his business. I lowered myself onto a bench outside the door and sat there more or less stupefied until my breakfast was brought. I still felt most distinctly unwell. Upon attempting to eat, nausea again racked me. I drank a little coffee and soon called the man out again to ask what I should pay.

I did not hear his answer, for a blow of the utmost severity had fallen upon me. I had no money. Fingers scrabbling from pocket to pocket encountered nothing more valuable than a large bug with struggling legs which had substituted itself for silver and gold. I had been robbed. Blood turned to water. I said 'I have no money'.

He did not take this news kindly. Whilst he jabbered and threatened I sat with my eyes closed and my back supported by the café wall. My mind, like my pocket, was utterly empty. I now possessed nothing but the clothes on my back. I wished I had not stirred the fellow up with my foot, for my superiority could not now be paid for as I had intended, in money, and by his language he was plainly determined to exact payment in kind. After a while he went away, but when I opened my eyes I found that he had only gone to collect his friends. Soon an extensive semi-circle had formed with myself as its focus, and this of course attracted further viewers; evidently people were getting up early in order to come and stare at me, and my creditor himself was soon so busy making and serving coffee for these sightseers that he had time only to shout at me as he hurried to and fro with trays. I remained inert, my eyes closed, until I felt fingers catch hold of my jacket. This was beyond bearing. I caught the rascal's hand—it was not the café owner's—and threw it from me. Again the fingers returned to take up a pinch of the tweed of my suit between finger and thumb. The fellow then made me a panto-mime of taking off his own greasy cloth jacket.

I understood.

As soon as I realised that they envied my clothes I concluded that I would do well to sell my whole outfit here, where I had a market and a crowd gathered, rather than to part with it piece-meal as need arose. Better still—the thought came to me—raise enough money to purchase a ferry ticket. To what destination? Well, at least to Europe. Perhaps my priorities were unsound, but my suit seemed of no more use to me today than my gentle-manly instinct had seemed of use yesterday.

In the course of very lengthy bargaining in front of this large assemblage—for I had acquired an advocate, rather on the prin-ciple of the dock brief taken by young Hopeful in an English court, who argued the merits of my clothing article by article—I disposed of jacket, hard collar, socks, braces, boots and waist-coat in return for my lodging, my breakfast, and 50 silver *piastres*. My advocate sold off my necktie too, but I had to repurchase it at a loss to keep my trowsers up. I also bought, for two *piastres*, a length of dirty white cotton sufficient for a cloak.

I could not help being infected by the atmosphere of good humour which had arisen amongst the crowd, so that although I was still uncommon seedy, I felt a strong appreciation, in a distant sort of way, of the joke of the thing. Also, and more curious, I felt an affection for the Turks which I had never felt before. I was certainly upon a more level footing with them than

I had ever previously been—for had I not relinquished every attribute of the superior race and class which had made me separate?—and they seemed better fellows looked at eye to eye. I was surprised at this, until I seemed to make out, in my hazy state, a kind of parallel with the fun I had found in Ben's company once I had learned to tumble down and get up again as carelessly as he did.

I gave three *piastres* more to my advocate—a Jew, I need hardly say—and got very carefully upon my feet to undertake, in my plucked state, the journey of some 150 paces to the quayside where a ferry must before long make its appearance.

I must have reckoned that my house at Emirghian was a bolt-hole. I do not remember. Nor do I recollect how I contrived to buy my ticket or to embark, but I would take an oath that I must have been aided in my character of a cross-bred derelict, in a way that I had never been aided in my rôle of English gentleman. I recall one lucid moment upon the boat, where I found myself propped against the rail hard by the gangplank (no doubt placed there by a charitable hand) and sat contemplating my trowsers, at such variance with my bare feet and cloth wrapping that I wished I had sold them with the rest . . . I do not know how I got off the boat, or to the door of my house. I think that the motley servants engaged by the dragoman must still have been there, for I retain the impression of having climbed to the top floor, seeking peace, as though climbing the Tower of Babel itself. Or perhaps the warring tongues were in my head. At all events I must have made my way into Maryka's quarters, for I was there, lying upon bedding on the floor, looking up into the indifference of her gaze as she sponged my face, when next I experienced a lucid interval.

Nor do I know how many days passed in this fashion. The round plain face of Maryka—the moon face prized in Asia, cold as the moon too—calmly rose and set over my bed, and rode through my sky, at an infinite distance, shedding no warmth. At first I feared being in her power. But there was no need, for as to whether I lived or died she was utterly indifferent, nursing me with no more emotion than she would have showed at laying out my corpse. Nor did I care myself whether I lived or died. My vision had been affected by the illness, and I looked out upon a scene which was full of dark spaces, blind spots I suppose, as though the world were a jig-saw puzzle I had yet to complete before sense could be made of it. What lay ahead was hidden in the blank spaces which swam into my vision if ever I tried to focus upon the future. Into these dark spaces I kept falling, however careful I tried to be, and there was no way of climbing out. It was only restful to lie still with closed eyes; more restful still to lapse into stupor.

XII

A Journey begins

I AWOKE AT last in the chill of a dawn absolutely in charge of myself. I looked ahead and saw by that cool light that the blank spaces in my vision had not lied : indeed I had no future. Indeed I had nothing. Only one thing troubled me, as an irregularity in order ever troubles the invalid mind, and that was the sole possession remaining to me : Maryka. Of her it seemed I could not rid myself. But there came into my mind a possibility; could I persuade her to return to the earliest stage of our intercourse, when she had sat in the window and told me her history? I believed that it would then be possible to persuade her one step back from that innocent beginning—to persuade her to take her freedom and give me mine. I determined to commence by asking to hear her history again, in hopes that innocence might be recreated from this beginning. I looked along the floor to the hump of her body curled in its bedding in the early light. I would not wake her, but in the morning I would beg her to begin again.

How soon it was that I found myself awake, and Maryka with her back to me as she placed a tray on a low table, I do not know. My resolution was fresh in my mind. I do not think I had spoken except in delirium since reaching the house, but now I heard my own weak tones murmur out :

'Tell me the history of your life.'

She turned, smiling with joy. But the smile, the joy, was not upon Maryka's cold features. They were upon Rachel's. It was Rachel who set down the tray and rushed in a whisper of light clothes to bend and kiss me with gladness. Those soft lips, warm breath, the brilliance of those dark eyes—it was Rachel!

'My poor love!' she cried out softly, 'to hear you speak sense

199

at last!—if it is sense to ask to hear the history of my life! And if you wish it, yes, yes I will, you shall hear it all.'

I cannot well describe the sweetness of those days. From that instant my health turned upward, yet I enjoyed awhile the languor of the invalid rather than suffering the impatience of the convalescent, and in the long cool days, in empty rooms lit with the light of the sun upon the Bosphorus, our happiness was complete, and in our completeness we were happy. For a time I asked no questions of Rachel because I asked none of myself. The fact that she asked me none led me to suppose that I had talked so freely whilst delirious that she required no further answers. But as my strength returned so curiosity returned with it, and one evening I asked her:

'Rachel, when first you came to this house who did you find here?'

'A Greek woman who said she was your housekeeper. Two or three other creatures, old women too, Greeks I daresay.'

'All living downstairs were they? No one up here, besides myself?'

'My dearest you were so alone! So very far away!' She stirred in my arms, and turned her face round to me to be kissed. So we lay, hour upon hour, enjoying in one another's arms that completeness of life which I had learned of from Maryka in our first days together. There interposed none of the difficulties which had used to part us, neither the difference in our wealth nor the difference in our sex, for what we had was held in common. Presently I asked:

'How did you make them go? The parcel of Greeks.'

She laughed. 'There is no difficulty in making servants go if you do not pay them! Their wages expired just as I came, and when they asked me for money I said I had none.' She laughed again. 'It is true, too, or almost. We are practically beggars!' At this we both laughed.

It seemed to me certain that she had not come across Maryka. In some manner—for some reason—Maryka had accepted her freedom. I asked no more questions. I kissed close the dear large eyes.

I had already learned how she had come to Emirghian. After a few days in the Pera hotel with her father—he terrified for

200

his safety, she alarmed (so she said) as much on my behalf as on Ben's—her father had announced to her that they were to sail next day for Liverpool, and had ordered her and Nanny to be packed and ready by a certain hour. When she had asked what was to become of Ben he had replied with a smile 'that a bargain had been struck'.

'With Archie?' Rachel had asked. 'You surely haven't paid the ransom?'

'My life no, never fear! I have struck a good bargain though, more than the boy's worth.'

'What have you obtained?' (Rachel told me she had asked.)

'Aside from the promise of settling Caper's hash, hey? Freedom to trade here, my dear. Arms, that's the article nowadays, arms and yet more arms till the fine gentlemen of Europe blows themselves sky-high!'

Rachel told me that she had from that moment had no intention of leaving Turkey with her father, or of leaving it at all until she had established what had been my fate and Ben's. So to Emirghian she had travelled next morning with a valise of clothes and what money had remained at the hotel. The first fellow of whom she had asked directions for 'the Englishman's house' had sent a child with her to point it out and carry her bag. Our possessions at the Pera Palace, already packed into trunks by Nanny, she had instructed the hotel to keep in store. So she had come to me, forsaking all. I did not doubt but that her father and Nanny had left for England. To be free of Nanny was a wonderful thing: I had come to recognise in her a type of female—as nursemaid, matron, chaperone or whore (for the whores favoured by the English upper class resemble nothing so much as debauched nannies)—a type of English female who preys upon and emasculates the male. Now, thank Heaven, she was gone. That Ben was safe—was returned to his own kind as a cage-bird to its jungle—I was able to assure Rachel.

'So we are free,' she said simply, using the same cheerful tone in which she had described us as beggars.

I dreaded only one happening: the reanimation of horror in that gloomy house across the creek in which had lived—and perhaps lived still—that deformed monster, my shadow Moostapha. No sounds came from the shuttered dwelling, no hammer-strokes from its yard, no boats rocked at its water-stair.

Yet I could not make myself quite easy in the garden overlooked by its presence, nor could I admire the wax-white flesh of the magnolia flowers, tinged with green and scented like a catafalque, quite as freely as did Rachel. It seemed to me that the flagstones below the tree sweated up darker and more horrid drops than their neighbours in the autumn weather which had now begun. I found it hard to believe that I had taken my punishment and could go free; I expected that maxim, in common with all the other misguided notions acquired with it as a job-lot at school, to prove false in the real life I now confronted.

Then one day Rachel came home from buying fruit and fish, the diet we fared upon, and said that she had spoken to the person from the house next door. My blood ran cold.

'Oh?' I said. 'Was he a——?'

There was a silence. Then she said 'I think he is a——'

With an effort I supplied the word : 'A eunuch?'

'Yes, a eunuch,' she repeated, 'poor little man. But he seemed friendly. Grateful.'

'Grateful?'

'Yes,' she said, 'you see he fell off his bicycle and I held it for him to get on again.'

His bicycle ! I remembered Watkins' cap perched on that hairless skull. Alas poor Watkins ! Still, from the moment I heard of Rachel having helped him to remount the Starley Rover, I ceased to fear that the horror of 'my shadow' might reclaim us. Whatever his exterior he was a fellow who, as I well knew, repaid favours most handsomely. Yes, we were free : as free as it is possible to be.

What use should we make of our freedom? There was nothing to be gained by our going back to any point upon the road we had come. All that I cared for was that we should start afresh from where we stood now. The destination did not signify. Rachel had begun a new novel, the first being now set up in print in London, and I would come upon her bent over her manuscript when I entered a room, or I would see her writing at the window when I looked up from my book in the garden. Although she at once laid down her pen when I came in—or, rather, when she noticed that I had come in—I wished that I had a part in these excursions of hers into the country of her imagination; so that when she said that she wished she could see Persia the better to describe it in her book, I seized on the opportunity for us to travel together.

It was decided. We would catch a steamer to Trebizond, and there put together what was essential to a journey over the mountains of Ghara, past the Ararats themselves, and so to the Western Tigris and Mosul. Murray's Guide informed us that such a tour might be undertaken by a lady accustomed to the saddle, and an Englishman may travel where he pleases in Asia, chiefly because the Asiatics have persuaded themselves that he is preserved from harm by the Black Arts. From the consulate at Trebizond could be obtained permits of travel made out to the *mutesarifs* and *valis* along our route. Travelling in such lands is so cheap that we, though paupers in Europe, would have ample means for all our wants in Asia.

I already yearned to see the white-fronted houses of Trebizond clustering among figs and laurels, their red-tiled roofs descending in terraces to the sea, for it was a scene I had carried in my head ever since those earliest travels which Rachel and I had made together out of picture books and atlases and our imaginations. All that was needed was to decide; we could leave by the first boat to the Black Sea.

That evening, finding Rachel's manuscript placed ready to be put into her carpet bag, I let my eye fall upon the first sentence. As I live, her new tale began thus : 'I was born into a family of poor fur merchants in the small town of Kuchuk Derbend, not far from the borders of Rumelia and Thrace. Those days were hard for our people, for the tax-gatherers ...'

The story was Maryka's. I took in the implications of this fact. I stood there for some time thinking of it. I must wait for the last chapter of Rachel's story to be written before I would learn whether the heroine came into the possession of an Englishman upon the Bosphorus. Would Maryka have considered that latest chapter worth including in her history? Had it happened? I tiptoed away from the pile of manuscript as if from a nest of snakes best left unstirred.

Next morning we stood together on the deck of a Russian boat as it left the channel of the Bosphorus and steamed into the unbounded horizons of the Euxine. Passing the white water which breaks ceaselessly upon the Cyanean Rocks I thought of Jason's passage between them, and of the rich man's passage through the needle's eye, and I embraced Rachel, for truly we were each other's only possession . . . No, I thought, there must always in human affairs be a reservation from the absolute. In this case Rachel carried with her the manuscript of her story, and I, to counter that, carried the intention of writing a story of my own, my own version of the truth, as soon as I found myself (all too soon, alas, expecting massacre here at Diarbekr) with leisure to begin.

As the ship responded to the livelier swell of the Black Sea, Rachel and I steadied each other upon its deck with an embrace, she with her manuscript, I with my intention. So we stood in the freshening wind and sea, the shores of Christendom receding. Alas, it was not long before Lord Byron's lines came forcefully to mind :

> There's not a sea the traveller e're pukes in
> Turns up more dangerous breakers than the Euxine.